Evil's Niece

'If you learn nothing else here, Judd, you'll know better than to taunt a woman who's smarter and larger than you!' barked Mrs Frike. 'Now drop your pants, and don't give me any sass about it!'

Judd's face paled and his Adam's apple bobbed with a hard swallow. He was teetering on his toes, glancing frantically towards Chapin but, when the housekeeper led him to the chair, he realised he was bested. He turned towards the wall and, with quivering hands, he lowered his pants past his bubble-shaped behind.

The room was silent: the two maids peering around the kitchen door – and the two in the corner – were too delighted by this spectacle to make a peep. Chapin could only stare as the housekeeper he'd grown up with flipped his new valet across her broad lap. She took her time positioning him, so the gravity of his predicament could sink in as part of his punishment.

'Palms to the floor,' she ordered. 'And by God if you kick me or wiggle around, I'll have the girls hold your feet. Understand me?'

'Y-yes, Mrs Frike.'

'Fine.' For effect, she paused again, pulling his shirttail up over his back and then fingering his buttocks to determine the best point of attack. 'Mr Schuck, you have such a fat ass, this spoon will have no effect at all. I'll have to use my hand.'

Other Books by the author

Demon's Dare
Devil's Fire
Satan's Angel

Evil's Niece
Melissa MacNeal

BLACK LACE

Black Lace books contain sexual fantasies.
In real life, always practise safe sex.

First published in 2003 by
Black Lace
Thames Wharf Studios
Rainville Road
London W6 9HA

Copyright © Melissa MacNeal 2003

The right of Melissa MacNeal to be identified as the Author of
the Work has been asserted in accordance with the Copyright,
Designs and Patents Act 1988.

Design by Smith & Gilmour, London
Printed and bound by Mackays of Chatham PLC

ISBN 0 352 33781 8

Contents

1 **Taken by Surprise**

New Orleans, 1897

New Orleans kept her secrets like a sultry Creole courtesan, leaning over wrought iron railings to lure her lovers down narrow streets with French names, into secluded Spanish courtyards where curious eyes couldn't follow.

Or so it seemed. Ever since I'd married Chapin Proffit, I'd been amazed and amused by his city's flamboyance. As I walked along Rue Dumaine, past shuttered brick buildings with an air of ancient mystery, I had to wonder about a place where one could pass a convent school, and then enter a voodoo temple where a dark-skinned priestess poked pins into dolls. Born and raised in St. Louis, I was ever aware of being the outsider here. A square peg trying to fit in the inner circle of the New Orleans elite.

Of course, Madame LaRue was all too happy to have my business. I'd just finished my final fitting of several new gowns – too ostentatious for my taste, fashioned of flashy fabrics and daring designs. The seamstress, however, insisted that, as the wife of a man who sat on the Cotton Exchange and lived in the Garden District, I should set the trends rather than follow them.

'You must dress the part,' she intimated in her French accent. 'Everyone judges Mr Proffit's success by the way he adorns his wife.'

I detested being a social ornament, on display to

enhance Chapin's reputation, but I was at least living well. Extremely well. That I was strolling the streets of the Vieux Carré alone was something these snooty aristocrats would simply have to live with.

On a whim, I detoured down another block to where I thought the Beau Monde Club would be – my husband was lunching there, with men who had political ambitions for him. As a woman, I would never set foot in the Club's hallowed halls, where I imagined gentlemen puffing on Cuban cigars and sipping expensive brandy after a lavish meal. But I wanted to see it, just to gain a sense of place; to root myself more thoroughly in this city which, after seven years, still felt foreign to me.

And there it was: a tall, corner building of whitewashed brick and maroon shutters, its balcony outlined with the wrought iron that gave this French section of the city its distinctive flavour. I was studying the railing's curlicues when the door opened, and out stepped my husband. As he glanced around, I found him handsome in a golden sort of way, with blond waves highlighting his chiselled face and a light linen suit cut to complement his slender physique.

I almost called out to him – just as a young lady stepped from behind the alley's oleander bushes, smiling saucily. He kissed her hand with something more than Southern courtliness, and my heart lurched. I stepped behind the nearest building, afraid to observe them further but too curious not to.

A clutch of men emerged from the club, their expressions inquisitive.

'Allow me to introduce my niece, Savanna,' Chapin piped up. He then named the three men, who bowed as they took in Savanna's alluring figure and revealing red dress.

Niece, indeed! I'd never before seen this pretty blonde, much less heard of any Savannas in the family. A sudden queasiness made me cling to the cool brick of the building I hid behind: my assumptions of a stable marriage were dissipating like the steam rising from the street.

As the men went their separate ways, Chapin quickly escorted his companion in the opposite direction. I decided to follow. I didn't want to know where they were going, but an aristocrat's wife had to gather information about her sheltered, narrow world from wherever she could.

I never dreamed I'd be watching my husband cheat.

He ducked down an alley that led to a gated court-yard – an oasis of wisteria and hibiscus among the closely constructed buildings, sequestered from the prying eyes of passers-by.

But not from mine. When that gate swung shut, I slipped up to see what Chapin had in mind for this 'niece', who'd been clinging to him like the ivy climbing these houses. His hours away from home, when I assumed him to be conducting the Proffit family's business, took on new meaning for me – the unassuming wife, who believed such indiscretions were only other women's concerns.

Chapin kissed Savanna hard on the mouth, and then spun her around to face a banana tree in the centre of the courtyard. She was panting, the hussy! No stranger to this illicit trysting, she grabbed the trunk of the tree and encouraged her lover to lift her crimson skirts. Her bustled behind and swishing silk petticoats blocked my view, but my husband was unfastening his pants like his fly was on fire. Need smouldered on his patrician features until his eyes glowed like prisms.

It was that glow that hurt me most; that fire in his

loins that scorched my heart. Anger consumed me, for I was being betrayed in the worst way, but as I gripped the iron bars of that gate, it was a deeper wound he cut with his infidelity: *envy*. Envy so green and bilious, I covered my mouth to keep from screaming.

Savanna was thrusting her backside at him, and he entered her with such force that her gasp camouflaged my own. With her eyes squeezed shut, she didn't notice the banana tree's phallic red bloom hanging just above her – an ironic piece of scenery. The ecstatic look on her young, flawless face was the last straw. As she panted out what she wanted him to do, and how hard she wanted him to pump, I had to turn –

But I was trapped against the gate!

A large, male body pressed me so close against one of its iron poles that my breasts bulged around it. When he rubbed a rock-hard erection against my hips, that place between my legs got so aroused by the hard bar that I saw shooting stars.

I choked back a cry. Bad enough that I'd caught my husband with a lover; now a total stranger had captured me with the same intent!

'Shh,' he whispered, stifling my cry with a large hand. 'Can't let them know we're here. We might get quite an eyeful.'

A molasses drawl tickled my ear, along with warm breath that smelled of brandy. The leathery palm covering my mouth rubbed my lips suggestively, but I wasn't about to kiss it. It protruded from a white French cuff held together with a gold stud, and the coat sleeve was unrelenting black – like my captor's sideburns, when he brought his face around to mine.

That dusky Creole complexion and renegade grin belonged to Dewel Proffit, Chapin's bastard half-brother.

His shirt collar was a blinding white that made his eyes stand out in the shadows; eyes of a dazzling blue that I would have found extremely attractive had they not belonged to a man of such dubious reputation. The very man my husband had warned me never to associate with, much less trust.

Dewel turned my head, so I once again beheld the spectacle in the courtyard. Chapin grimaced as his body rocked against the backside of his conquest, whose expression matched his own. Together they struggled towards release, rutting like dogs in an alley despite their fine clothing.

And, as a strangling sound erupted from my husband, I could only stare in disbelief, with a raw, rasping sadness.

So that's what a climax looks like. That's how I'm supposed to feel when Chapin ... if he would ever take me with such passion.

I shook these thoughts from my head, for they were every bit as disturbing as the man behind me. With a low chuckle Dewel undulated, making that iron bar cut heavily into my chest. My breasts rose high and tight in my corset, protruding lewdly through the gate's openings with my nipples in the lead. A brandy-scented hand caressed my mouth, and powerful thighs forced mine apart for unspeakable intimacies with that unyielding spindle. I felt extremely vulnerable and unladylike. Far more aroused by my captive state than I cared to admit.

My husband was ravaging his playmate again, and the sight of them inflamed my private parts. I furtively positioned myself so my clothing rubbed that desperate little nub, carried away by the soft moans and gyrating of the rake behind me. My eyes closed and the sensations became so intense I quivered, my need rising beyond decency – beyond the inhibitions that had previously prevented me from –

I jerked backwards as though struck by lightning, overwhelmed by such a dazzling jolt.

Dewel chuckled. 'You're shakin', sugah. Is it from rage, catchin' your man with his little tidbit? Or do you want me real bad?'

I didn't dare answer that, much less try to talk between this bastard's fingers. His other hand had snaked around my waist and roamed upward, until he was squeezing a breast – as though he had the right to take any favours he pleased! Once again I butted against that shameless erection, trying to shrug out of his muscled arms. When the lovers pulled apart, this brazen Proffit had the audacity to steer me into the nearest alley with his hand still across my mouth.

'They've gotta get out through that gate,' he explained. 'If Chapin can have his little secret, we might as well have ours, Miss Eve.'

I broke free and slapped him. 'You indecent, despicable –'

'Yes, and yes, I am.' Dewel's Creole features glowed with mirthful pride. 'But I've kept you from betrayin' yourself to your husband and causin' a nasty little scene.'

'He told me he was attending a luncheon at his club.'

'And so he did. I sat at the same table.'

'But he said it was political,' I blurted. 'He introduced that little floozy as his *niece*, when she's no relation whatsoever. And who knows how long she'd been there? Like a puppy awaiting its master!'

Dewel's smile waxed indulgent, and then he listened – until the clank of the gate announced their departure.

His lush lips curved into the arrogant, egotistical grin I'd associated with this younger Proffit ever since I'd met him at my wedding. His black suit made him look undeniably wicked, showing off the sturdy frame of a man who managed a sugar plantation – an estate he'd inherited from his daddy, much to Chapin's chagrin.

He was night to Chapin's day; dark and moody and sensual – a legacy of the Creole whore who bore him. And he knew how to control a moment with exasperating aplomb.

'My sweet, naive Miss Eve,' he began. 'Young ladies with rich *uncles*, so to speak, often wait for their benefactors to emerge, hopin' to share a few stolen moments. It's beyond your comprehension, I know, but if you're as smart as I think you are, you'll tuck these things away for when the information can be most useful.'

'Is that how you inherited the cane plantation? Using – or making up – information to influence your daddy's decision?' I blurted.

All of Chapin's warnings concerning the illegitimate heir to the Proffit's estate on the bayou came to mind as I watched the man in front of me. No one in her right mind would trust him! He had the sparkling blue eyes of a playful angel – like Chapin, and their father – but his burnt-sugar skin and raven hair snapped with a Spanish accent. His arrogance topped everything, however. Dewel Proffit acted *entitled* to the lion's share of his father's fortune!

'Our daddy had good reason to bequeath me the plantation, Miss Eve,' he said in his most polished drawl. 'His legitimate son remains the figurehead of the family, with a mansion in town and a seat on the Cotton Exchange, and all the privileges that go with his station. But just as Chapin has told you only negative things about me, he will never reveal *why* Daddy settled his estate this way. It's not in his best interest.'

'So what am I supposed to do about this ... this new *situation*?' I demanded. My brother-in-law was the last person I should ask, but my exasperation was burgeoning like the erection that tented his trousers. 'I can't stand idly by as though nothing has happened!'

His smile grew catlike, and he shrugged with the nonchalance of the very rich. 'Perhaps *you* need a niece, Mrs Proffit.'

I slapped him, outraged at his impertinence. But I was angrier because he was right: in this Southern aristocracy, ruled by good old boys and their connections, a wife either stayed in her place or found herself without one. My world was a prison gilded with gentility, but its invisible bars stood as rigid as the one Dewel had pressed me against. He would no more assist me than he would divulge those family secrets he'd alluded to.

And, damn him, the beast had caught my wrist and was running his pointed tongue along the strip of skin between my glove and my cuff, delighting in my distress. I tried to pull away – tried harder to ignore the sheer carnality of this intimate contact – but Dewel was no gentleman. He only held me tighter, unbuttoning my cuff so his tongue could tease further up my forearm.

'Let me go, you disreputable –'

'Yes, perhaps it *is* a niece you need,' he whispered, bringing his face mere inches in front of mine. 'Or perhaps what you really want is a good fuck.'

I was stunned speechless, my arm still suspended in his grasp. And then, to my horror, I burst into tears.

Dewel had cut too close to the truth, had guessed the humiliating secret about my marriage. And about me.

'All I ever wanted was for Chapin to handle *me* the way he ... I ... shouldn't be exposing myself to you –'

'All in good time, sugah.'

'– but when he ... he whirled her around and entered her, like a dog humping a bitch in –'

'Made her moan, didn't he?' Dewel whispered in his hypnotic baritone. 'Did it make you horny to watch, Miss Eve? I bet your drawers are drenched. I'd love to lick that honey from –'

Again I slapped him. But all I got for my efforts at self-defence was my backside against the brick wall of the house, where Dewel swiftly positioned me. 'I should never have assumed you'd understand my plight, much less care about my feelings!'

'Oh, but I do, darlin'. More than you know.'

His eyes, as blue as the midsummer sky and twice as hot, targeted mine. 'You probably aren't aware, but had I not spotted you, during that trip to settle our daddy's affairs in St. Louis, Chapin wouldn't have had the balls to propose. How he landed you is no secret, but why you've stayed with him is a mystery to me.'

My family received a generous settlement in exchange for my hand in marriage – which I saw as a dutiful daughter's contribution to her family's finances, after Daddy's market speculations went bust. So I was intrigued enough by Dewel's allusions to stop sniffling, but not bold enough to question the secrets lurking in his bottomless blue eyes ... eyes so similar to my husband's, yet far more compelling.

What did he know about Chapin that he wasn't telling? Why had he assumed I'd find my marriage intolerable enough to walk away? My parents had passed on. I had nowhere to go.

The pounding of my pulse drowned out these questions, however, and my heart was a frantic bird trying to escape its cage. And yes, my drawers were drenched, clinging to my inner thighs. I had come under Dewel's spell despite my best intentions, and it was a dangerous place to be.

He tilted his head, gauging my reactions, lowering slowly towards me as though – was this rogue about to kiss me?

But he stopped, near enough for his brandied breath to feather my upper lip. I had never wanted a man so badly in my life, but I was too appalled at my improper thoughts to give in to them.

'Why have you confided in *me*, Miss Eve?' Dewel crooned. His voice rang low and seductive, making me quiver to the core. 'What do you want to happen now?'

Oh, the answers I could give him! The wayward sensations that drove me to close that tiny space between our lips and taste my doom!

But propriety saved me, after a fashion. 'I want my husband to take me the way he ... he nailed that damned niece,' I replied, impassioned by a cause that might backfire. 'If I were a better, more desirable wife – if I knew how to flirt and ply my feminine wiles – maybe Chapin would seek his satisfaction at home.'

I swallowed hard, caught up in the maelstrom my courtyard discovery had spawned. Prodded by yearnings as forbidden – and insistent – as the ridge in Dewel Proffit's pants. 'And if anyone can teach me how, it's you.'

His face tightened and his nostrils flared. He pulled me against his hard body, intent on carrying out my desperate demands – or on snaring a witless chicken, like a fox allowed into his half-brother's hen house.

'Like Eve with that apple,' he murmured. He searched my face for signs that I'd back down – or recover my right mind. 'My God, woman, how could any man resist your charms? Or your challenge?'

2 **A Peek at Miss Picabou**

What have I been missing?

As Dewel Proffit handed me up into my waiting carriage, his playful swat to my backside made me glare at him, standing there in the door, watching as I sat down and arranged my skirts. But who could remain angry with a handsome man who smiled with such debonair decadence?

'We'll meet again soon,' he promised with a wolf's grin. 'I never keep a lady waitin'.'

Thank goodness my driver, Rémy, pulled away – perhaps because Chapin had warned him, too, about Dewel's nefarious nature. And yet, as the carriage clattered down the brick streets, I wondered if I'd been in the dark because of my husband's hatred for his half-brother, or because of my own ostrich-like tendencies not to see what was going on right before my eyes.

We passed the tall, imposing facade of the Cotton Exchange, and my doubts assailed me afresh: was my husband in there conducting his business? Or had he slipped off to another secluded niche with his 'niece'?

Niece, indeed! How long had he been seeing her? She looked ten years younger than he, even though Chapin, at thirty-eight, appeared quite youthful and cut a fine figure in his custom-made clothes. Why did he seek out her company? Lord knows I was available at all hours of the day or night, with precious little to occupy my time.

My head began to spin with the implications. Had I

allowed myself to go to seed? Or was my very availability – and social acceptability, as Mrs Proffit – competing with the seductive shine of forbidden fruit? Other ladies referred to their husbands' boredom in the bedroom, but I never dreamed it was my own man's affliction. Chapin had never showed much interest in sex, even when we were first married.

God, you tempt me. How could any man resist your charms?

Dewel's words made me flush all over again as Rémy handed me down from the carriage, at the side entrance to our house – a grand residence on Prytania, in the elite neighbourhood known as the Garden District. The place had belonged to Chapin's parents, Robert E. Lee and Virgilia Proffit, before we married. Dewel had always been forbidden to come here: this declaration was made by Chapin's cheated-on mother when she learned of her husband's illegitimate son, and had been carried into this generation by Chapin himself.

Yet now that I'd had a very personal encounter with the family's black sheep, I saw things differently. He'd raised questions, about Chapin's secrets and personality ... about the nature of the Proffit family's relationships. And about me, as a woman worthy of affection. A female who inspired desire.

Because Dewel saw me in a redder light – and he'd persuaded his brother to court me in the first place – the rake had revealed several new layers of meaning surrounding my marriage.

Mrs Frike, housekeeper for Chapin's parents as well, took my gloves and hat. 'Will you be dining upstairs tonight, missus?'

'Yes, thank you, Fanny,' I replied without thinking.

And then it struck me, how much of my life was so habitual these days – and how much of it didn't include

my husband, because he was seldom home. He'd redec-
orated the house in sweeping shades of maroon and
royal blue to please me when I came here as his bride –
had given me the most spacious suite, with French
doors to the gallery overlooking the gardens in the
back. We entertained lavishly, if seldom; we belonged
to all the right social groups and supported the arts. But
did he think of me – really *see* me – any more than I
thought about him?

I ascended the spiral staircase, aware now of things
that were missing ... things I'd not questioned until
Dewel Proffit's blazing blue eyes forced me to. I passed
Chapin's chambers and for the first time in weeks I
actually looked inside. His cherry furnishings and collection of Impressionist prints remained the same as
when I'd come here, because this suite had belonged to
his beloved mother. Yet I saw his rooms differently
now.

Would I find anything besides his fashionable clothing, if I threw open his armoire? Would his secretary
drawers reveal his secrets? Letters to that young lady,
perhaps?

Anger engulfed me, a betrayal that cut to the bone.
How *dare* that man cheat on me? I was the wife who'd
accommodated his every desire – and now realised he'd
expressed so few of them. How had I provoked his
infidelity? And why did I know that, if challenged,
Chapin would point out *my* shortcomings rather than
his own?

I suddenly wanted to explore his sanctum, to rip his
room apart in search of evidence. But I didn't dare. Far
safer to continue to my own suite, where the pastel
pinks and sunny yellows soothed my soul; where a
brazen male like Dewel Proffit would feel totally out of
place.

Or would he? Just knowing my husband rarely graced these rooms might be motive enough for Dewel to slip up the gallery's outside stairs without anyone being the wiser. But these were foolish thoughts! Chapin's illegitimate half-brother knew not to come here –

All the more reason for him to defy family rules. To rub his brother's nose in it!

I stepped into my elegant bedroom and leaned against the door, as though I could shut out my illicit feelings about the man I'd met today. He was every socially unacceptable thing Chapin was not: gossiped about; nonchalantly libidinous. An entrepreneur known for shady dealings with bankers and brokers – and their wives.

Yet it had been Chapin in that courtyard, sneaking around with a young lover. And it had been Dewel assuring me that my own inadequacies were not to blame – indeed, that I had no feminine shortcomings, as far as he could see. He'd raised my spirits with his attentions, with his audacious suggestion that I, too, needed a niece.

I laughed out loud. A younger 'nephew' – now *that* might set a lonely wife's pulse to pounding. But it would remain a fantasy I'd never live out.

Why not, Mrs Proffit? They say taking a lover brings the bloom back to the lily, and adds a new dimension to one's days: a juicy, delicious secret to savour in moments alone.

Yet it was not a younger man that came to mind as I felt myself growing wet between the legs. Again I saw Dewel's dark face, with that roguish grin and those defiant blue eyes ... the raven hair that beckoned my fingers to run through it. And again I felt his weight pressing me against the iron gate, refusing to back down, or to allow me that opportunity. Dewel was a man who took what he wanted and played by his own rules.

And he smelled good too, like brandy and fine tobacco – and the musk of a male predator sniffing out a mate. My husband preferred expensive French colognes to the earthier scents I associated with his half-brother.

I swallowed hard; felt the vein in my neck fluttering with my unspeakable ideas. Dewel was forbidden fruit, plain and simple. That was his only allure – the fact that I'd been told not to associate with him, much less believe anything he said.

But my heart heard things differently, now that my eyes had seen a new truth. Although *everything* of importance had now come into question, I had to live as though nothing had changed.

Or did I?

The next morning found me writhing beneath Dewel's dark body, arching to receive the erection I'd wanted since the moment I'd felt its presence. I no longer questioned how he had beguiled me: he was giving me the attention I craved but didn't know how to coax from a husband who slept in his own bed, kept his own counsel, and had placed me on a pedestal too high to climb down from.

Was I not a woman who inspired sexual desire? Lord knows I *wanted* Chapin's affection. Yet seven years of disappointment disappeared at the touch of Dewel's bare skin.

'I'm gonna bury my cock deep inside you, sugah,' he breathed against my ear. 'Then I'm gonna pump you nice and slow this time, so I can feel your pussy purrin' ... I'm so long and so hot, I'm gonna have you clawin'' at me for release and then yowlin' like a she-cat when you come. And you *will* come, sweet Eve. Again, and again.'

I moaned at his implicit promise, for never had a man spoken so openly of what he intended to do to me. This was a different sort of arrogance, this cocksureness, for it spurred me into taking what I'd wanted for so long. My husband's occasional fumblings in the dark had fallen short of even my sheltered, virginal expectations. And now I knew why.

'Take me,' I begged, opening my legs like a shameless hussy when my dusky lover positioned himself above me. 'Bury it deep and rub me hard, high up against the bone, where you drove me so insane before. I want you to –'

'Begging your pardon, missus, but you'd best wake up. Someone's here to see you.'

'– pump me until we both convulse with ... dammit, Dewel, was that someone talking to me? Can't they see we're –'

'I tried to tell her you were asleep, but she strutted up here like a house afire and I –'

I awoke so suddenly I sprang upright in my bed, to find a total stranger fixing me with a minxlike gaze. Her hand was on my breast! And then I saw I was totally naked – and exposed! – because I'd kicked the blankets all over the bed. Poor Fanny, the grey-haired housekeeper, hovered behind this unexpected guest, wringing her hands as though I might fire her on the spot. I yanked the sheet over myself and backed the stranger away with my glare before anything else unseemly took place.

'It's all right, Fanny,' I rasped, although nothing was further from the truth. Dewel and I were still humping in my head – or at least the remnants of that fantasy made me wonder if he was somehow responsible for this intrusion. 'I'll handle it from here. Please fix my breakfast now – and enough for our guest as well.'

With a puzzled nod, the housekeeper departed, leaving me alone with a young woman the likes of whom I'd never seen. Her midnight hair was gathered atop her head in wild disarray, with only a white ruffle of a maid's cap to suggest her occupation. Her charcoal dress fell halfway down firm, slender thighs and her side-buttoned boots came to her calves. She wore a pristine white pinafore, yet when she leaned towards me again I detected the bobbing of her loose breasts beneath it – a movement I found unnervingly alluring.

'Who on earth are *you*?' I demanded, grasping my sheet up around my armpits. 'If you've come looking for a position –'

'Oh, the position you were in looked just fine,' she purred, winking suggestively. 'Legs spread so pretty – *ooh-la-la!* with that wreath of red curls around a –'

'I beg your pardon!' I'd never laid eyes on this will-o'-the-wisp of a French maid, yet she was describing me in intimate detail as though she'd been here when –

Oh, my God, I'd not only been dreaming of Dewel, but acting it out as well. Perhaps even talking aloud, so she and Fanny could hear what I'd been demanding him to do. By the look on her face, she'd been ready to join right in.

'No need for pardon, madame. Monique Picabou understands a woman's dreams – her needs. And I'm here to service you.'

Blood rushed to my face, and I couldn't find words to cover my embarrassment any more than my night-gown, crumpled on the floor, could hide my nakedness. 'I – I don't understand. I never sent for –'

'Ah, *oui*. You haven't read Monsieur Proffit's note, because I have it right here.'

She fished a slip of paper from beneath her dress, her grin waxing wicked as she touched herself. 'It says he's sending me here on loan from his own household, because you need a niece. Your wish is Dewel's command – and here I am, madame, just the woman to teach you about seducing that man you married.'

I buried my face against my bent legs. Dewel would be laughing like a hyena, certain this impertinent girl with the lilting voice would catch me unawares – and probably flying high on a fantasy about *him*. How could I have fallen prey to such an egocentric bastard?

Therein lay the key, the fallacy that had led me to this moment of exposing myself not only to my housekeeper, but also to a wild young wanton whose ideas went beyond my comprehension. I was in charge here: the wife of a prominent New Orleans gentleman, ensconced in my fine home on Prytania. No one could make me do anything as outrageous as this wayward female was suggesting.

With that in mind, I composed myself. Not easy, because when I looked up, determined to send her away, Monique was rifling through my closet. She'd thrown open the louvred doors to assess my dresses – feeling the fabrics and checking the cut of the bodices, shaking her disheveled head before flicking each one aside.

Mustering all my tact, and trying to ignore the shimmy of her backside beneath that indecent uniform, I addressed her firmly. 'Contrary to Mr Proffit's high opinion of his abilities, what woman in her right mind would ask such a scandalous man for help with her marriage? He's a known –'

'Right mind? Left mind?' she replied, playfully tapping each side of her head as she grinned at me. 'Both brains fly out the window when Dewel focuses those baby blues on you, *oui*? You might as well play along, Auntie Eve. But he always wins, you know.'

I nipped back a retort. This outrageous young lady would remain loyal to her employer, so I needed another approach. Something to sidetrack her from this talk about my private affairs.

'Who did you say you were again?'

'Monique Picabou, madame. At your service!'

Peekaboo, indeed! She looked far too eager to render services I couldn't even imagine. And since she'd come from Dewel's house, I could guess what sort of servicing went on between those two. I was naive, but not blind.

'So you're French?' I ventured, hoping again for a safer avenue of conversation.

'*Non, non, non*, madame – Cajun,' she replied with snapping brown eyes. 'My family lives in the bayou behind Monsieur Proffit's cane plantation. I suggest we start by getting you new clothes, Auntie Eve. No wonder your Chapin's chasing after a hot young pussy!'

My face must have fallen again at this reference to my personal dilemma, for then Miss Picabou scurried to my bedside, her eyes wide with apology. Even so, I sensed she – like her employer – knew more about my husband's private life than she would ever let on.

'You're a beautiful woman, *cherie*,' she crooned, tilting her head to study me until I thought her disorganised black topknot might topple out of its white ruff. 'Pretty face, and shiny hair that glows like fire in the morning light. Curves in all the right places, while most women your age look like one big lump from shoulders to hips, *non*?'

I was about to protest her remark about my age, for

this careless little wanton was probably only five years younger than my thirty. But she prattled on.

'Some men, they require more *ooh-la-la*, you know? The neckline down to here,' she said, tugging at the top of her uniform, 'and the bosom perched high, up here.'

My jaw dropped when she scooped out her own cleavage to illustrate her point ... with two rosy brown points bobbing on soft mounds of flesh, hanging over the top of her pinafore.

'And the skirts slit up to –'

'I beg your pardon!' I snapped.

Monique paused, her hem hoisted to her hip to reveal a bare thigh bisected by her black garter strap. She studied me with mischievous eyes, yet her flippant air disappeared.

'Never beg, Auntie Eve,' she stated seriously. 'It's bad form to show desperation. And if you beg Dewel, *well* ...'

The maid rolled her eyes with the coquettish charm of a French floozie. 'Dewel never lets you forget what you owe him, for granting your request.'

Another truth I ignored at my own peril. After all, I had begged him to show me the ways of seduction. I was damn lucky it was his maid at my bedside, rather than the rogue himself.

'You understand now, *oui*? So, *ma tante*, if we visit the dressmaker –'

'I am not your aunt, dammit!'

I tossed aside my sheet to confront her, until her crestfallen expression made me realise I'd never been in control of this conversation. What sane woman allowed a total stranger – even if she was a zany, charming, exotic stranger – to instruct her in the ways of winning back her man?

But then, hadn't I asked my scandalous brother-in-law for the same advice? In his inimitably irritating way, Dewel had granted my request, and I must face the consequences of talking before my brain was engaged.

At that moment, I was facing the shapely posterior of his Cajun maid, who'd leaned over to grasp the sides of my padded vanity bench. She backed towards me, her rounded bottom shifting beneath the black straps stretched taut to hold her dark stockings. Her black boots flexed with each step, accented by the subtle tapping of her heels on the floor.

She stopped at my bedside, plopped down to make the white pad wheeze, and then crossed one ankle over the other knee. As she pulled something else from her bosom – a cheroot! – I noticed how firm and smooth her parted thighs looked, with skin resembling velvet.

She wore no drawers.

I averted my gaze, to watch her bite the end from her slender cigar, strike a match across the bottom of her boot, and then light up, with the air of a professor about to give her scholarly opinion of my situation. When she focused those coffee-coloured eyes on me, I was rendered speechless by this striking young woman and her array of contrasts, now wreathed by a ring of smoke.

'Madame,' she intoned, her cheroot resting demurely in the fork of her fingers, 'I've been sent here on a mission, a rescue mission, by Monsieur Proffit himself. It's a duty I take most seriously. No matter what you may think about Monique Picabou and her Cajun ways, she has your best interests at heart. I know things you cannot understand at this moment, but I'll prepare your heart and your soul to change, so your body can follow.'

I nodded, for what else could I do? Dewel had been playing puppeteer ever since I'd given him permission to take me over. I dared not doubt his maid's intent – nor his – and this thought made me quiver with a curiosity that burned in my cheeks and my chest … and in that place between my legs that hadn't gotten nearly enough attention these past seven years.

My gaze wandered beneath Monique's brief black skirt. 'Where's your underwear?' I challenged, realising how matronly and disapproving I sounded.

'I don't own any.' Her lips twitched with a smile. 'I like the feeling of freedom, and I like to defy society. But mostly I enjoy knowing that Dewel, and my beau, Tommy Jon, think about me being naked down there. They consider the possibilities constantly – for that's what men are all about, Auntie Eve.'

Another draw on her cigar, another puff of smoke, and Monique became a seductress extraordinaire. Her legs fell languidly apart to display a neatly trimmed black bush with a pink nub protruding from it. I could smell her sex, so intriguing, with a riper pungency than mine.

I swallowed hard. Never had I seen another woman's private parts, much less my own.

And why not? my thoughts suddenly demanded.

'Time for our first lesson, *oui*?' she asked, stroking my sleep-mussed hair from my forehead. 'My new Auntie Eve has much to learn, and she'll make me a fine pupil. Your wild, erotic dreams of Dewel are only the beginning, *cherie*.'

3 An Inquisition, and My Christening

As we went downstairs to breakfast, the aromas of fried ham, Andouille sausages and sticky pecan buns sent my mind into a tailspin. Why was I allowing myself to be cajoled this way? And how would I explain Miss Picabou to Fanny, a housekeeper who was the soul of propriety? I was ravenous for the morning spread this motherly woman always prepared, yet deep down, somewhat below my growling stomach, a forbidden hunger demanded to be fed as well.

Dangerous, this illicit dare I'd taken. Monique smiled demurely, keeping pace as I rounded the outside spiral of the staircase – until, with a girlish giggle, she hefted one hip on to the mahogany balustrade and deftly slid the rest of the way down. With a neat little hop, she hit the vestibule floor and then grinned up at me.

'Smile, *cherie*, look happy,' she entreated, her olive complexion alight with her smile. 'Today you become as free as Monique!'

An alluring thought; an idea that inspired my envy, for when was the last time I'd had *fun*? When had I last indulged in doing as I pleased, the devil – and high society – be damned?

I hooked my arm through hers, and together we marched down the short hallway to the dining room. I felt ready to burst into some rollicking song, for the sheer joy of it –

But there sat Chapin.

He glanced up from his breakfast, regarded my top-knotted companion with a raised eyebrow, and then rose from his chair. Always the proper gentleman, my husband. 'And whom do I have the pleasure of meeting?' he prompted in a tight voice.

I quickly unlinked our elbows. Why did I feel like a child who'd been caught at something naughty? 'May I present Monique, my – my new lady's maid – since you've told me so many times I should hire more staff,' I added in a rush.

Then I turned to the woman beside me, who stood with her hands clasped before her. Her prim smile camouflaged what she knew about my husband and his extramarital activities. 'Monique, this is my husband, Mr Chapin Proffit. Although I've taken you on as my personal assistant, you will, of course, be responsible for any tasks he assigns you as well.'

'Of course,' she echoed, with only the slightest hint of derision. Her curtsy appeared extremely graceful, considering how the tops of her gartered stockings showed when she lifted her skirt. 'It is an honour to work in your home, for your lovely wife. I will give her excellent care, monsieur.'

With a quick, efficient nod Monique then disappeared through the kitchen door – the proper move on her part, to carry out the role I'd assigned her on a moment's notice.

But it left me alone with a man who now inspired questions that squelched my appetite. How could I sit here as though I'd seen nothing yesterday, with a man who didn't usually eat breakfast? Was I to interpret this odd behaviour as his atonement? A way to spend more time with his neglected wife?

Chapin was not the only one going round the proverbial mulberry bush – or whatever he called it, on his 'niece'. I, too, had to dance around his covert courtyard activities, acting as though I hadn't seen his wild abandon as he approached her from behind . . . that grimace of ecstasy as they muffled their cries of delight.

He pulled out the chair beside his, going through the perfectly proper motions, as he studied me with unaccustomed candour. When I perched on the edge of the seat, however, he scooted me forward until my midsection pressed the table – an unusually aggressive move. 'What were you doing with Dewel yesterday?'

My heart stopped and I nearly choked. 'I'd been to Madame LaRue's for a fitting,' I squeaked. 'He happened along and, as a gentleman, he escorted me to the carriage so I wouldn't walk alone –'

'A gentleman does not swat his brother's wife on the butt!' Chapin snapped, his hands still gripping my chair. 'That bastard's up to something. Now what is it?'

Had my husband always had a cruel streak, or was I just now seeing this side of him? After a few uncomfortable moments, and my protesting gasp from being pressed so hard against the table, he released me and reseated himself. Chapin Proffit was the picture of Southern gentility in his crisp suit of ivory linen, with a white shirt and pale yellow cravat, and his golden, collar-length hair flowing back over his ears. He was his mama's fair-haired boy in every sense of the word – but Virgilia died before his father, so she'd had no control over how the family properties were divided.

This bone had always stuck in my husband's craw, and he was picking at it again. His pale blue eyes pierced mine, demanding an answer. His fingers drummed the table beside his plate, making his crested signet ring glisten in the light from the crystal chandelier.

I took a few terse moments to lay my napkin across my lap. 'You misinterpret what you saw, Chapin,' I hedged, my voice deceptively low and calm. 'When my shoe wobbled on the carriage carpeting, he reached up to keep me from falling backwards. You would do the same for a lady in a similar circumstance.'

I held his chilly gaze, and then turned my attention to the platters of food that no longer enticed me. After all, what did *I* have to explain, after what I'd seen *him* engaged in? As I chose a sausage and a bun that spiralled around its sweet pecan filling, he let out a dissatisfied sigh.

'And where did you procure Monique? She's decidedly crude and unsuitable.'

I should've pricked him with my fork, to deflate that puffed-up tone of his! But I caught myself: what did he know, really? What had he seen, both with Dewel and when I entered this room arm-in-arm with Monique? I couldn't create any connections between his half-brother and my new maid, so I summoned up a province over which he had little control.

'Madame LaRue recommended her,' I fibbed, pointedly filling my mouth with food so I wouldn't have to answer him further.

'And you asked for no references?'

Damn this man, had he always been so difficult? *Years* I'd managed his household, and he'd never been so picky! I continued to chew, slowly and methodically, while looking him straight in the face. I was thinking up a logical reply, of course, and having a hard time of it.

'I've had no occasion to question my dressmaker's taste,' I replied. 'Why are you so testy this morning, Chapin? Did you not sleep well? Or is there something you need to tell me? Some crisis in the family finances, perhaps?'

He wouldn't reveal what he'd been spending, nor with whom, but my question had the desired effect: he became so interested in his meal, all I heard for the next several moments were the delicate clatterings of our fork tines on the bone china plates – a civilised sound that echoed in this cavernous chamber with its long, polished table and gilt-framed mirrors.

Guilt-framed, to be sure, I mused as I forced down food I wasn't hungry for. But I refused to cave in. I'd had my share of illicit fantasies and unexpected adventures in the past twenty-four hours, but they were *nothing* compared to what I'd caught Chapin at.

I'd have to be careful, though. Being too smug about my new-found knowledge would cost me if I forgot these little lies I'd been weaving. Like a spider's delicate web, they'd collapse if I made a wrong move or gave conflicting details.

Finally he rose from the table and, as an afterthought, he clasped my hand. 'Our finances are fine, Evie – never stronger, as demand for cotton increases on the market. Not that you ever need worry your pretty head about such matters,' he added with a protective smile. 'And I'm pleased you've taken my advice about increasing the household staff, for it seems I've been placed in the running to become the next mayor of New Orleans.'

What wife wouldn't feel excited about such a surprise? 'Well, congratulations, Chapin!' I said, as pleased about this new topic of conversation as I was not to be the centre of it.

'Thank you, Evie. I'm rather tickled myself.' His smile lit up his entire face, making him one of the most beautiful men I'd ever seen. 'It behoves us to engage the rest of our new staff from a reputable clearing house. We'll be hosting parties for the city's most prominent political forces, and I can't abide any social blunders, or suspicions about stealing the family silver – or, God forbid, any jewellery belonging to our guests. I'm sure you'll do your best, Miss Eve.'

'Yes, of course I will,' I murmured, accepting his peck on the cheek with a tight smile.

He strode to the dining room doorway, and then fixed me with a gaze that camouflaged his former animosity. 'Please accept my apologies for that unpleasantness about Dewel. I suppose being placed in such a public fishbowl has made me very aware of whom you and I are seen swimming with, my dear. He may be my half-brother, but I'll tolerate no more of playing second fiddle in this family. Nor will I allow him to wreak havoc on my campaign, just for the fiendish joy he'd get from it.'

'I can certainly understand that,' I said with an emphatic nod.

'I knew you'd see it my way. Have a fine day, dear wife.'

'And you as well.'

The quiet clatter of his custom-made boots bade me a genteel farewell as he crossed the vestibule. I exhaled the breath I'd been holding, with a touch of mockery.

'Crude and unsuitable, am I?' came a lilting whisper behind me. 'Well then, we'll procure the master a household staff from only the *finest* school for domestics, Auntie Eve! Or shall we call you ... Auntie Evil?'

I turned to protest and correct her, yet I began giggling. Monique stood with her fists planted in her hips and her bared breasts shoved above her pinafore's placket again, making them jiggle lewdly. With a cheroot between her teeth and that riot of raven hair tumbling loose on one side, my new maid was the image of impropriety – and other things I didn't even know how to think about.

She responded to my shaking head with an unladylike snort. 'What's sauce for the goose is good on the gander, *oui*?'

I couldn't argue with that. Monique obviously had some unique form of retribution in mind, and it would be a tasty change to watch Chapin simmer in this pot he'd set to boiling.

less contemplate such activity with another woman – and in a room where my seamstress might walk in at any moment!

'I don't think –'

'That's right – don't think!' Monique released me, pivoting to fetch the bolt of fabric. Knowing the effect she was having on the body of a woman who swam far out of her depth and feared drowning in this sea of new-found sensuality. 'This lace, it'll give you a whole new perspective on clothes. After today, you might never wear anything else, Aunt Evil.'

With deft motions, Monique unwound a long length of the soft, raven lace, making it shift and whisper in the little room. Smiling, looking so decidedly French, she then pulled it tight over my breasts, walked around me to catch the starting edge, and then tossed the final length of it over my shoulder.

'*Voila!* A dress fit for a naughty queen – or a mayor's wife on the make,' she added with a chuckle. 'Attend a party dressed in this – nothing more! – and you'll be the belle of the ball, madame.'

I glanced in the full-length mirror and sucked in my breath. My bare shoulders glowed with excitement above the filmy black wrapping of lace, which flowed to the floor yet left my nakedness clearly visible beneath the swirling pattern of roses and ivy.

Before I guessed what she was about, Monique came up behind me and plucked the pins from my hair, sending it in an unruly auburn cascade past my shoulders. Then she turned her own hair loose, casting aside the white wisp of a cap by tossing her head, to stand before me with the most brazen expression I'd ever seen.

'It's all in the details, *oui*?' she murmured. She shifted the lace at my shoulder so it draped more dramatically, and arranged the main layer so clusters of roses stretched strategically over my aching nipples. 'A simple clasp at the shoulder, to hold it in place, and you are covered, *cherie*. Yet so very, very revealed.'

'I couldn't possibly wear this in front of guests!'

'*Non?* Then add little black panties – they're all the rage. Or a garter belt like mine.'

'But they'll show through the –'

'But of course!' she cried with an exasperated wave of her hands. 'And if that husband of yours doesn't take you under the nearest table immediately, he *will* when he thinks someone else will beat him to it. Competition is a good thing, *non?*'

My head was spinning with the airlessness of the room and the brazen way this young lady talked. Again she adjusted the cowl of black fabric that draped over my shoulder, with the look of a Parisian artiste – except then her palms slithered lightly down to brush my breasts, lingering there as she looked me in the eye. Monique's face was mere inches from mine, her rouged lips parted and her dark eyes wide. She was the rudest, most abrupt, unpredictable person I'd ever encountered.

And I was quivering. Holding my breath as I wondered ... feared ... anticipated what she might try next. One of her hands slithered down the lace along my waist, past my hip towards my inner thigh. And then she *slapped* it.

'Foot on the chair!' she commanded, and at once my body obeyed.

'Now look at the effect. The dress parts at the edge, allowing a view of shoe, and then stocking, and then ... bare thigh the colour of sweet cream, draped in black see-through roses, madame. I swear to you, I've never seen a more provocative sight.'

She was studying my reflection in the mirror as

avidly as I, yet her eyes lingered at the top of my thigh, where a hint of auburn peeked through. As though in a trance, she knelt before me and slowly pushed aside the filmy curtain of lace with a single finger, so close her breathing warmed the place between my legs. As though entranced by this maid's magic, my folds tingled and parted and my foot slipped forward on the chair. Liquid dribbled down my leg, and I thought I'd wet myself with this uncontrollable excitement.

Never had I been so open, or so intimately studied, for Chapin had never ventured down this path. And never had I felt so – evil, indeed! – deliciously wicked, despite the fear making my pulse pound below my belly. I drew in my breath, watching in the mirror as Monique moved closer.

At the first sign of her pointed pink tongue, I almost bolted. Monique clamped her hands around my inner thighs, and with a low moan she moved in. Her face, from that angle, looked positively alive with lust – something I'd never dreamed of inspiring, or accepting, from another woman. Yet I'd heard about this sort of kiss, and wondered . . .

The touch of her tongue made me gasp and, for want of a way to brace myself, I clasped the sides of her head. My fingers wove into her warm hair, feeling the pulse above her ears pounding as rapidly as my own, while Monique eased upward. She lapped as delicately as a cat, closing her eyes so those long lashes shivered at the tops of her cheeks, as though she'd never sampled such ambrosia.

I wanted to close my eyes and scream with the sensations coursing through me, but I didn't dare bring Madame LaRue running in – nor did I want to miss that marvel taking place beneath my springy mass of curls. In the mirror, I watched her dark head bob between my spread legs, saw her lips parting mine for intimate kisses like I'd never dared imagine.

'Open yourself, *cherie*,' she whispered. 'Let Monique catch every drop and show you how it feels to shatter from the inside out.'

I flexed, and the spasms of desire shot like lightning through me. Was all that moisture coming from her tongue, or my . . . sex? The wet, rhythmic licking sounds filled the little room, kicking up a salty scent I found extremely heady. My hips were rocking forward to meet her advances, making the black lace tickle my thighs. Those same hot longings Dewel had inspired at the courtyard gate were cresting as she followed the edges of my folds and then ran her tongue hard up the centre, pushing my mound higher with her fingertips to open me even further.

My God, I felt lewd, yet I was beyond stopping. A panting sound surrounded us and, when I glanced at the mirror again, I realised it was me. Humping and breathing so hard, chasing after an elusive rainbow of pleasure I couldn't yet define –

And then she thrust her tongue inside me.

I lurched, and my grimace was that of Chapin's blonde as she neared completion. 'No,' I rasped. 'No more! I can't take any –'

Faster she licked, high against that hot little button where every nerve burned. I swore I smelled smoke. I tried to pull away, but Monique grabbed my backside, kneading with strong fingers that cut into my flesh like the iron bars of that gate – driving her tongue upward and so furiously, we were both quaking.

'Monique, please!' I panted, grasping for that last straw of sanity even as I realised an uncontrollable madness ruled me. I felt ready to soar, and when her fingers slipped beneath the lace to pinch a nipple, my insides lurched as though I'd fallen from a cliff.

As I convulsed, she stood to kiss me, stifling my scream. I clenched my eyes shut. My jaw dropped with the extreme need to cry out, made more intense by the wet, slippery lips that covered mine as she thrust her fingers into me. My body shuddered as though someone had shot me through with a lightning bolt – going far beyond the shocking sensations I'd allowed myself when Dewel pressed me against that gate. The current grabbed me and *shook*, until I collapsed into the chair like a wet rag.

My maid fell forward against its upholstered arms, her hair flying wildly around us as she caught herself. She wiped her mouth against the back of her hand with a glutton's gusto, and then she giggled. 'Your first time, *oui, ma tante*?'

I blinked, struggling to regain rational thought. 'Why, of course not! Chapin –'

'You can't fool Monique,' she said in a voice that brooked no argument. Then she lowered herself to straddle my lap, wrapping her arms about my waist. 'Men are too caught up in their own frenzy to make us come that way, and Chapin's no different. But now you know how it's supposed to feel. How did you like that fine climax?'

For a moment I could only rest with my arms around this minx, wondering whether I should be more upset by her impertinence, or by the sad fact that she was right.

I was thirty years old and had just felt my first orgasm.

And I'd had it with a woman.

And the wetness around her pert nose and lush,

parted lips made it clear I'd gushed all over her because I'd ... lost control of myself.

I swallowed hard, pondering this. There was no comparison to Chapin's fumblings in the dark, which at first had ended with his stickiness all over my thighs. Then, as the years went by, our encounters became fewer and further between.

But then, I'd assigned Monique the small bedroom between my husband's suite and mine. She already knew about my love life.

What she couldn't understand was the aching in my heart, as I recalled the lust that had driven those lovers in the courtyard yesterday ... the surging, yearning, all-consuming need that overtook them, with an intensity my handsome husband had never shown for me.

'Yes, it was my first climax,' I finally sighed. Not knowing what else to do, I stroked her hair back from her face. 'It's been an enlightening day, Monique. I never anticipated –'

'Ah, but that's the best part.' Her cheeks coloured prettily. 'We get too serious about the loving and forget that fucking should just be fun! Get dressed, *ma tante*, and we'll see what your seamstress has put together for us. We'll take it home, so Monique can design a new wardrobe – your secret weapon, to ambush Monsieur Proffit and his cock, *oui*?'

I smiled, hoping she was right.

'Then I'll get you those servants, like he insisted.' My maid stood up to rub the wrinkles from her short black skirt and pinafore. When she saw the wild disarray of her hair in the mirror, she laughed, gathered it on to an untidy topknot and wrapped the frilly white maid's cap around it again.

'It's best to give a man what he demands – what he thinks he wants,' she continued as she helped me up from the chair. 'But together, you and I – Evie and Monique – we'll take Chapin for a ride that'll leave his head spinning! He'll have much more to answer to than he bargained for, when we're through with him.'

Even in her zany Cajun sing-song, her words sounded more like a threat than a promise. Once again, I sensed things might spin out of control. 'Perhaps I should interview candidates Madame LaRue recommends –'

'You've heard of the School of Domestic Endeavor, *oui*? Run by Honore Delacroix?'

I looked up from folding the length of black lace, to gauge her expression. 'Of course! They have an impeccable reputation for training well-disciplined domestics, suited to the choosiest of families. Or so I hear.'

Monique bowed, and then retrieved my corset from the floor. 'Training and discipline,' she echoed emphatically. 'Only the best for my Aunt Evil and the man she loves. Leave it all to me, *cherie*.'

I bit back a protest and then turned, so she could lace my corset. I was fooling myself if I thought I had any control over this game, or would ever know all the rules.

Then I smiled, for nothing had changed, really. Hadn't women been living this precariously all along, with every man they ever met?

5 A Picabou Party

'The nerve of that woman! Can you believe she charges a fee for her maids?'

I raised up on my elbows, still groggy from sleep, to watch Monique bustling about my room in the dimness of early morning. 'Miss Delacroix? Why, of course she does,' I remarked with a long yawn. 'How do you think she makes her money?'

'But without a trial period, we won't know they're suitable – *non*? I wasn't even allowed to assess the trainees,' she said, wildly waving her cheroot. 'Something about Miss Delacroix having to be there for the interview, *after* I pay the fee!'

Had I not been tired from lack of sleep – from fiddling with my slit whenever my thoughts drifted to Dewel, or this young woman's wonderful tongue – I would've laughed. My maid was flapping about the room like a bird searching for an open window, frantically parting the drapes to yank up the sashes.

'So we'll go today, and I'll pay the fee, Monique,' I said pointedly. 'It's standard procedure. Just as it's customary to inform your employer if you won't be reporting for work. Where have you been these past two days?'

The young woman caught herself before flinging a flippant remark my way. With a fist at her waist, holding her little cigar, she resembled a teapot with steam coming out its spout. 'Dewel needed me. Mama needed me. And Tommy Jon, he needed me most of all.'

'Tommy Jon?'

'My beau. He's got a cock so big it won't all fit inside –'

Mrs Frike's shocked expression as she stopped in the doorway halted our conversation. 'You'll be wanting breakfast downstairs this morning, missus?' she asked, her forehead puckered with disapproval. 'Shall I set for the two of you?'

'Yes, please, Fanny. Is Mr Proffit not in then?'

'Left for the Exchange an hour ago, ma'am.'

I had my ideas about what sort of exchange would take place at dawn. 'Thank you, Fanny. That will be all until we come down for our meal.'

Her stiff little bow bespoke rheumatic knees and a distinct dislike for my new maid. After years of service in this household, Fanny Frike knew her place, and knew how to keep others in theirs, so it would be interesting to see how Monique fared over the next several days.

I set these thoughts aside to raise an eyebrow at the raven-haired beauty beside my bed. Her hair stuck out in two long, bobbing pigtails, which, with her lacy white pinafore, made her look like an overgrown child. 'You were saying?'

Monique's grin lit up with a giddy sense of conspiracy. 'Ah, *oui*, Tommy Jon Beaumont. Now *there's* a man you must meet, Auntie Evil. And he wants to meet you, after I told him about licking you in the dressing room at –'

'You told him *what*?' I threw aside my covers to confront her. 'I have my limits, Miss Picabou, and you have just pushed beyond them!'

'Ah, *oui*, I pushed, madame!' she gushed. 'T-Jon, he stood behind me to pump me with his dick – and he held on to my hair like . . .' She grabbed her pigtails and

43

threw her head back, as her hips arched backwards to imitate her recent activities.

It was all I could do to keep a straight face, but this little wanton had to understand what sort of behaviour – not to mention discretion! – I expected of her. 'Stop it! You owe me an apology, Miss Picabou, and I cannot tolerate such lewd carryings-on. What if Chapin were in your room, with his ear to this wall?'

Monique's face fell like a bumped soufflé, but then she belligerently sucked on her cigar. 'Maybe he'd learn something,' she retorted. 'I'm sorry my Auntie Evil doesn't appreciate me this morning. But she must understand that I –'

'It's not that I don't appreciate you, Monique, but –'

'Then you'll come tonight? To meet T-Jon at the Picabou party?' Her dusky face brightened. 'We'll have music – a Cajun band! – and food like you have never eaten before.'

Such an invitation was the last thing I'd expected, after her initial tirade about Miss Delacroix. 'I don't think –'

'*Oui, cherie*. No thinking – and no telling Chapin! Just let Monique show you a good time.'

'I'm not sure I'd fit in with –'

'It's the next lesson,' Monique insisted, grasping the low, ruffled neckline of my peignoir. 'Tommy Jon, he wants to show you his special talent. He'll make sure everything . . . *fits in*!'

I paused, speechless, as those cow-brown eyes riveted mine and then gazed pointedly at the dual peaks beneath my nightgown. 'And what does Tommy Jon do?'

'Makes the finest boots – and toys – Auntie Eve has ever seen.'

'Ah. Yes.' What else could I say? This maid refused to

44

be refused, and would somehow always have the last word, wouldn't she? After all, she'd just coaxed my breasts to attention and could probably guess, by the scent, what I'd been playing with during the night.

'Ah, *oui*, indeed,' she whispered, and with a giggle she kissed my cheek. 'Now get that pretty ass out of this bed. I'm ravenous!'

Disappointment tingled between my legs as she flitted towards the door. I had hoped she might be hungry for –

And then she turned, flashing me a brilliant grin. 'Was the house too quiet while I was gone, Auntie? Did you miss your sweet Monique?'

A week ago I would've fainted dead away – or ordered her out of my house – for such a presumptuous remark. But I couldn't lie, for it was much more than that licking I'd thought about during my long hours in this huge house, with just Fanny for company. I sensed my life was about to have the rug yanked out from under it. A dusty, faded rug that *needed* a good shaking.

So I gave her the smile that had been in hiding ever since her abrupt arrival. 'I did miss you, my dear. More than I can say.'

That night, as Monique led me by the hand towards the bayou, I felt more joy than I'd known in years. The stars came out to play, while the cicadas sang their lazy songs as the twilight fell around us like a veil, lush with promise. We had parked at the back of the plantation house and, as lights came on in Dewel's downstairs windows, I wondered who lit his lamps ... whether he was even at home on this fine night. Surely such a lusty man wouldn't spend an evening alone – and wouldn't have to, for any woman would gladly have him.

Pick me! ran through my mind, and I shoved that

wayward thought aside. I was a married woman, merely out to meet my new maid's family – checking her background, I could call it, if Chapin asked. As luck would have it, he'd gone to a dinner meeting of political backers and wouldn't be home until late.

Or so he said.

Monique's laughter lifted me out of my suspicions. The heavy scents of water and thick vegetation told me we were nearing the bayou: swamp, some would call it. For the Cajuns who'd made it their home for generations, however, it was a world unto itself. A world with its own wildlife, its own rules – and its own secrets. As my maid helped me into a pirogue and then began to paddle, I entered another time and place; a setting normally unexplored by society types.

Monique rowed the slender boat expertly between cyprus stumps; beneath live oaks, where Spanish moss hung from the branches like mysterious moonlit shawls. Night birds called around us, their cries echoing in the canopy of trees. Otherwise, there was only the lapping of the water against our boat, and the fluid movements of Monique's tight body beneath her flowing peasant-style skirt and blouse.

'You feel happy, *non*? It's perfect for you, that pretty dress. Like a gypsy's.'

I grinned, hugging my knees. 'I feel loose and – well, lewd.'

'Ah, *oui*. The freedom of leaving the corset in the drawer.' Monique's eyes followed the slope of my bared shoulders along the opening of my loosely gathered blouse. 'Tommy Jon, he's going to eat you up, *cherie*. I may have to sneak him into the trees to get my share tonight.'

My face flushed with pleasure. From a distance came the twanging of a guitar and the sawing sing-song of a fiddle being tuned, and the spicy aromas of a Cajun buffet. Something inside me stirred, for tonight I wouldn't be concerned about appearances, or saying the proper things to the proper people on my husband's behalf. Tonight was just for me. To enjoy. To explore. To discover!

We pulled up to the shoreline near a cabin on stilts, a simple structure with a sloped roof and a gallery porch. Monique had no more than set foot on land when a swarm of children rushed out to greet her.

'Etienne! Marie-Claire! Et toi, ma jolie Ginette!' Her voice rang out over their French chatter. 'Miss Eve has come to dance and sing with us tonight. Make her welcome, mes petits.'

Those three grinned at me – with that same openly curious gaze I'd first seen on Monique's face – while more children rushed around the corner of the cabin. 'Your nieces and nephews?' I asked, squeezing the hands that reached for mine.

'Oui, quite a flock of them. My brothers, they love their wives!' She grabbed my hand, and we proceeded towards flatter ground, where long tables were covered with fragrant pots of food.

'Maman! Everyone!' she called out, 'Miss Eve has joined us tonight. Make her welcome. Make her happy!'

And how could I not be happy, among such smiling faces? Groups had already gathered around a bonfire and a barrel of beer, while others poured from pitchers of wine with slices of lemon and orange afloat in them. They looked up from their heaped plates, their joy contagious as they motioned me to the tables.

I followed Monique to the serving line, listening intently as she spooned food on to her plate. 'Crawfish étouffe ... jambalaya ... Maman's special recipe for red beans with rice ... mashed yams ...'gator pie –'

47

'What?' I dropped the serving spoon as though a long set of toothy jaws had emerged from the bowl.

Monique laughed, plopping a generous spoonful of the pie beside my dirty rice. 'The 'gators that come ashore to check our chickens don't make it back for seconds, if my nephews catch them at it. Eat or be eaten, *ma tante*. Or both, if you're lucky.'

Her eyes caught mine in a playful gaze, and I glanced around to see if anyone was watching us. The last thing I needed was to be involved in such word play – or the sex play it might lead to – among total strangers. I doubted it would get back to my husband, but still ...

My maid let her plate land on the table, to throw her arms around a man who'd apparently been waiting for her. He caught her up in an exuberant hug and then kissed her firmly, moving his mouth over hers with low moans that made my insides tighten. Standing there behind Monique, I could see every flutter of his closed eyes, every possessive shift of his lips as his hands splayed across her bottom. I didn't know whether to turn away or to take notes on the most intimate, full-body kiss I'd ever beheld.

When he finally let her slide down to the ground again, I was met with a gaze that made me wonder if I were next. 'I didn't mean to stare at –'

'Yes, you did.' His voice was as sultry as a Louisiana midnight. 'You loved every minute of it. You were wishing Tommy Jon Beaumont would do *you* that way!'

'All in good time, *non*?' Monique laughed. 'At least give Miss Eve a chance to eat before you stalk her like the wolf you are.'

'Wolf' did not half describe the lean, male face and the feral intent in dark eyes that penetrated my defences. I didn't think wolves roamed this far south, but Tommy Jon's gaze was changing all my previous, naive beliefs. It was a predatory hunger heating up his features, from the set of his square, shadowed jaw to the subtle shifting of lean hips in black pants a size too tight. That cock Monique had mentioned formed a blatant ridge along his fly, and I swore it throbbed as I tried not to watch it.

'All right, I'll give you ladies time to prepare yourselves,' he said with a quirk of his thin lips. Dimples danced alongside his mouth, making him appear even more audacious as he ran his fingertip along the side of my face.

I sucked air, mesmerised – although his bravado was for show, for Monique was clearly his lady of choice. And after another sensual kiss for her, he joined a group of men gathering on the cabin's gallery with their instruments.

We sat beside Monique's mama, a sturdy woman with features her daughter would inherit over time, and sisters-in-law who chattered amiably in their rolling Cajun dialect. I took one bite of the fragrant food and attacked my meal as though I hadn't eaten in weeks. So many spices and textures. Such a contrast to the formal fare Mrs Frike served up. I was soon doing the unspeakable by dragging a crust of bread through the last spicy drops of that alligator concoction, eating with the wild abandon of my companions.

The band began to play then, with an older, nearly toothless fellow strumming a battered guitar while his friend chimed in on a fiddle. It moaned at first, and then got caught up in some catchy syncopated rhythms, duelling with the guitar. Then Tommy Jon picked up a concertina.

'A squeezebox is the perfect instrument for my beau, *non*?' Monique quipped. 'In and out, in and out! He'll make that thing wheeze like a bitch in heat.'

Another man stepped up then, and when he began to sing, I sat in awe. He wailed in a high, clear tenor like a human siren, in a catchy cadence only a Cajun could master. The crowd clapped in time, nodding and singing along, letting his voice soar above theirs.

I took a long draw on my wine punch and felt it tingle all the way down, felt the happy music swelling inside me until I laughed out loud and joined in the back-beat clapping. It was contagious, this harmony – this happiness borne of simple times and simpler means. I envied the love these Picabous shared, and decided to enjoy it while this magic moment lasted.

As the moonlight spilled through the treetops, some of them jumped up to dance. The song now was a driven, spinning thing, where the men whirled their women so quickly it made me dizzy to watch them. Monique grabbed my hand.

'But I don't know how to –'

'What's to know?' she called out above the music. 'Let your body go, *cherie*. Here on the bayou, there is only the laughter and the song – the wine and the food.'

She spun me around and let go, aiming me towards a young man who released his partner and caught me. The clearing was filled with couples and small groups of children, who danced in a ring, all of us riding high on a wave of sheer delight. Hand to hand I was passed along, sometimes grabbed around the waist and sometimes I twirled like a top in a clutch of women.

More wine … more of that Cajun whine – lyrics I didn't need to understand to love – and more of Tommy Jon's suggestive squeezebox ringing out with the fiddle and guitar. Two of the older women took the children's hands to lead them in a line that snaked towards the house. Bedtime, but how were they to sleep? The musicians paused to swill their beers, but showed no sign of letting up.

And then the dancers began to peel off shirts wet with sweat and the colourful dresses that swirled above the ladies' knees. I caught my breath, to be sure the wine punch wasn't affecting my eyes. They were taking off their clothes! Along the edge of the trees, pants and skirts and underthings piled up, and then the dancers filled the clearing again, answering the siren cry of the singer and the fiddle that vied for second place.

Thank goodness they got so caught up in their dancing they didn't press me to disrobe as well. It was one thing to show myself to Monique, but another thing entirely to cavort in the all-together among total strangers. I watched their glistening, moonlit bodies, trying not to stare at bobbing breasts and jiggling hips and coarse, dark hair curling around sex lips or emerging erections.

'See anything you like, sugah?'

I jumped when someone squeezed my shoulders, as that voice registered in my mind. 'Dewel! You scared me half to –'

'There'll be nothin' halfway about it, once I get you warmed up.'

He turned me in his arms. His face was shadowed by the trees, but those eyes ... sparks danced in them like the bonfire's flames, which sent heat surging through me. 'You look so free and easy in those clothes, Miss Eve. Even if you are overdressed.'

'You're fully clothed yourself, Mr Proffit,' I replied, grasping at any straw to remain sane. His hands followed the tops of my shoulders, as though he might tug my blouse down over my breasts. 'Do you always wait for this crowd to get carried away before you appear? Afraid the plantation master might dampen the night's activities?'

'I was dancin' with these people before I was born,' he replied, lowering his face so I could see every flicker of his lips by the firelight. 'It didn't matter that Mama carried me out of wedlock, nor did they think less of Daddy for it. Even if I hadn't inherited Bayou Belle, I'd be welcome here.'

I lowered my eyes, feeling stupid. 'I stand corrected.'

'Stand closer instead.'

Dewel's hand found my hip, pressing me against a body hot with animal desire. His mouth covered mine, driving away my protest, for I'd longed to feel this moment – this man – again, in something other than my dreams.

I leaned into him, letting him fill me with his longing. His moan resonated in my throat and the kiss deepened, becoming more carnal. It was the wine, I told myself, for my rogue brother-in-law had nothing but trouble to give me, and I'd had enough of that. His lips burned into mine, parting them for a tongue thrust so disorienting I had to grab him to keep my balance.

Dewel released my mouth with a savage sigh, running his lips down my neck to burrow into the top of my blouse. Did I let him claim my breast, or did it offer itself up? When his teeth teased my nipple, I came back to my senses.

'Dewel – we mustn't! I can't give Chapin any more fuel for the ... He *saw* us the other day!'

He released my breast to look me in the eye. 'Saw us what? Spyin' on him?'

'*You*, swatting me on the bottom. He must've come around the corner at just the wrong moment.' My body throbbed, recalling my guilt. Or was it something else at work here – perhaps the ridge Dewel was rubbing against my front?

'And what did we see *him* doin', sugah?' he drawled. His dark hair fell forward, casting a rakish shadow over a face alight with wicked intent. 'You've done nothin' wrong, Miss Eve. You're still a wife faithful to her vows, and I'll respect that – until you tell me not to.'

It sounded like a foregone conclusion; only a matter of propriety cast to the wind. I clung to his muscled arms, shaking. I had nowhere to go, nor did I have the inclination to escape.

Behind us, the music shifted into a mellower waltz, where the singer let the instruments woo us. Tommy Jon was stepping off the porch, too. He took the out-stretched hand of his naked lover and they slipped into the trees.

Dewel chuckled. 'Ah, young love. Bodies rushin'` to fulfil their needs, only to create more. I want to dance with you, Eve, but you'll have to be naked. Only skin-to-skin will do on a night like this.'

He unbuttoned his shirt with efficient flicks of his fingers, never letting his gaze leave mine. White silk gave way to skin, dark and smooth in its mystery, more tantalising for the swirl of black hair on his muscular chest. His trousers drifted past his hips and by the time I realised he wore nothing under them, he'd stepped out of his boots too. Naked and unashamed – no, downright brazen – Dewel stood before me, ruler of all he surveyed.

And he'd never stopped looking at *me*.

He untied the ribbon in my peasant blouse, which he gently shoved past my shoulders. I didn't try to stop him, for every thrum of my pulse told me it would do no good – and that I wanted what he was doing to me. I watched, spellbound, as the rest of my clothes drifted down my bared body into a puddle on the ground. When a couple dancing past us paused so the man could hoist his pretty partner, impaling her on his erection, Dewel grinned. His ravenous kiss left no doubt about what he intended to accomplish tonight.

Then he moved us into the graceful sweep of that Cajun waltz. His steps were confident, accommodating my shorter strides and leaving me in no doubt about how to follow his lead. Few men were so easy to dance with the first time, and I found myself stepping closer, revelling in the heat of our bare bodies as we moved among the others yet remained in our own alluring little world. His skin ignited mine. He smelled like wine and desire, and a light sweat that intensified his musk.

Yes, he was rock-hard, and when his cock brushed my bare midsection I closed my eyes against a surge of need. When had a man ever seduced me this way – in a naked crowd, all of us swaying like lovers about to fall on to a bed? I was vaguely aware of couples disappearing into the trees or simply sinking to the ground around the clearing, but Dewel danced until the last note floated away to blend with the gentle lapping of the bayou's waters against the shoreline.

Then, with a sorcerer's grin, he guided me towards the woods. 'Tell me what you see,' he whispered, 'and tell me what you want. What Chapin doesn't know won't hurt him.'

When Dewel turned me to face away from him, hugging me against his hot, hard body, my eyes widened: on the ground, not fifteen feet away, my maid Monique lay with her legs and arms wrapped around Tommy Jon. They were humping so furiously they didn't notice they had an audience – but then T-Jon raised up, as though to give us a better view.

'Oh, my,' I murmured, for his attributes were every bit as impressive as Monique had hinted.

'Describe his cock.' Dewel's breath warmed my neck, in rhythm with Beaumont's forceful strokes.

'It's so long and thick, I don't see how she takes it all,' I wheezed, aware of another erection prodding my back. When his hands came up under my breasts to cup them, I found myself thrusting forward, greedy for his touch. 'Are they always that dark at the top?'

'When a man's aroused, sugah, he goes from pink to red to purple. Just imagine how her sweet little cunny must feel, gettin' filled and then emptied. In and out, like a piston, he's pumpin' it.'

My own cunny – for I could think of it that way now – burned with the same longing I heard in Monique's moans. I clenched and became very wet. When Dewel moved one hand seductively down my stomach, I shuddered.

'Part your legs, darlin'. I'll give you a samplin' of what you see – unless you want me to take you full-on.'

I closed my eyes with the effort of refusing him, for his own tip was thick and insistent as it slipped between my thighs. 'No, we'd better –'

Two fingers eased through my curls, to find the folds that so needed their attention. 'Now look how he's anglin' her ass on to his lap, so he can dive even deeper inside her.'

'And when she puts her heels on his shoulders –'

'Our young stud not only gets a fine view of her bouncin' breasts, but he's got a straight-on shot. I'm guessin' he'll explode any minute now.'

Indeed, Tommy Jon was clasping his lady's ankles and throwing back his head as he thrust in a desperate rhythm. Dewel, meanwhile, had slid his shaft into my outer wetness and was holding it against my slick slit, with his hand completing the sheath. He bent his knees behind mine, bumping forward, creating an illicit friction ... so close to sliding inside me that my slightest shifting would've captured him.

The thought of that coupling, going at it like dogs in an alley, excited me beyond belief. Chapin had never ... or at least not with *me*, he hadn't.

As though sensing this break in my concentration, Dewel rubbed against me with unmistakable need. 'You're drivin' me crazy, Eve. I've wanted you for so long, sugah. No one would be the wiser if we –'

Monique babbled in wild French, her body shaking crazily. It spurred Tommy Jon to climax too, and their bodies made wet, slapping sounds that had me reaching between my legs for Dewel's cock. I held it between my palms, rocking my clit against it to reach that same sweet surge my maid had given me with her tongue ... pressing frantically against the shaft that poked in and out beneath my springy hair.

The sight of his purple tip, coupled with the bumping of his large, male body, carried me off the cliff. I doubled over with the first spasms, and Dewel slipped his fingers deep inside me until I gushed, mindless with the pleasure ... oblivious to everything except the sensation of flight. When I looked down again, his seed was spewing from between my thighs, white and shiny in the moonlight. Two long spurts and then a third, and then he held me hard to catch his breath.

Monique and T-Jon grinned and gave us a little wave. A few days ago I would've felt filthy, ashamed to show my face, yet this open sharing of passion gave me ideas about what might happen among the four of us at another time. Something in Beaumont's expression as he stood and helped his lover up, and something in Dewel's possessive kiss, told me I was branded now. A wanton – at least until I got caught at it.

A sobering thought.

'I'd better get home,' I fretted, struggling in vain towards my clothes. When had the music stopped? When had the others disappeared into this night I would never forget?

Dewel held me against himself, spreading my honey up my stomach. 'And I'll take you there, sugah, as soon as –'

'No! What if Chapin's out looking for me? He'll see –'

'His half-brother, escortin' his dear wife safely back to that house on Prytania. That house where he leaves her unsatisfied. Untouched, most likely.' He penetrated my soul with his gaze. 'What sort of a lover would I be if I left you to face him alone, Eve?'

I swallowed hard. 'You're not my lover, Dewel. I appreciate your gallant –'

'Not yet. But I always get what I want, which is precisely why my big brother can't stand me.'

He released me, but while I hurried into my clothes, that maddening man told Monique and T-Jon to run along – leaving me no choice but to let him escort me home. He wasn't the least bit concerned about the hour, or the way my late arrival wouldn't escape the house-keeper, or my husband. He dressed calmly, all the while watching me fuss with my dishevelled hair and dirt-smudged blouse. He glowed with the confidence of a man who cared nothing about appearances, or what others might think. Like a lion, Dewel assumed the rest of the jungle revolved around him, the king of beasts.

As we left the clearing, still littered with remains of the Cajun feast, Dewel poured us two last glasses of wine. Then he dipped his fingers and ran them along my face and beneath the top edge of my peasant blouse. I was so startled by his wet fingertips skimming my skin, I could only drop my jaw.

'Chapin will think ... I'm going to smell like a bum.'

'Better than smellin' like me,' he drawled. Then he kissed me, heading immediately into that ravenous realm of possession where I couldn't think or act. I could only shiver with the thoughts he planted in my poor muddled head, and fear for my future.

We finished the wine during the ride in the pirogue: while Dewel rowed deftly between cyprus stumps and lumps I suspected were alligators, I tipped the glass to his lips. This meant I sat close enough to feel the deep strength of his body, rekindling our heat with his every pull on the oars. When the claret liquid sloshed on his white shirt, he laughed. After he pulled us ashore, we walked towards the plantation house in the moonlight, swinging our clasped hands between us like carefree children.

The carriage ride into town was another example of pleasure a married woman should never allow herself: Dewel took every advantage of those twenty private minutes to fondle me into submission again. Dazed by his potent kiss, I sprawled across his lap as his hands roamed beneath my clothes. He went straight for my wet cleft.

'No underthings,' he remarked with a lascivious grin. 'Such a wayward wife.'

'Monique talked me into –'

'No, ma'am,' he countered, his wine-scented breath sending shivers of need up my spine. 'Your body was preparin' for *me*, even before your mind realised it.'

'And how did I know you'd be there? Monique invited me to a family gathering,' I retorted, playfully slapping his shadowed face.

He grabbed my wrist, and then ran the point of his tongue around my palm. 'You and I *are* family, Miss Eve,' he teased, but then his eyes darkened. 'I knew the moment you set foot on my property. Watched you girls scamperin' to the pirogue, from my window. And I started plottin' your fall.'

I stared at him in the dimness, fearing his seductive powers yet enthralled by them. The carriage slowed as we headed up the driveway towards the house. 'Don't come in. I don't think Chapin's home, but I can't take any chances.'

I reached for the latch of the carriage door, but Dewel drew me back for a final kiss – an elixir far more potent than the wine he'd baptized me with. 'Take care of yourself, Miss Eve. Till we meet again.'

Reeling, I stepped from his carriage and hurried through the kitchen door where Fanny took deliveries. I listened for signs of anyone being around, but all I heard was the sonorous striking of the clock in the hall. *Bonggg … bonggg … bonggg.*

I could *never* recall being awake – downright electrified – at three in the morning. I removed my shoes with a smug smile, and then moved quickly through the dark pantry, deciding the back stairs were the quietest route to my room. I delighted myself with how silently I climbed – this sneaking around was easier than I'd imagined!

I topped the stairs, my door in sight –

But then Chapin stepped from his suite, fully dressed and ready for me. His face was pinched with anger, almost demonlike in the light from the hallway table lamp.

'And where have *you* been, Mrs Proffit?' he asked in a sinuous whisper.

6 **Chapin Takes Me**

He was scowling at my untied blouse, my messy hair, my rumpled skirt – and he'd caught me sneaking up the back stairs – so there was no point in denying my whereabouts. Chapin Proffit had ways of finding out what he wanted to know, and his clenching hands reminded me who would pay for my lies.

'Monique invited me to a party with her family,' I replied as steadily as the wine would allow. 'I saw it as a chance to confirm her suitability for –'

'Mrs Frike told me you left with her hours ago, wearing these ... *inexcusable* clothes!'

His tone didn't surprise me: I was prepared for a dressing-down. I was not ready, however, for him to grab the gathered neckline of my blouse and rip it off me.

'You've been with Dewel, *haven't* you?'

He punctuated this demand by yanking my skirt down, and then sneering at the colourful puddle of clothes around my ankles. 'For *years* I've tolerated that bastard – let him mind his own business while I minded mine. But now that I'm being groomed for the city's most prominent position, he comes out of his cave. To cast me in a dubious light by chasing after my wife!'

'The party was on his land, because the Picabous are his friends. What right have you –'

'Had his whoring mother known her place – and had my mother outlived our father – he wouldn't have a pot to piss in!' Chapin pulled me into his face by grabbing my camisole. 'Beware a man with friends in such low places, Evie. He's dragging you through the muck, and I'll have no more of it.'

His fine-featured face now resembled a rabid mongrel's, contorted with jealousy that had festered into a full-blown infection. I didn't dare reply. I was too busy taking each breath, fearing it might be my last, for I'd never seen my husband this carried away by his hatred for his half-brother.

'You smell like cheap wine and cigars. And sex!' he said, driving his hand between my legs to test my wetness.

'And *you* smell like perfume!'

The heavy sting against my face was a delayed reaction, after the loud clapping sound that echoed in the upstairs hall. I'd known better than to make that remark, but his feminine scent and all that Cajun wine had overwhelmed me. I didn't wait for him to slap me again.

'Yes – run to your room and hide, little harlot,' he cried after me. 'But don't think I've finished with you!'

Where had such rage come from? I slammed my door and leapt on to my bed, sobbing at the swift deterioration of a marriage that was at least civil, if not the affectionate fantasy I'd entertained as a young girl. Chapin and I had experienced difficult days and trying nights, as all couples did, but I'd never foreseen *this*.

I curled in around myself, muffling my frightened whimpers in my pillow, wondering what recourse I had. Fanny was obviously reporting to her employer, while Monique, Tommy Jon and Dewel were too far away to help me. It was a huge house, with plenty of nooks and hidey-holes, but Chapin knew them far better than I. What a shame that such thoughts were now paramount in my mind as I struggled to catch my breath.

What struck me, however, was that my brief encounters with Dewel – and the evening with Monique's fun-loving family – had shown me what I'd been missing: the company of people who befriended me for myself, rather than for my contribution to their success. The price I'd paid to keep my own family solvent seven years ago suddenly felt much too high. I'd never heard the amount Chapin placed in that bank account, but if Daddy knew what I'd just endured, he would *not* tolerate it.

And neither would I.

I swiped the tears from my throbbing cheek. Packing a valise would only take a few moments; I could stash it beneath my bed, and be gone after Chapin left for the Cotton Exchange in the morning. I could lay my hands on enough jewellery and cash to buy train fare to –

The door to my room opened, and then closed. I remained motionless, peering through the dimness to determine Chapin's mood.

He was naked.

This alone caught me off-guard, for I couldn't recall the last time I'd seen him unclothed. He was fondling himself, in a patch of moonlight where I could see his slender cock extending beyond his hand, which was a first as well. The soul of sexual repression, my husband. Or so I'd thought, until I spied him with that 'niece'.

'He got you drunk, and then he fucked you.'

No, and no! I wanted to cry out, yet his language waved a white flag, and his shaft was its pole. Monique had told me most men rose to competition, and her prediction was coming true: I'd *never* seen Chapin this aroused! He radiated a heat that threatened to consume me, and it seemed I was attaining my original goal in a most roundabout way.

'So, while I can't hold you totally responsible for your actions, we can't pretend they haven't happened,' he continued in a voice tight with desire. 'And you can't tell me you didn't like it!'

His arrogance set me on edge, but I kept quiet. It was enough to know he'd taken his anger in hand ... a rather fascinating sight, watching my husband stroke himself. I'd never dreamed a man's member could withstand such frenzied attention, and the sound of his rapid rubbing renewed the wetness between my legs. I shifted slightly, wanting to touch my slit.

'I've spared you the marital relations you found so messy and inconvenient, but no longer,' Chapin declared. 'I thought you'd come around – if only to have the children we once longed for. But my indulgence has been a mistake.'

He walked slowly towards my bed, casting a long, lurid shadow on the wall behind him. 'You're my wife, Evelyn, and you vowed to love, honour and obey me. It's time you accepted the responsibility that comes with this fine life I've provided you. So – will you submit? Or must I take what's rightfully mine?'

I hadn't uncurled from my original position atop my bed, and my crocheted counterpane cut its pattern into my palm as I clutched it. This was the first I'd heard of Chapin's eagerness to be a father – or that I'd considered sex messy and inconvenient. Lord, when I married this man, I knew next to nothing about my own body, let alone what to do with his!

Although I pulsed with desire, part of me wanted to lash out, to tell him where he could stick that thing he now pointed at me. But in Southern society, a woman had nowhere else to go – at least not without a well-planned strategy in place – if she defied the man who supported her. I stretched tentatively, considering my options.

Insisting that Dewel and I had done nothing would be the wrong approach. Correcting my husband's notion about my feelings towards sex wouldn't be in my best interest either, because his accelerated breathing told me that, ready or not, he was going to come.

Best to play Chapin's game for now – or at least make him think I was. After all, I *wanted* my husband to enter me as eagerly as he had Savanna. I wanted to feel like a desirable wife … a woman he craved.

'I've always been yours for the taking, Chapin,' I whispered, rising up on my elbow to better display my breasts. 'Kiss me now. Let's put this nastiness behind us and live like lovers.'

He inhaled as though to continue his lecture. So when he opened his mouth, I rolled forward to hook my arm around his neck – to pour my heart and soul into a kiss. He was so startled by this move that, while our lips were still locked, I rolled backwards to coax him between my legs.

He broke the kiss to inhale, rubbing his cock against me. 'Get the rest of your clothes off, before –'

'*Take* them! Put me in my place, Chapin, open and willing, beneath you.'

'Bitch!' He yanked down my drawers while placing his other hand behind my head, holding me hostage. 'High time you showed some interest –'

'Forget the past,' I insisted again, arching up until the tip of him nuzzled my slit.

So many other retorts, about how seldom he was home and how disinterested *he* had always seemed, danced madly in my mind. But this was not the time to air such grievances. It was a slim, faint hope that by behaving this way I could inspire his affection for me – that we might change the course of our downward-spiralling marriage, here in my bed. For I did want to love this man. I wanted us both to be happy.

Chapin surged like a man possessed. In and out of me he slammed, grunting and rutting as though overwhelmed by his animal passion. I wrapped myself around him, thrusting up to meet him, thinking that yes, this was the enthusiasm he'd shown his little blonde lover. He was trying to satisfy me that same way. I looked up, to bask in the flames I envisioned in his pale-blue eyes.

But they were closed.

Chapin's lip was curling and he was hurtling towards climax. Even to my inexperienced mind, he appeared lost in a mental vision ... calling up all the cues and images that produced the desired results. He shot into me, and just that quickly he disengaged. He chose to recover at the foot of the bed.

'I'll be leaving at first light for St. Louis,' he announced between breaths. 'And while I'm conducting our family's business, you shall be hiring more servants for the parties to promote my campaign. I want them settled in and working upon my return.'

He focused on me then, his expression brooking no argument. 'I strongly suggest you dismiss Monique, as she's the devil's apprentice. And there will be no more parties on the bayou, and no more trysting with Dewel. Is that understood?'

Of course I understood. We hadn't been making love: he'd been marking his territory. Mapping out my future as the wife of the next mayor of New Orleans.

* * *

'And was that the husband's carriage pulling away this morning? With luggage on top?' Monique flung the draperies wide to let in sunshine that rivalled her bright smile, her Cajun sparkle. 'This means we can do as we please, *oui*?'

'He caught me last night. Fanny told him I'd left with you, and he was lying in wait like an animal, to pounce on me.'

'And did he?' Her dark, arching brow lent her an air of sexual sophistication I could never hope to achieve. How was it some women were naturals at seduction? And why didn't she look as muzzy as I felt?

'It wasn't the least bit satisfying, but it took the edge off his anger.' I sighed, shivering with this chilly memory. 'He feels I need more responsibility – namely children. And he expects new servants to be working when he returns from St. Louis.'

'And what does Dewel expect?'

Blood rushed up into my face, both from her implied knowledge of what went on between Dewel and me and from what I could *imagine* going on. 'He's staking his claim on me too. In a much different way.'

'Well! How exciting for Auntie Evil, to have *two* such prominent men vying for her –' She slipped her hand beneath my sheet to tease my slit with a playful finger, laughing when I jumped. 'You see? Things *happen* when Monique comes around. And who will win?'

Just that fast she'd gone from teasing to point-blank. In my headachy state, I could only stare at her face, riveted by eyes as hot as black coffee and lush lips pressed into a determined line. Her hair was again a tousled topknot with a total disregard for decorum, but I could never, never underestimate this young woman's power.

'Who will win?' I echoed, for it was the ultimate

question concerning my current situation. And my future. 'Chapin is determined to become mayor, with me as the perfect society wife on a pedestal beside him. But Dewel . . . Dewel wants my very –'

'*Non, non, non!*' Monique chattered, waving a finger in my face. '*You* will win, Miss Eve. And I will help you.'

My well-meaning maid couldn't possibly understand the *hatred* between the Proffit half-brothers. Nor did she know Chapin well enough to comprehend my predicament: the wife who wanted his affection, yet who was almost afraid to accept it. But she refused to back down.

'I will run your bath, Auntie Evil, and then I'll go back to Miss Delacroix's School of Domestic Endeavor. When I return, you can instruct the maids I bring you, and all will be well. You are with me, *oui*?'

My self-appointed saviour was bustling around my room, humming cheerily as she pulled my brightest paisley-print dressing gown from the armoire. She turned on her way to the bathroom, awaiting my reply.

'*Oui?*' she demanded, tapping the toe of her high-heeled boot. 'I have experience in handling new staff, and you must abide by my rules for their training. Otherwise, we'll cross purposes and all will be lost – *poof!* –'

She clapped her hands together and threw them above her head, raising the hem of her uniform well above the tops of her stockings.

'– and Monsieur Chapin will get pissy again. And Dewel won't be happy at all. And believe me, *ma tante*, when Dewel's not happy, nobody's happy.'

67

7 Pretty Maids, All in a Row

My maid returned that afternoon with three young ladies who passed her muster. 'They're waiting in the front parlour, Miss Eve,' she said, her topknot bobbing as she entered the kitchen.

When Mrs Frike and I looked up from the week's menus, the housekeeper's face furrowed with disapproval. 'And why do we need more staff, missus?' she asked with a sniff. 'Are you implying my services no longer –'

'Mr Proffit himself has requested it,' I assured her, for despite her tale-telling she'd been excellent help over the years. And this was the wrong time to cross her. 'With the pre-election parties he wants to host, think of these girls – and Monique – as servants to do the menial labour while you, Fanny, remain in charge of the overall preparations. Just as you've always done so capably.'

Her feathers were smoothed, but the housekeeper's doubtful glare followed us out of the room. Once we were in the hallway, Monique snatched up my hand with conspiratorial glee.

'You should see them, Auntie,' she whispered. 'Three very pretty maids Mr Proffit – and *you*, of course! – will adore. Eager to please. Ready to do our every bidding.'

'And how much experience –'

'Green as the grass, *cherie*, but this way we'll train them up right. Discipline is everything, so they'll be ready for our important guests, *oui*?'

How could I refute her? Monique's Cajun features sparkled with the excitement of a little girl who'd received three exquisite dolls for Christmas, and couldn't wait to play with them!

'All right, I'll follow your lead,' I murmured as we approached the parlour. 'But they *must* be ready before Chapin gets home. And how did you pay Miss Delacroix's fee?'

'*Shh!*' she said fiercely, her finger at her lips. 'You must never, never let them sense your doubts. You are the mistress of this house. You must exert control at all times.'

I'd had little experience at managing staff, since Mrs Frike had overseen the hiring and firing of other domestics for two generations, with the Proffits' blessing. So Monique made a valid point: high time I assumed the role that was rightfully mine. High time my decisions were taken seriously!

She patted my collar into place, letting her hand stray to the swell of my bosom. 'I will remain your favourite niece, of course,' she teased in her low singsong, 'but these girls were born to serve, *ma tante*. The higher your expectations – the more you make them toe the line – the harder they'll work for your approval. Now, let's go whip them into shape.'

She led me into the sunny front parlour, where the gold-flocked wallpaper and furnishings of royal blue and maroon set a rich yet intimate tone. The three girls sat straighter when we entered, and when one stood up – she had russet hair and a complexion tawnier than my own – the other two followed with tight, anticipatory smiles.

Their dove-grey uniforms had high, buttoned collars and fell just above sensible black shoes, and their white aprons bore the school's monogram – SFDE – on the upper placket. They all looked about twenty; prettier than I expected of girls going into service, with a coltish air I attributed to their inexperience.

'May I present your new mistress, Mrs Chapin Proffit – most likely the wife of our next mayor!' Monique added with a flourish. Then she waxed more serious. 'You may call her Miss Eve, as is our Southern custom. You will find her fair, yet exacting. You've landed yourselves quite a plum for a first post, *oui*? So if you don't meet our expectations –'

Smack went her hands as she focused on each of them.

'– Mademoiselle Delacroix will hear of it immediately!'

The trio of maids nodded as though they'd heard this admonition from the headmistress herself. Their gazes followed Monique to the umbrella stand at the vestibule doorway. Had that slender cane always been there? My Cajun maid plucked it up with obvious purpose shining in her jet-black eyes.

'And this – *this* is how we correct those who go astray!' she exclaimed. 'You must avoid having a backside too sore to sit on, *oui*?'

Their heads bobbed as they glanced quickly at one another – and then at me. I was maintaining an air of highest propriety, but I'd never disciplined the help, nor did I want to start. Monique, the little imp, had now established this behaviour, so I couldn't refute it without contradicting her – or myself, as the mistress she presumably spoke for.

'And now Miss Eve wants a word.'

I returned their avid gazes, and for a moment the four of us blinked in the bright light of Monique's implied punishments, for crimes I hoped they'd never commit. 'Good afternoon, girls, I –'

'Good afternoon, Miss Eve,' they chorused. Their eyes were alight with expectation, until the subtle tapping of that cane on the parquet floor caught their attention. Straighter they stood then, each of them smoothing her uniform as though to gain my favour.

'I'd like to know your names and a bit about you, and then we'll begin cleaning upstairs, in my suite,' I said. 'We'll work our way into the main rooms of the house this week, and meanwhile we'll discuss your roles at the upcoming soirées for my husband's friends and political backers. You first, please, Miss – ?'

The girl with the russet upsweep and tawny eyes curtsied prettily. 'My name's Annabelle, Miss Eve,' she said in a soft drawl, 'and I am *so* pleased to be here, ma'am.'

I liked her immediately. Clean and pretty, yet modest in her speech and manner. 'Tell me about your family, Annabelle.'

Her lower lip quivered. 'They've all gone to heaven, ma'am. Victims of a fire, on a night I was ... assisting a sick friend.'

'I'm so sorry!' I gushed – and then, catching Monique's raised eyebrow, I guarded against further familiarity. 'I hope you'll find that time and honest labour ease your grief. I'm sure you'll do us all proud, Annabelle. And you?'

The centre candidate teetered on the heels of her pumps when she curtsied. She appeared to have Spanish – or perhaps native Indian – bloodlines, for her dark hair was knotted at the crown, to flow stick-straight past her shoulders. With her darker brows and high cheek bones, she looked quite exotic.

'Chloe at your service, Miss Eve,' she said in a lower, almost reedy voice – the oboe in a chorus of woodwinds.

'My father ran off, so Mama and us girls came to the city to make our own way. It's a pleasure and a privilege to be here, ma'am.'

I nodded, aware of how petty my own grievances appeared compared to these girls' stories. 'I'm pleased to meet you, Chloe. I'm sure your training with Miss Delacroix will make your future a great deal brighter than your past. We all have our misfortunes to rise above, don't we? And you, Miss –'

'Oh, I just can't *tell* you how pleased I am to – why, everyone knows how splendidly successful Chapin Proffit has been –'

Three taps of Monique's cane didn't deter this lithe, expressive blonde as she clasped her hands rapturously before her.

'– following in his illustrious daddy's footsteps! I just can't *believe* my good fortune –'

Three louder taps, and my maid stepped forward. 'A simple introduction! We have work to do, *oui*?'

The poor thing paled, then stared at her feet. Then she stepped towards me and kneeled, as though I were her queen. 'Begging your pardon, Miss Eve, for my tendency to run at the mouth. My name's Sylvia, and my chatter was so bothersome, even to my own family, that they cast me –'

This time Monique rapped the cane sharply, right beside Sylvia's shiny black shoe. 'Miss Delacroix, she warned me of your *chit-chit-chit*,' she said, quickly pinching her fingertips against her thumb to mock the girl's mouth. 'You'll work twice as hard as the other two, to control this bothersome habit, *oui*?'

'I'll strive like no maid has striven before, yes, mistress.'

'Yes, *who*?' Monique crossed her arms beneath her breasts, letting the cane swing from her fist.

Sylvia quivered like a trapped rabbit. 'Yes, Miss Eve,' she said with a bow to me, 'and yes, Mistress Monique. I'm duty-bound, and my welfare's in your hands.'

'Come along – all of you!' Monique said, briskly clapping her hands. 'We'll begin in Miss Eve's suite, and we'll show her how quick and efficient we are, *oui*?'

'Yes, Mistress Monique,' they chanted. Their voices differed in pitch, but their expressions looked the same: awed, and fearful.

As she waved them towards the stairway, I was struck by hunches I couldn't put into words, mostly involving this trio's response to Monique. As though some sort of ritual were being carried out between a trainer and her ... slaves.

I couldn't argue with my maid's technique, however, for in mere hours she'd accomplished a miracle: she'd procured help from the city's most talked-about domestic service – without paying Miss Delacroix's fee, I suspected – and she was already putting them to work. And Chapin wouldn't even be in St. Louis yet! By the time he returned, his house would be in order. I'd have another chance to prove myself worthy of his name; an opportunity to win back his favour, and transform our marriage from a relationship arranged around finances to one that revolved around ... fucking.

That naughty word made me grin. Why shouldn't I put a secretive smile on Chapin's face as he campaigned? Think of the citizens who'd benefit from having a gratified, *satisfied* mayor at their helm. Monique's lilting Cajun dialect was more demure now as she instructed the three new maids in my room. Almost as though she were sweet-talking them into cleaning, purring as only my 'niece' knew how.

My thoughts wandered to those moments in Madame LaRue's dressing room, when Monique's pink, pointed tongue found my nub ... perhaps the black lace we brought home might provide a few moments of private pleasure. I could slip into my bathroom, near enough to keep track of what the three new girls were doing, while I investigated Monique's ideas for costumes.

Once behind the closed door, surrounded by shiny white walls, I opened the box from the dressmaker's. The folds of black lace rustled seductively as they fell open, revealing the delicate web of roses and ivy intertwined ... looking downright decadent draped across my leg. Filled with an illicit thrill, I let my skirt and shoes and stockings fall haphazardly to the floor, and my blouse and corset followed.

It felt absolutely indecent, disrobing where I could hear the three maids' subdued voices as they spoke with Monique. I caressed my breasts, then cupped them out towards that adjoining wall – and I suddenly imagined a window there, where I could be on display like a mannequin in a store front. And what would Chloe and Annabelle and Sylvia think about *that*? Seeing the lady of the house naked, wrapping herself in filmy black lace as though she were a present for them to open.

This thought so inspired me that I tied the lace in a very large bow over my breasts. The rest of my body remained bare, yet titillated by the furtive whisper of the fabric. And how would it feel, down there?

Taking the longer piece hanging down from the bow, I gave myself a tentative caress. Why this sensation drove me, I didn't know, but I shuddered so hard I fell back against the sink's rim. I didn't often engage in such wanton activities alone, for what did such stimulation accomplish? What proper lady aroused herself, just for – *just for her own enjoyment? Because she can do it better than anyone else?*

I'd never pondered such things. Or at least before I met Monique, I hadn't. The fantasy of standing in a store window, with Monique joining me now, licking me all over while those new maids watched us, sent my pulse into a trot. With quick fingertips I rubbed the lace against my coarse curls, parting the folds to caress that nub Monique had found with her tongue ... as though it were a common thing for two women to share, like a new dessert recipe.

Eat or be eaten. Or both, if you're lucky!

Desire sparkled like diamonds inside me. I rubbed fast and high, breathing in little gusts, feeling the dew pool at the rim of my hole and then run down my thighs in rivulets.

Fearing I'd fall and attract attention, I leaned against the wall between the sink and the tub, sticking my hips out with my legs parted. I was panting. I imagined the three maids catching a glimpse of me and then coming to the window to watch. In their chaste grey uniforms, they seemed mesmerised by the lines my fingertips made around my slit.

'Look at her clitty – how it juts out to be sucked.'

'Oh, she smells delicious – I wish she'd give me a taste.'

'I get her first –' this from Annabelle, the redhead *'– because I know just how to stick my tongue up her and make her spray all over my face!'*

Where had such thoughts come from? Never had I mouthed those filthy words or discussed such subjects! A lady simply didn't –

And isn't it fun, not to be a lady at every moment? You have a secret life now!

My head dropped back. My fingertips spread my moisture over territory that fascinated them, driving me insane with new-found need. My hips began to rock and wiggle and my insides flexed. I didn't know whether to bring it all off with a burst, or to savour this stolen moment for as long as I could make the pleasure last.

I was ready to let go, ready to succumb to my frantic fondling, when Monique slipped in and shut the door behind her. My God, she *had* seen me through the –

'I wondered if my Auntie Evil wasn't well, staying in here so long,' she murmured. 'But this – ooh-la-la!'

She focused intently on my writhing, lace-wrapped hand. Her own fingers slipped beneath her short uniform, and then she slapped the rim of the tub with one booted foot, standing only an arm's-length away.

'It's exciting to watch, *non*?' she breathed, flicking her own clit to attention with the thrum of her fingertips. 'We can play follow-the-leader. Do what I do, *ma tante*. Open your hole with forked fingers – this way – and then stroke your clit from the underside.'

Her sharp intake of breath told me the sight affected *her* too. I'd never watched a woman fondle herself, yet Monique was clearly experienced at it – baring her most private parts with pale fingers separating rose-coloured flesh from short black curls, to give me a lesson in technique. Surely Dewel couldn't have guessed she would –

That's precisely why he sent her, came my mind's reply.

The memory of his hot weight, pressing me against the iron gate as he rubbed his cock against my backside, made my desire spike like a fever. Monique was wet now, making juicy, secretive sounds as her fingers quickly drove her to my level of arousal. Her slit turned a deeper pink. Her agile body rocked in rhythm with mine, and with the moans that escaped her.

'Oh, *cherie* – such a sight you are. Such a pretty

piece,' she coaxed. 'I'm on the edge – so very close – come here and fuck me – *mon Dieu!*'

And then Monique was on *me*, straddling my lace-draped leg so her folds could rasp against the black pattern. Her flexing thigh pressed the fabric against my clit, and I grabbed her hips when the pain and frenzy fused into white-hot pleasure. Together we thumped against the wall, searching for those moments of perfect contact ... the completion of this secretive act we shared again.

With a gasp, she landed against me. I'd have felt very awkward if one of the new girls came in and saw us, despite the way I'd previously imagined performing for them. But my fantasies – and my needs – went beyond reason sometimes. I didn't have answers for questions I'd just begun to ask.

'Why can't it be this way with Chapin?' I murmured. Words I wouldn't have dared express ordinarily, yet I sensed Monique understood.

'We can't always have what we want, Auntie Evil.' She was wetting a towel, and then gently wiped between my legs before she cleaned herself. 'But sometimes, if we try for it anyway – finding ways to be happy, staying open to joy – we get what we *need*. Maybe not where we expected to find it, *non?*'

Wise beyond her years, Monique, yet wickedly innocent. Her childlike view of the world set my own circumstances into perspective and, when she left me to get dressed, I knew Dewel had placed my budding sexuality in very capable hands. I could only hope Chapin would appreciate my new-found knowledge, even if I had to hide the way I was acquiring it.

'*Mon Dieu*, what is this I see?' My maid's shrill voice penetrated the tiled white wall. 'I left you for only a moment. I asked you to arrange Miss Eve's new gowns in the closet above her new shoes. And I find – *this*!'

Feverishly I buttoned my blouse. What catastrophe merited such an outburst from the woman who'd been a purring pussy moments ago?

'Downstairs! This minute!' she barked, and I envisioned a fist against her hip while she pointed towards the door. 'Not here two hours, and already I've caught you playing on the job. Like sneaky little girls dawdling in mama's closet. Out! Out!'

Absolute silence then; the maids knew better than to sass back. As I was smoothing my hair in the mirror, Monique peeked into the bathroom. 'We request your presence in the front parlour, Auntie Evil. I hope you're ready for the ... the *spectacle* they've made of themselves.'

As she closed the bathroom door, and the purposeful tattoo of her boots went towards the stairway, I sensed Miss Picabou was not as angry as she'd led our new domestics to believe. This was part of her act, and she relished every second of being their superior.

Far be it from me to intercede. I smoothed my navy skirt and tucked in my blouse, a natty nautical design with a sailor collar, as was coming into fashion now. Looking at it, no one would guess what I'd been doing to myself in here – and with a length of black lace! I folded the fabric back into its box, smiling at what I might want to do with it next.

I descended the stairs, pausing outside the parlour to compose myself. I was the lady of the manor, the wife of a prominent politician, and I had an image to maintain in front of new employees: the dignity and breeding of Southern gentility must prevail if these maids were to properly perform their duties in the coming months.

When I saw them, however, my hand flew to my mouth.

The three domestics stood in a row, hands clasped before them, looking mightily afraid of the punishment to come. Chloe had let her straight black hair down and sported a thick coating of kohl around her exotic eyes; she'd rouged her cheeks and lips as well, and she looked like ... well, like a tart in uniform. Beside her, Annabelle fidgeted in my new gown of turquoise tulle. She'd wound my longest strand of pearls into her red-brown hair, so it dipped dramatically over one ear. And Sylvia ... Sylvia had removed her apron and grey uniform, presumably for a better view of the stunning new shoes that graced her feet. Shoes I'd had specially designed of an iridescent fabric with a shine like glass, to match my fanciest new ball gown.

But it was Monique catching everyone's eye. She'd stripped away her dress and pinafore – not a shred of innocent pretence remained about this virago clad in a black corset, with a matching garter belt and stockings above her calf-high boots. She surveyed the trio of maids from behind a wickedly thin black mask, and was pulling on velvet gloves that flared above her wrists. She retrieved her cane from the umbrella holder with a zeal that had *me* flinching, even though I'd done nothing wrong.

'What a mess you've made of your first day, *non*?' she crowed in that relentless Cajun rhythm. 'Your sole purpose in life is to make my aunt look good. And *look* at you!'

Her tone would've withered a hardened criminal, and the way she clicked that cane on the parquet floor as she paced, pantherlike, intensified her wrath. 'What if Mr Proffit walked in? Why, he'd kick your foolish butts out to the street. And then he'd complain to

Miss Delacroix – and you know what *she'd* do to you!'

The girls shifted nervously as their gazes fell to their feet.

Tap, tap tap. 'What do you get when you cross Aunt Evil? That's who she is, you know – my Aunt Evil. And for good reason.' Monique continued in a rising cry. '*What do you get when you cross Aunt Evil?*'

Silence rang around the parlour, until Chloe's red lips quirked. 'Cross her with what?'

An unladylike snort escaped Annabelle, and then her dangling pearls quivered with her effort to stop giggling. Poor Sylvia looked mortified enough to wet herself.

'You three are the most pathetic . . .' Monique gripped her slender cane in an effort to keep from hurling it at them, a chorus line of dilettante domestics. 'You deserve a spanking, and you know it. Now turn around and bend over that couch. Dresses up! Drawers down!'

Could I believe what I was seeing and hearing? I opened my mouth to suggest –

But, as the girls assumed the position she'd ordered, Monique turned to point her cane at me, shaking her head. I stepped back, abashed yet fascinated: the three girls, although clearly frightened by the corporal punishment they faced, prepared themselves as though they'd done this before. Three skirts and white shifts were hiked slowly over three backs that bent low over the settee, revealing ruffled white panties that billowed demurely over their hips – the latest rage in underthings. Three sets of hands reached back to three waistbands, and slowly began to lower the frilly undergarments over firm young backsides.

To my horror, Fanny Frike then entered the room, to see what sort of commotion my maid was causing now.

Taking note so she could tattle to Chapin, no doubt. The housekeeper stopped to stare, with the most amazed expression I'd ever seen.

'Saints preserve us,' she whispered. 'They've all got balls!'

8 **A Trio of Queens**

'Space yourselves! Spread those legs!' Monique commanded. 'Don't make me tell you twice, you naughty maids!'

The three maids – if one called them that, considering the anatomical parts I now saw with utmost clarity – separated themselves along the couch, and then leaned over it for the punishment to come. I had followed Fanny's gaze and stood gaping, my pulse galloping like a runaway mare, for surely the fusty old housekeeper would call a halt to this charade – and tell Chapin all about it the moment he got home.

Yet she stood stock-still, gripping her hands in front of her stomach. She had yet to blink.

Tap, tap, tap, went the cane's tip on the floor.

Did I imagine it, or did all three miscreants lock their knees so their asses protruded more prominently? I couldn't stop staring, for between each pair of muscled thighs dangled a set of testicles, each with its uniquely coloured haze of hair. A blonde, a brunette and a redhead. Displayed as though for my enjoyment; angled so I could watch their cocks starting to stiffen.

'So you want to be queens, *oui*?' Monique went on, so caught up in her role as disciplinarian, she was heedless of the housekeeper and me. 'Well, even royalty pays the price for overstepping the line. Humiliation is the very *least* you deserve for your behaviour this morning, *non*?'

There was a murmured reply; a shifting of tight backsides anticipating the cane.

'Yes, *what*, you pathetic pansies?'

'Yes, Mistress Monique,' came the chorus.

'Maybe you'll improve in your role of serving girls, as befits this fine household, if you have royal names to live up to,' the virago in black intoned. 'No doubt you were the ringleader, Annabelle.'

She gave the redhead in the centre a preliminary whack, making the fleshiest part of the maid's ass jiggle and blanch before a pink stripe appeared. 'And dressed so divinely, in Mrs Proffit's prettiest pearls and turquoise gown. You fancy yourself French, *oui*? Marie Antoinette, perhaps?'

Again the slender cane whished through the air, producing a stripe above the first one.

Annabelle jumped, stuttering, 'Yes, mistress, Muh-Marie Antoinette cut a stunning figure as queen.'

'Toinette it is then!' Monique gleefully landed another whack on the centre of that attractive backside, watching the flesh shimmy and shine pink above those quivering balls. 'Try not to lose your head again. Even Marie only got one chance at it.'

Warming to her role, Monique paced behind them for a moment, to intensify the anticipation. The clatter of those tight boots, punctuated by the cane's *tap, tap, tap*, was enough to make me pity whomever she humiliated next.

'Dabbling in Auntie Evil's cosmetics, were we, Chloe?' she then demanded, and with a deft flick of her wrist the cane bit into the darker maid's shapely backside.

This minx had the nerve to wiggle, making those balls swing seductively around a cock that prodded the couch. She stifled a cry, however, when Monique made her whip sing a surprise second verse – louder and harder this time.

'With those dark features and that midnight hair, you belong in Egypt, *non*? Cleopatra, queen of the Nile?'

'She ruled, yes! Her legend shines through the centuries,' the newly named maid boasted. But her crowing rose to a howl when the whipping continued with two more quick whacks in succession, and then a third. This time the stripes were patterned in precise X-shapes, growing rosier as we watched.

'*De-nial* is no place to float your boat now!' Monique quipped. 'You have no business trying Aunt Evil's beauty secrets, trying to be as pretty as she. You are her servant! Her slightest wish is your command, *oui*, Cleopatra?'

'I was only – *yess*, Mistress Monique!' the sinner cried out when the cane met her dusky butt with a vengeance. 'Just as Cleopatra served Egypt, I live to do Miss Eve's every bidding.'

The parlour got quiet, except for the ragged breathing coming from the couch ... and from the stout housekeeper who stood riveted by this performance. I'd never known Fanny Frike to fixate on anything the way she gazed at the three asses and sets of privates so blatantly displayed before us.

'They're young men, in the prime of life,' she breathed, taking in every curve of their cushions, every sinew of the thighs that ended in a froth of white ruffles at their knees. 'Yet I was certain they were girls. Jesus, Mary and Joseph!'

Religion was the furthest thing from my mind, however, for only one penitent awaited her due, and her creamy, rounded moons were already aquiver. White thighs framed a neat little pair of nodules adorned by hair so pale it was nearly invisible, yet I had no trouble imagining what stuck out in front, high and hard: Sylvia had shifted to allow it room to grow. Her panties ringed dainty knees and white-stockinged legs, with fine-boned ankles and feet just made to fit my beautiful see-through shoes. While it irked me that Sylvia had chosen my newest, most expensive footwear, I had to admire her taste.

'And *you*, silky Sylvia!' Monique's voice crescendoed. 'Carried away with straightening Miss Eve's pretty slippers, even after I warned you, *non*?'

Whisss-smack went the slender cane, and the maid's outburst wrenched my soul.

'Please, Mistress Monique,' she pleaded, her ankles wobbling on the high, narrow heels. 'I was trying to do my best job –'

'You tried on every shoe in the closet!'

'– of placing each pair beneath the dress they complemented best, and –'

Tap, tap, tap.

'– Miss Eve has such a *lovely* assortment, I couldn't always decide –'

Whisss-smack, and again Sylvia yowled like a whipped kitten, reaching back to shield her ass with her hand.

I was ready to step in, but Mrs Frike took my elbow. 'Obviously needs watching, that one,' she intimated, shaking her head sternly. 'Better to let her – him – take his licks now, and understand what's expected in this house. I can tell you *I* won't tolerate any such foolishness about your clothes and shoes when it's me they answer to!'

Her vehemence gave me pause: in my years as Mrs Proffit, I'd known Fanny Frike to run a disciplined household, but not with a cane. Not by punishing some poor servant's bare backside! Yet I sensed the thrumming pulse in her grip had nothing to do with this spanking spectacle. Something about having three young men with interesting idiosyncrasies under her roof was giving the housekeeper a whole new outlook on staff management.

'All right, Cinderella!' Monique continued, slapping the curved handle of the cane against her palm. 'It's down to the cellar with you – to let your sisters get all the glory – if you misbehave this way again, *non*?'

'But I didn't mean to –'

Whisss-smack, and yet another piteous yelp, and another shining pink stripe across that ripe, white backside.

'It's just that ... well, Cinderella wasn't a queen,' Sylvia protested. 'She was only the misfit princess in a fairy tale!'

'Enough whining. All of you – up. Up!' Monique banged the cane's tip on the floor to hurry them along. 'You will apologise to Miss Eve for using her personal effects for your own enjoyment. You will spend the rest of today wearing only your aprons, with your panties around your knees. And you will answer to your new names – cheerfully, *oui*?'

'Yes, Mistress Monique,' they replied as they turned to face me.

Cleopatra in her kohled eyes, and Toinette with her pearl headpiece, and Cinderella in her glasslike slippers without a prince to rescue her from such piercing shame. It took all my effort not to giggle as they made their apologies. Each maid in turn came forward, begged my forgiveness, and swore to behave with perfect decorum from here on out. And, as they peeled off their outer clothing, leaving their panties down around their knees, I realised the point of Monique's punishment: their rosy rears would be on display for all to see, a reminder of their morning's shortcomings.

'What a bunch of sissies!' Monique hissed – although,

even with her wicked mask and fierce black attire, I could see she was enjoying herself immensely. 'Back to work – all of you! And if you whine like whipped pups at what I make you do, just wait. This afternoon you'll work with Mrs Frike!'

The heavyset housekeeper couldn't hide a smile. 'That's my cue to have some tasks ready,' she remarked with a final scrutinising of the three maids. 'But I don't mess with a silly little cane, girls. I've got a broad hand and an arm that never gets tired – hear me?'

Cleopatra, Toinette and Cinderella scurried towards the stairway as best they could with their white skivvies nipping at their knees, not daring a last look at the dour housekeeper who exited the parlour. When Monique and I stood alone in the centre of the room, I took a deep breath. What did I say – what did I think? – about the scene I'd just witnessed?

'Must you be so –'

'Strict?' The black-clad mistress tugged at the fingertips of her gloves. 'They must learn in a hurry, *non*? If they are to meet Mr Proffit's approval – and make *you* look good? And never, never forget that Miss Delacroix, she trained them this way.'

Monique stepped closer then, to peer at me with those provocative dark eyes still surrounded by a mask of black satin that went up into pointed corners.

'These girls who are boys?' she asked in a confiding tone. 'They make the *best* servants, Auntie Evil. Sissy maids live to follow orders. They're born to serve. They *choose* this path, because to attend the School of Domestic Endeavor, to be trained and then recommended by Honore Delacroix, why – they can attain no higher life!'

Sissy maids. I'd have to take this new bone and chew on it, for I'd never been presented with such a philosophy, nor met anyone who knew of it. I simply could not fathom a healthy, normal young man becoming a – a maid. In skirts!

But again my personal servant – very unorthodox in her own ways – corralled my stampeding thoughts with a fingertip on my cheek, forcing me to focus on her unmasked face. She was flushed and lovely from her exertions, truly the queen of my staff. And once again her subtle charm cast its spell.

'I'm planning a special surprise for tonight,' she murmured, grinning as she thought about it. 'Tommy Jon, he's made you a gift, *ma tante*. And he wants to deliver it personally.'

My mouth went dry at the memory of her well-hung lover pumping her, but then reality set in. 'I don't think he'd better show up here –'

'*Non?* You can refuse that handsome man and his special talent with –'

'If Fanny tells my husband about these goings-on, I'm hanged!'

Her laughter filled the elegant room with a gaiety seldom shared in this sombre house. 'Fanny'll be busy watching those sissy maids,' she explained with sparkling eyes. 'And if the housekeeper's so excited by their little secret, she'll keep *your* secrets too, *non?* For if she tells Mr Chapin what's under those aprons, he'll send them away. Then *everyone* will be unhappy.'

My head spun with her skewed Cajun logic, but I was enjoying it too much to argue. It was indeed an ironic advantage that our stodgy Mrs Frike had found a new light in her life.

'And, Auntie Evil, you know what they say – about when the cat's away? The mice, they should play.'

Monique wiggled her nose like a mouse – a fetching little mouse in black who snatched up my hands. 'T-Jon, he's all excited about making your present. He'll be *so* disappointed if you refuse him. And there'll be no fun for me if my man's not happy,' she added pointedly.

With that, she headed for the door with feline finesse – probably so I'd notice the way her bared hips swayed beneath that tight black corset, while her footfalls set the pace for my pulse. She pivoted, to lean against the door jamb in profile, one leg bent with a foot to the woodwork as she slipped a little cigar from her stocking top, and then a match.

A spark flew from the bottom of her boot, and then she placed the cheroot between her lips, her movements exaggerated to full effect, making me watch until she was ready to take her leave. With sensual slowness she inhaled, her cheeks hollowing, until she reversed the procedure to blow her smoke. Then she smiled as only Monique Picabou knew how, a mixture of lazy lust and childlike charm radiating from her entire body.

'Leave your suite's gallery door open, Auntie. We'll come like thieves in the night, to steal your innocence ... your inhibitions,' she whispered. 'To teach you about seducing your husband when he gets home, of course.'

Of course. It would be true because this young woman declared it so, before leaving me with a flounce of her fully exposed behind. I could only listen and obey. And wonder who was really the servant here.

9 **Confessions of the Caned**

The more Monique helped me follow my husband's orders, the more tightly I got wound into her naughty, treacherous web. What a shock, to see young men who made such pretty women. Being utterly fooled by their voices and looks and mannerisms. I felt downright drab and uninventive, when I considered the efforts it took to carry out their deception.

Monique had obviously known their gender all along – and surely had her reasons for procuring them – but Chapin would see *nothing* funny about what hung in their panties. He would banish my Cajun maid himself when he learned she'd brought them here. The entire blame would lay on my shoulders for, as Monique had reminded me, I was responsible for the conduct and deportment of my staff. Thoughts of Toinette appearing in my pearls, or Cinderella coming to our masked ball in my spun-glass slippers, made my head spin.

Yet my curiosity was more than piqued. And with Monique gone for the rest of the day, I had the perfect opportunity to get acquainted with my new employees; to find out *why* three attractive young men chose to live as women and work as servants.

They stood at the table along the kitchen wall, their bare backsides exposed as they polished flatware for Fanny. My hand went to my mouth. Those stripes radiated heat and pain I could not imagine, for even though my parents had used the occasional willow switch, they'd never made *welts*. Everything within me railed against whipping them this way, yet Monique was right: if I contradicted her discipline now, my sissy maids would play us against each other. If Chapin found this out, there'd be even more hell to pay.

I could, however, show some compassion – in exchange for information. Walking alongside the sink, I picked up Fanny's jar of bag balm: it was formulated for the udders of dairy cows, and it soothed human skin as well.

'Good afternoon,' I spoke, hoping to sound firm yet friendly. 'I think we'll all be happier if I apply some salve to those stripes. It hurts me to look at them, so I can only imagine how awful you must feel.'

The trio glanced over their shoulders with a mixture of expressions, while Mrs Frike, kneading dough for bread, rolled her eyes as though she thought I was pushing my case a bit.

'We'll be fine. Really,' Cleopatra assured me.

'Not like we haven't had our bottoms whacked before,' Cinderella chirped.

I twisted the lid from the jar of balm. 'So, Miss Delacroix condones canings at her school?'

'Oh, she lives for them, Miss Eve,' Antoinette informed me. 'She insists that the pain and humiliation make us better domestics. More penitent, and likely to strive higher next time.'

'And do you agree with that?' I then wondered if I should have asked. After all, I wasn't paying my staff to have opinions. I scooped up a dollop of the cream on my fingertips and touched it to his crisscrossed bottom.

Antoinette sucked in his breath, and then stuck out his butt. His tawny eyes looked anything but penitent. 'Not unless I respect the person cracking the whip. Some mistresses set behaviour traps for us, to satisfy their spanking habit. If you don't mind my saying so, I think it's a crock. A way for superiors to pick on those who have no choice but to take it.'

I gently smoothed the lotion over his pert, rounded backside, fascinated by the hard muscle beneath skin that radiated such heat ... the give of the flesh at the fullest phase of his moons. 'And your family perished in a fire? You went into service when you were orphaned?'

The weight of that stare made me glance up, into a face that looked hardened despite a feminine hairstyle and carefully applied cosmetics. 'The authorities believed *I* set that fire, Miss Eve,' he stated. 'Miss Delacroix's school provided me the cover to get on with my life, even if I'd rather not parade around like a lady.'

My hand stopped, cupping his warm, slippery underside. A surge of adrenaline, shot from his eyes to mine, made my pulse race. 'And did you? Set that fire?'

Lord, the last thing I needed was an arsonist in my house! The kitchen felt airless for a few interminable seconds, as Antoinette challenged me with a taut-jawed gaze: it was the look of a hoodlum or a harlot, which no amount of powder or rouge could disguise.

'No, Mrs Proffit, I did not.'

His whisper sounded strangely seductive, coming from a servant confessing a checkered past. 'I was thirteen. Had gotten crosswise with the local constable, so I was the first person he suspected – despite the fact that I lost my *mother* and three sisters when that ratty old tenement went up like wildfire. So I ran – smack into Honore Delacroix when I rounded a corner.'

'And she took you in?' I began to rub the other half of his ass with the bag balm, filing away these fascinating details for later. Toinette sounded quite sincere, yet I sensed an undercurrent of defiance and rebellion against authority.

'She cut me a deal. Honore never fails to see the dollar signs in any situation.' He sighed, letting his eyes go half shut. 'Rub lower, please ... yes, right there.'

My ploy was beginning to backfire – for what woman in her right mind fondled the help, expecting to maintain the proper decorum? 'She's taken advantage of your hardship then? Profited from your misfortune?'

'Who hasn't?' Antoinette replied acidly. "When you're born on the wrong side of the tracks – wrong side of the sheets – it's a way of life. But I'll warn you before you rub that stuff any lower.'

I looked up, my face unsettlingly close to one that could be my double.

'The fire never goes out, Miss Eve.'

With a flick of the fork he was polishing, Antoinette drew my attention to the apron tented against the table. He was long and hard, leaving no doubt that in the right circumstances, he'd be hefting me up there and spreading my legs, and there'd be nothing of the sissy maid or Marie Antoinette in the way he claimed me.

I was flattered, yet flustered, and reminded myself to remain firm. 'See that you never singe either of us,' I replied, loudly smacking his slick backside with my hand.

The servants on either side of us were trying not to snicker as they studiously polished their silverware. 'And you two – as accomplices – shall be held accountable as well,' I added brusquely. 'Monique may have procured your services, but I won't hesitate to notify the authorities of what's going on here, and at that school.'

I had no intention of following through on that threat, for it would only get me into deeper trouble with my husband. But they should know that Miss Eve would remain in control, no matter what their black-clad whipping mistress had implied. No special favours for Antoinette, simply because he'd opened his soul and flashed his manhood at me.

I stepped behind Cleopatra then, who still bore koh-led circles around her obsidian eyes. 'And you went into Miss Delacroix's service when? Because your mother gave you up?'

Again I scooped up a gob of the balm, to spread over the olive cheeks sticking out beneath his apron strings. And again my gesture was met with a slight sigh and an air of cooperation I found heartening.

'I sugar-coated the truth, if you must know,' the dusky young man replied. The voice I heard was more masculine than when we'd met, yet it retained a timbre and pitch I would've attributed to a female, were I not witnessing the rise of his erection. 'My mother sold me into service because, yes, there were too many mouths to feed. But I was prettier than my sisters, so I brought the nicest price when she put us on display at the French Market.'

My eyes widened. 'Your mother *sold* you to – ?'

'It's more common than you might think, among the poor,' he sighed. 'And since it was the illustrious Miss Delacroix checking my teeth and face, and then finger-ing my ... privates, Mama drove a harder bargain. Honore represented a future for me, and her money fed the rest of them for quite awhile.'

My brow furrowed as I smoothed salve across Cleo-patra's stripes. He was taller than the other two, with glossy black hair pulled back at the crown, to hang past his shoulders. His skin was soft and hairless; his sinews more evident, now that he wore only an apron. With a male haircut and clothing, he would cut a striking figure even among the crowd Chapin associated with.

What a shame that he'd had no better choice as a child! Yet I sensed he was – like my husband – a man who would always revere and respect his mama. Even though he was living as a woman because of her, he would never stop longing for the mother who sold him.

'How long are you required to remain with Miss Delacroix?' I ventured, rhythmically rubbing circles around his firm young buttocks. He was leaning into it now, craving the contact of my hand as much as I enjoyed applying the ointment. 'Surely there's a limit to –'

'We may leave when we're twenty-one,' Cinderella piped up. 'But few of Miss Delacroix's students really want to. Her methods are harsh, but her reputation and high fees assure us of work in the finest homes. On our own, we'd be hard-pressed to land such prestigious positions.'

Cleopatra and Antoinette nodded, picking up new spoons to polish. What didn't fit, in this picture? Had life with a wealthy man made me forget the stigma of falling on hard times?

My own circumstances weren't terribly different from theirs, since my marriage to Chapin had offset my parents' debts. But I had agreed to this arrangement as an adult; I'd bartered myself into Southern society because eligible suitors in St. Louis weren't pounding my door down, and because it seemed the prudent thing to do. These three had entered into some dubious relationship with Honore Delacroix as children and, by the sound of it, they'd become her ... whipping boys. Maybe even her slaves.

When I glanced over at the fair features of my third

servant – the one who'd mewed so pitifully when Monique whipped him – I sensed a different story, however. Cinderella had an air of high breeding the other two lacked; a poise and carriage and deportment denoting good lineage.

'And what of you, Princess?' I asked as I stepped closer, spreading the first dollop of balm on her pitifully crisscrossed backside.

Cinderella flinched, more from emotional pain than the fire in her stripes. She picked up a knife and began to polish it with sudden fervour.

'My father declared early on that I would never meet his expectations as an heir,' he replied in a high, tight voice. 'I was an embarrassment to him, and a source of disgust to my mother, when they caught me wearing my sister's shoes. "Why did *Lucy* get pretty kid slippers while I had to stumble around in clunky old boots?" I asked them.'

The blonde's breath caught in her throat, from the moment's emotion but also because she loved the caress of my lotioned hand on her backside. 'I wasn't yet seven when they took me to Miss Delacroix's, on the advice of a family friend,' Cinderella went on in a fragile drawl. 'I suspect they made a large donation, for the privilege of sweeping me under her rug.'

My God, could I ever look at these three again without feeling sorry for them? I'd unwittingly opened a Pandora's box that infuriated me, and incensed me, and insulted me. I knew them for the cross-gendered men they were now, as well as for the helpless boys they'd been before coming into Honore Delacroix's School for Domestic Endeavor and, as I quickly completed massaging Cinderella's balm, my thoughts collided.

I was ready to rail at Monique for getting me into this situation. Ready to lash out at Mrs Frike for the way her avid gaze followed my hands over those three attractive asses: she was old enough to be their grandmother, after all, and had all the allure of a lumpy mattress. And I was determined to meet with Miss Delacroix for an explanation of just what went on at her esteemed school, for it appeared Domestic Endeavor was her *least* concern when she accepted applicants.

I was also unspeakably horny. That was my own fault, so I left my new maids to their work before I succumbed to the temptation of grasping Antoinette's randy shaft with my lotioned hand.

'Thank you for your candour, and for the conscientious work I know you'll do,' I murmured, and then I went up to my room.

I'd had an eventful morning, and I needed to prepare myself for whatever the evening might bring. With Monique, I never knew. And if that handsome rebel lover of hers had a gift for me, the possibilities for pleasure would wag their finger in a come-hither gesture I couldn't ignore.

My own fingers, slick with bag balm and still hot from massaging my male maids, found their way to my desperately wet sex, and I let imagination have its way. Thank goodness Chapin was out of town. He would never understand any of this!

The evening found me gazing expectantly into the moonlit gardens, from the railed gallery that spanned the back of the house. The maids had settled into their large dormitory room above mine, on the third floor, and Mrs Frike might well have slipped up from her quarters alongside the kitchen to tuck them in. Nothing would surprise me at this point.

The house was quiet. Not unusual, since Chapin was often out this late. Yet my pulse thrummed with the awareness that three young men now lived here. Perhaps I should check on them ... just to be sure Fanny wasn't harassing them, of course. But then a pebble clanged against the wrought iron and bounced on to the smooth porch floor by my bare feet.

I looked down, into the shadows of magnolia trees and manicured boxwood hedges, and saw two grinning faces framed by hair the colour of the night. Monique's laughter reached me with her wave, filling me with her contagious sense of joy. My maid and her tall, muscular man stood naked and ready to play! Right out there in my garden!

I trotted down from the gallery, my feet barely touching the iron stairs. What would they do if Chapin had come home – or if Fanny saw them cavorting out here in the altogether? I was ready to demand. But Tommy Jon caught me around the waist to toss me against his chest while his other hand muffled my squeal.

'You thought we forgot about you, *oui*?'

Monique was whirling like a dervish, her hands outstretched to catch moonbeams while her hair rippled in a black cascade behind her. Her breasts bobbed and her body flexed with each step, providing a breathtaking vision of young loveliness – which my captor couldn't ignore.

'She's talked about you all night.' As Tommy Jon set me on the ground, he stole a hungry kiss while keeping his eye on the woman he loved. 'She told me what happened in your bathroom this morning – about feeling your juice through that black lace ... how it whispered against your tight, red curls. She told me how you stared at those boys' bare asses, watching their balls jiggle above their white silk panties when she spanked them.'

I swallowed hard. I should've realised Monique and her T-Jon would have no secrets – even if they were supposed to be *my* secrets.

'She tells me you want my cock, Miss Eve.'

And there it was, rising to greet my pointed stare. I'd never seen *anyone* so well endowed as Tommy Jon Beaumont.

He knew this, of course. So he stood with his arms akimbo, his lean hips easing forward and a devilish grin on his face. His erection swayed to its full length as though it loved putting on such a show. Maybe it was the interplay between shadows dancing on the breeze and the light of that big moon above us, but I swore that cock bobbed its head, bowing to me. A drop of dew glistened at its tip, and then ran down the thick, rounded crown until it dropped off.

I sucked air, and my insides got hot.

'So – here it is, lady. Take it.'

Had there ever been such a blatant invitation? While I could envision earlier Proffits trysting here in the garden, where the fountain burbled and the azaleas and crepe myrtle provided nooks made for such nesting, I doubted any of them held a candle to this naked pair. My hand extended, as though pulled by a magnet from within the alluring man who'd challenged me. Tommy Jon Beaumont stood like a statue of a Greek god, with the planes and curves and cords of his body carved into the moonlit night.

But the museum statues I'd seen didn't have such a shaft sticking out! I was getting up my nerve, taking that first fateful step, when Monique sideswiped me as she whirled to the music of the cicadas.

'Strip, Auntie Evil!' she ordered. 'Then maybe I'll share him. And then *maybe* you'll get your gift.'

10 **A Taste of Wild Honey**

I sent my silk dressing gown drifting down my bare body, for I'd suspected this wild pair might stage such an outrageous rendezvous. How gratifying, to watch Tommy Jon's eyes focus so intently as my breasts, and then my midsection, and then my sex were revealed. He had his own diversion, after all – she crouched before him, steadying herself between his sturdy legs as she kissed the tip of his cock.

I held my breath as she took him into her mouth. Did women *do* this? Did men enjoy it as much ... as much as I enjoyed such attention from Monique?

His quiet moan told me. His fingers speared into her glossy, unfettered hair, moving her head at the tempo he wanted. Monique's lips remained in an O that followed his shaft forward and back – pushing and then pulling to make him longer – while she cupped his sac. She was an impish little thing, so where all of that piston went, inside her mouth, remained a mystery. A mystery I longed to taste and feel for myself.

Feeling bold, I bumped her out of the way. My maid, however, merely bumped me back with a swing of her hips that sent me sprawling in the grass. Then she laughed and grabbed Tommy Jon's hand.

'It's in the fountain, Auntie,' she teased, leading her lover in that direction. 'You must find it before we let you play.'

Who could resist her playful challenge, or her squeal of delight when Tommy Jon scooped her into his arms?

I followed them, laughing when the agile Tommy threw her in. With a scream and a splash she landed in the fountain's basin, popping up like a porpoise to blow water from her mouth.

'Look what I found!' she crowed, waving it above her head. 'Let's play catch, T-Jon. Keep-away – from Auntie Eve!'

The object she tossed him was dark and long and ... as it tumbled through the air into his outstretched palms, another giddy jolt passed through me. Tommy Jon Beaumont had made me a leather cock! He looked my way, and then lobbed it into an arc above the fountain's spray.

'Maybe, Monique, she can use two of them?' he teased. 'Hot and hungry as her pussy gets, she might *need* this extra one. But I made this toy especially for her pretty Aunt Eve ... the lady with the lovely cunny. I want to push it up inside you myself –'

I could stand no more. Sprinting towards the fountain to join them, I revelled in their dark, sleek wetness as they stood nude in the moonlight, with rivulets of water running down their bodies. T-Jon caught the dildo and waggled it just beyond my reach before tossing it back to his lover. As it sailed over my head I sprang up, my arm fully extended, but Monique gave me a playful push and caught the leather cock herself.

I splashed to the bottom of the fountain and then found my feet; shot upward, sputtering in mock protest. How many years since I'd frolicked in water? Never nude in a fountain, to be sure! And although my hair was sagging in soggy lumps hung up on hair pins, I felt like a child. What freedom, to splash in the water without clothes – to shiver with the chill of it until my nipples went hard and goose bumps covered me. And then to look at the two other wet bodies cavorting on either side of me, and feel their absolute approval that I'd joined them – not as the lady of the estate, but as a friend.

And how long had it been since *that* happened?

Monique tossed the leather prick to me and I caught it – but I was then drawn backwards against Tommy Jon's hard, male body.

'And now I'll show Miss Eve how this feels ... how hot she'll get from rubbing herself in all the right places, like I want to do with my cock,' he murmured against my wet ear. 'I moulded this over my own prick, you know. Fashioned the soft, wet leather over my hardness, and sewed the folds with special ridges, to excite you.'

He ran little kisses down my face then, holding me against himself with that arm beneath my breasts. Driving me insane, the way he undulated against my backside to further excite us both. 'Open for me, pretty woman,' came his whispered command. 'T-Jon Beaumont's gonna show you what you've been missing.'

Had he, too, guessed that Chapin was a less-than-attentive lover? Or was it his Cajun ego, touting his proportions and stamina, as every male was wont to do?

Not that it mattered. With his knee spreading my legs from behind and that dark, hard shaft of leather gliding down my stomach towards my wet curls, I was too spellbound to care. Monique watched us, wiping the wet hair back from her face.

'This is going to be so good,' she said in a husky voice. 'Rub the tip around her clit, T-Jon. Let it glide between her lips ... up and down in her dew – ah, *oui, cheri!* – and then press in with it ... ooh-la-la. You've got her squirming now!'

I let out a shameless moan, falling back against his

body, succumbing to the magic of both his wands. Raising a foot to the rim of the fountain, I opened myself – gasping when that slick leather tip found its way below my aching clit, to tease at the rim of my hole.

'Push it in,' I whispered. 'Oh, please, Tommy Jon, I've never had such a –'

'Long ... solid ... eager cock shoving up you?' he finished.

And when he made good on that, guiding the dildo with slow but relentless pressure, I froze against him with my mouth open. In and then out, with a rhythm that remained steady yet accelerating, until the hard leather shaft danced up and down as he twisted it, to put those ridges into play. I was squirming, helpless, unable to stop my body's gyrations. Tommy Jon pumped with relentless intent as he held me spellbound with his expert attentions.

The madness peaked quite suddenly, and when he focused the pressure on my throbbing clit, I surged to my tiptoes with a high-pitched cry. The garden echoed with utter, mindless babbling that made perfect sense to my incited mind. My pussy was going crazy. I couldn't control my convulsing hips as I rode the cresting waves of my climax. Somehow Tommy Jon had tapped into a nerve centre and was still making me twitch with each caress, until he finally let me fall back into his embrace, exhausted.

'You liked that, *oui*?' he teased, kissing my temple.

'Oh my Lord, I never knew – never guessed –'

'The women, they all say that after they've been with me.' Then he gently turned me, so I could sit against the fountain's rim to recover. 'You're a good pupil, Miss Eve. If Monique wasn't here, I'd show you a few more moves. But she demands her turn, you know.'

I had to smile, for my maid always demanded attention.

'You were such a fine instructor, *cheri*, Monique wants to give *you* a turn,' came her sultry reply.

She hopped up into his arms to be caught like a little girl, wrapping her legs at his waist, although the kiss she gave him was anything but innocent. With her whole body she lit into that man, rubbing her breasts and slit against him while her mouth reminded him who he belonged to. Tommy Jon moaned and kissed her back, hard and possessive, before letting her slither down to the ground again.

There in the moonlight, silhouetted against the night sky, they made a beautiful sight with the jets of water falling in arcs around them. He coaxed her lower, letting his head fall back when her lips found the tip of his cock. I felt like an intruder, sitting that close to such intimate behaviour, so I slipped the dildo from T-Jon's hand and stepped out of the fountain. I felt no need to share Monique's lover while she was enjoying him. I'd gotten plenty more to think about from the myriad wild sensations he'd brought me during my own climax.

'Hope you saved a taste for me, sugah,' came a drawl in the darkness.

I searched the shadows around the hedge: there was no mistaking that molasses voice. My heart raced, for Dewel was not allowed to set foot on this property – but then, why would he follow his half-brother's rules? Trespassing in Chapin's garden, with Eve, took on a whole new meaning as he stepped from behind the massive magnolia tree that hid us from the house.

'Surely you're not surprised,' he continued in that velvety baritone, peeling away clothes he'd already unbuttoned. 'I'm here on a purely tutorial mission, of course. To show you the joys of returnin' a man's favours. Teachin' you how to drive him wild, like Monique there.'

His erection jutted above the trousers he shoved down, leaving no doubt about what he had in mind. A glance towards the lovers in the fountain was an education in itself, for my maid was obviously enjoying her work, driving her mouth up and down T-Jon's huge cock.

'I – I've never –'

'Then it's time you did, darlin'.' Dewel closed the distance between us with quick strides. 'Much as I love a hot, tight hole, a woman's mouth can do things her sex can't. And when she throws in some lickin', and suckin', why – I just have to surrender myself to her. Just like Chapin would, if he were here.'

His last words made him grin lasciviously. Dewel Proffit cut a proud, virile figure in this garden mottled with moonlight, and his cocky talk teased at my senses as much as the sight of him and the scent of fine cigars that lingered on his skin.

His kiss tasted of brandy and I was intoxicated before I could put up even a token resistance. But why would I? I wanted nothing more than to please this man beyond his wildest expectations.

'What do I – what if I hurt –'

'You won't, sugah,' he reassured me, guiding my hand to cup his sac. It filled my palm and felt tantalising, with those two separate nuggets inside the warm, loose flesh. 'Put your leg up and I'll give you a little incentive. Watch Monique and Tommy Jon ... tell me exactly what she's doin' to him, and you'll be well on your way.'

On my way to what? Learning another technique to seduce Chapin, or falling more deeply under his bastard brother's provocative spell? I had no choice but to prop my foot on the bench, facing the lovers in the fountain, because Dewel had already knelt in front of me to direct my moves.

'Oh, Eve, honey, you do tempt a man,' he murmured, his breath warm on my cooling thighs. 'Tight little curls, around folds that look like a flower ready to open ... around this little nub that's just calling out for me to tease her.'

With a single stroke of his tongue he made me gasp, rekindling the flames Tommy Jon ignited with his dildo. 'Dewel, please –'

'I'll give you all you can handle, you little beggar, but you've gotta talk to me,' he hinted, and then he lapped at me again. 'What's she doin' to him?'

Grasping the sides of his head for balance, I focused on the two lovers. 'Her cheeks are caved in, from ... sucking on his cock. My Lord, it looks a foot long, and so thick, and ... now she's slowly moving her mouth down the shaft.'

'Mmm,' Dewel moaned, leaning up into his work. He was massaging my bottom, and when the fingers of both hands found its crevice, they parted the two halves – which opened me up right before his eyes. He chuckled, kissing my nether lips.

I cried out again, then remembered to open my eyes. 'Monique's wrapped her hand around the base of it now, and she's pumping it up and down so her fist meets her lips ... so every inch of that cock feels her squeezing. Is that how you like it, Dewel?'

He drove his tongue into me and I lost control, grinding my sex against a mouth that made wet, sucking noises. How had he brought me to climax so effortlessly? Was it his own potent magic, or the way he'd made me watch those Cajun lovers? Tommy Jon hunched, his face tight with need, and I wanted to make Dewel feel that way too.

I stepped back, watching him lick my honey from his lips. 'Your turn,' I murmured. 'It's the least I can do, after all the ways you've pleasured me. How can you make me come so easily, when Chapin –'

I caught myself, but he already knew how the sentence would end. 'Practice makes perfect,' he quipped, and then he sat on the bench with an expectant grin. 'And, of course, that's why I'm here. So you can practise, for your dear husband's benefit. Not every half-brother would be so generous.'

I was about to warn him that Chapin might return at any time – might even be watching us from the upstairs window – but he ran his thumb slowly along the curve of my lower lip.

'We're gonna forget him for now,' he said, his blue eyes intense in the twilight. 'This is just for me, Eve. Because I *am* a selfish bastard, like he's always claimed. Kneel between my knees and suck me, sugah. Suck me hard and fast, because I need you – *now*.'

I obeyed his siren call, closing my eyes and inhaling the musk that hovered between his legs. His labour in the cane fields had honed his body to an enticing hardness – but that was nothing compared to the cock that pushed past my lips.

I opened for him, running my mouth over his hot, smooth tip and then down the ridged length of his rigid member. He tasted like skin and sweat, yet also like brandy. I couldn't help giggling.

'Like that little surprise?' he asked, thrusting against my tongue. 'Thought I'd make your first time a little tastier. Some women won't do this for a man, Miss Eve, but you're takin' to it like – oh Jesus, woman, but you've got a mouth on you!'

I continued swivelling my lips around him, running my tongue along the underside of a cock that filled my mouth with its throbbing. Slipping his fingers into my wet hair, Dewel guided my head faster, his moans more insistent now. He began to pant – a rasping sound that drove me to suck harder. His whole body tensed, and I prepared for whatever might come out.

And come it did, a torrent of warm, buttery silk; first one gush and then a couple more, as Dewel fought for breath. When I glanced up, his grimace was reward enough for the mouthful of fluid I wasn't sure what to do with. He shook his head to clear it, then smiled and kissed my cheek.

'You can spit if you want,' he whispered. 'Most men get a big thrill from watching their woman swallow – or from squirtin' all over her face. Never tried the stuff myself, but I'll understand if you find it distasteful.'

I held it, pondering my options. Not wanting to retch if it disagreed with my stomach ... not wanting Dewel to think I found anything about him distasteful. After all, he'd sampled my private honey and –

It went down before I realised it. And stayed. I wiped my mouth with the back of my hand. 'Not as tasty as, say, Fanny's chicken gravy. But not as awful as cod liver oil either.'

His laughter made me giddy, telling me I'd pleased him in many ways. When he pulled me up to kiss away the remains of his come, he made my head spin into a fresh wave of desire. I kissed him back, sharing his exuberance: being with such an exciting man made me feel like a whole different woman.

'You're a goddess any man would want, sugah, but you've had your share,' he teased. 'There'll be another time. Lots of them, now that I know just how luscious you are.'

Dewel smiled, looking brazen and disreputable with his dark hair falling over his brow and those dimples dancing alongside his mouth. 'But tell me before I disappear – how are the new maids workin' out? Monique thinks they show promise, now that she's ... whipped them into shape.'

In an instant my mood changed, for this was the man who'd insisted I needed a 'niece' – and Monique had imported the hornet's nest that would get us all stung soon. 'Chapin will go through the roof if he –'

'Because of the spankin'?' The younger Proffit considered this. 'He was always one for discipline. Certainly enjoys inflictin' pain himself.'

'– finds out what sort of servants Monique brought home,' I rasped. 'Not only are they young *men* – who make prettier women than I will ever be! – but their circumstances are unthinkable. Why, one of them's an accused arsonist, hiding from the law!'

Dewel's eyes widened, and he pulled me into his lap so we could talk more quietly. 'And how do you know this, sugah? Honore Delacroix supplies servants for the city's most persnickety blue-bloods, so I can't believe –'

'She – he – told me himself! And then Cleopatra – or Chloe, or whatever his real name is – said his mama *sold* him to the headmistress – in the French Market,' I rasped, my whispers rising with my frustration, 'because he was prettier than his sisters. And poor Cinderella –'

At this name, a dark eyebrow arched in disbelief, but Dewel kept listening.

'– was dumped at the school at a very young age – with a very large donation – simply because he showed a fondness for ladies' shoes!' I finished in a fit of disgust. 'If Chapin finds out Monique has brought such odd ducks into our home, I'm in deep trouble, Dewel.'

He thought for a moment, cradling me like a child yet making me very aware I was a naked lady on the lap of a lecherous man. 'And why are you tellin' *me* these things?' he asked quietly. 'What do you want to happen now?'

It was the tone I recalled from our first encounter by the courtyard gate, when Dewel had defined my discovery that Chapin was cheating: I must navigate another emotional crossroads and never look back. Once again, his primal power acted like a truth serum, making me behave in ways I wouldn't have dared, before I became involved with him.

'Well, besides the fact that *you* brought this on – I expect some answers from Honore Delacroix,' I replied. 'I'm going to that school, to demand an explanation from the headmistress herself!'

'Did the spankin' bother you, Miss Eve?'

I studied the planes of his face; determined that he was more interested in my welfare than in escalating the feud with his half-brother. 'Not so much as the trickery – the way Miss Delacroix makes these young men live a lie, to meet her own needs.'

Was it the moonlight? Or did Dewel assume the crafty air of a sly old fox? 'You're the lady of the house,' he affirmed with a nod. 'You should indeed quiz Honore Delacroix about your new servants. An instructor of such prominence and high moral standin' owes you these answers – and more.'

11 **Nasty Accusations**

'Ooh-la-la, Auntie Evil! You really had Dewel grunting and spurting – responding to your mouth – last night, *oui*?' Monique laughed as she threw open my curtains. 'You're ready to seduce Chapin now.'

'We need to talk, Monique. Please shut the door.'

Squinting at the sunlight, wishing she weren't so damn cheerful, I scowled more harshly than I intended to. She and Tommy Jon were probably out later than I last night, yet she looked as fresh as a just-opened rose – albeit a rose in a short maid's uniform, flashing her bare bottom as she bent over to pick up my clothes.

My maid's face fell, but then her expression grew more pensive. 'Did I do something wrong, Miss Eve? I thought you'd *like* playing naked with Tommy Jon and me. Thought bringing Dewel would be a nice surprise – the best way to keep training you for –'

She cocked her head, her smile decidedly conniving. 'Or has Auntie Evil changed her mind about this husband seduction? You want his brother instead, *non*?'

How I wished I could grin at her playful suggestion – or at that topknot of midnight hair bobbing untidily behind her white ruffled maid's cap. But this was no game, dammit. I didn't know if Mrs Frike had spotted us frolicking naked in the fountain, nor could I postpone speaking to Honore Delacroix about the new servants.

Not so much what Dewel had said, but how he'd said it, suggested things that were going on behind my back;

things he and his zany maid remained deeply involved in. It was no secret he wanted me, but I couldn't just toss aside discretion and common sense, now could I? After all, the bastard heir to the cane plantation had nothing to lose from these little scenarios he and Monique created.

'I can't go charging over to confront Honor Delacroix about these three maids,' I explained in a low voice. 'But I can't waste time getting answers either. Chapin came home late last night.'

Her chocolate eyes widened. 'But he wasn't gone long enough to –'

'I don't know what his story is. I just don't want him to overhear ours.'

Nodding, Monique fetched the breakfast tray Fanny had brought up earlier, and quietly shut my door. 'Let me fix your café au lait, *ma tante*,' she murmured, 'while you tell me about this. Did something go wrong with our two queens and the princess yesterday? Did Chapin *see* us in the garden?'

Her sincere concern settled some of my suspicions about strings she might be pulling – even with the best intentions. 'He didn't get home until after I came upstairs. But if Mrs Frike happened to see us, who knows what she might have told him about that – and about the new, uh, *girls*?'

I took a large bite of the pecan roll beneath the lid she lifted, and gratefully gulped half the cup of the milk-laced chicory coffee. It was best to address one issue at a time; to lead her along with questions and watch her reactions. 'First of all, did you know that Chloe –'

'Cleopatra,' Monique insisted. 'We must maintain his new image and expectations, now that he's away from the school.'

I bit into my roll, forcing myself to remain patient. 'Did you know Cleopatra's mother *sold* him to Miss Delacroix? At the French Market, no less? He was only a child, and she palmed him off like he was –'

'It is that way in poor families, Miss Eve,' she cut in with a slightly resentful flash of her long lashes. 'I myself went to work very young.'

'But Chlo – Cleopatra – didn't take a job, although he was the *son* and he could logically have done so,' I countered. 'His mama sold him because he was prettier than his sisters.'

'And Miss Delacroix paid her well, no doubt. That doesn't make him unsuitable as a servant on your staff.'

'And did you know that Cinderella's family *gave* him to Honore? With a large donation?' I continued grilling her. 'His family was very wealthy. They could've sent him away to boarding school if his taste for ladies' shoes offended them. I find this intolerable!'

My maid, perched on the side of the bed so she could pinch off a bite of my breakfast, paused to chew thoughtfully. She didn't want to abandon her plan, and her Cajun pride wouldn't let her admit a mistake. 'If their work is not satisfactory to –'

'And did you know Toinette is hiding from the law?' I pressed on, leaning over the tray to make my point. 'You recall the fire he mentioned, where he lost his family? He might have *set* it, Monique! He wouldn't give me a straight answer.'

The Cajun blanched, and then returned the last bite she'd snitched back to my plate. I'd seen what I needed: my well-meaning Monique couldn't have known these more sordid background details when she acquired our three unusual maids. Which meant her interview process might not have been as thorough as she'd claimed.

'It's not the maids' abilities I'm questioning here,' I

went on more gently, 'it's Miss Delacroix's scruples. Her basic sense of decency. And I'm more concerned about our safety – and what I'll tell Chapin, because he's sure to quiz me about them – than about how you came to choose these three. Did you get them from Honore herself? Because she recommended them for our household?'

Two bright patches of pink appeared beneath the big brown eyes she was batting. She pulled a cheroot from the bosom of her uniform and bit off both ends. 'Miss Delacroix's a very busy lady, so –'

'Have you even *met* her, Monique?'

Resentment flared with her match, and then she swatted away my question with the hand that held her cigar. '*Oui*, we meet – months ago – but she wouldn't recall little Monique Picabou. Brushed me off like a housefly! She was out of the school when I went to hire the maids yesterday, so I just *handled* it, Auntie.'

What she hadn't said spoke volumes: my maid hated to be ignored, so she was repaying the headmistress's offense in her own inimitable way. 'So you didn't pay my fee,' I said, which answered my question from yesterday and gave me a very solid reason for visiting the school. 'If Miss Delacroix didn't recommend these three maids, how were they selected?'

The maid's eyes brightened slyly. 'I conducted a very extensive interview –'

'May I see your list of questions? The written references you got from each one?'

'– by testing each student, and inspecting . . .' She sighed like a deflating balloon. 'Oh, all right! I had all of Miss Delacroix's students stand in a line and lean over.'

Only Monique would conduct such an interview! As this picture ran through my mind, I had to stifle a giggle in spite of my serious situation. 'You chose the ones with the best butts? Monique, I've tried to impress upon you –'

'Chloe, Annabelle and Sylvia were the most *motivated*,' she insisted. 'They're ready for the challenge of serving in a household. And now that we gave them new names – a whole new life – those three will not only serve you, Auntie Evil, but they'll love you so much they'll risk their reputations – their *lives* – for you! This is much more important than good answers to interview questions, *non*?'

She blew smoke out her nose, eyeing me like a dragon who might well be the one to test their loyalty – and mine – although I couldn't see it becoming a life-or-death matter.

You didn't foresee Chapin taking you in anger either.

A sobering thought. One that reminded me the time was passing, and that I had many proverbial fires to put out. Not the least of which might be set by the husband lurking somewhere in this house.

'Thank you for telling me,' I said, placing the cover over my breakfast plate. 'I'll visit the illustrious Miss Delacroix this morning, and pay my fee for these fine maids you've hired. I want to see what sort of woman I'm dealing with here, so choose me a dress that's suitable for such a visit, Monique. Something elegant, yet –'

'Powerful,' the little Cajun whispered. 'Honore Delacroix is another name for *power*.'

An hour later I went downstairs feeling ready to face the city's most formidable headmistress. I wore my new suit of forest green with a pleated cream-coloured blouse, and a fashionable hat that didn't diminish me to the frilliness of a debutante. A final check in the hall mirror bolstered my resolve: I would retain the maids

Monique had chosen, for I trusted her instincts. But I would also question Honore Delacroix closely: I suspected an inexplicable *something* about a woman who would acquire three young boys under such dubious circumstances.

'Going out, my dear?'

Chapin's genteel tone couched his suspicions about my destination – and the company I would keep. I turned to him, biting back my resentment – and wondering what things *he* hid as well. He was nattily dressed in a frock coat of brown and gold houndstooth that brought out the blonder highlights of his swept-back hair.

'How handsome you look,' I remarked, for he cut a stylish figure even when he didn't leave the house. 'And how nice to have you home. What changed your travel plans?'

He smiled tightly, and remained in the doorway of the dining room. 'My platform committee called a lunch meeting at the Beau Monde Club today, to plan our campaign strategies. And *you*, dear heart?'

Deer heart. Yes, that's how mine was beating – like the pulse of a doe in a hunter's gun scope. I'd caught his scent, but wasn't sure which escape route was safest.

I didn't dare quiz him about the inconsistencies of his story, as he could certainly ask questions I didn't want to answer.

'I'm going in to pay the acquisition fee for our three new maids,' I replied carefully. 'Now that I've seen them work and we've acquainted ourselves, I'm sure they'll perform quite well.'

'Excellent. I look forward to meeting them.' He reached inside his coat then, his expression getting edgier. 'Before you go, perhaps you can explain this.

The greengrocer's delivery boy tripped over it this morning.'

The blood raced from my face as he pulled out a long object of black leather, and then nailed me with his knowing gaze. Laced with red cross-stitching in strategic places beneath its mushroom-shaped head, the custom-made dildo looked even more incriminating by light of day than when Tommy Jon had brandished it in the fountain. 'I have no idea –'

'Oh, I think you do, Miss Eve,' he whispered, advancing towards me with the toy extended from his fist. 'But for propriety's sake, we'll say you're going to ask that Cajun maid of yours to keep better track of her personal possessions. Mrs Frike grew rather agitated when the boy asked her what it was.'

Chapin slapped the dildo into my hand and left with a smirk, donning his derby as though he'd once again proven me a wanton and incompetent liar. Damn that man! Playing cat and mouse with me. Talking of *propriety*, while making his silent accusations about how I'd spent my time.

Why hadn't he just lifted my skirts and rammed the leather shaft inside me? At least I would've felt something besides a cold, growing resentment as the door slammed behind him.

My visit to the School of Domestic Endeavor was as disheartening as my chat with Chapin: Honore Delacroix wasn't there. And her secretary wasn't any more inclined to give me a tour of the school than to answer my questions.

'When do you expect her return?' I asked, masking my impatience. The girl behind the desk was an insipid spinsterish sort decked out in a flouncy gown of yellow, with a disposition that sucked lemons.

She slammed her desk drawer, as though I might try to peek at her files. 'I don't expect Miss Delacroix any time today. She's making home visits, to ensure the suitability of the positions our girls are being hired into.'

'What an excellent practice. Might I find out when she expects to visit the Proffit home? I'm sure the three ... girls we've procured will be pleased to see her.'

'And you would be ...?'

'Eve Proffit – Mr Chapin Proffit's wife. He'll soon be hosting campaign parties, and –'

She stopped riffling through her ledger to stare up at me, above the thick lenses of her spectacles. 'And why have I not met you before, Mrs Proffit? I never forget a face.'

Once again my credibility was called into question – and I was damn tired of it! I placed my gloved hands on either side of her account book, so she would get a good look at whom she was dealing with. 'My assistant came here yesterday and procured three domestics, Miss ...?'

'Sully,' she replied with a rancour matching mine.

Quite sure no one would sully *this* unpleasant woman, I reached into my reticule. 'I've come to pay my fee. And to make an appointment for a home visit from Miss Delacroix, please.'

'Oh, I'm sure you'll be seeing her soon. She's not at *all* pleased with the way your *assistant* sashayed out of here with three of her own domestics!'

I arched an eyebrow, and then scribbled out a cheque for one hundred dollars. Probably not enough, for a deposit covering three maids, but I was beyond caring what this twit in yellow dimity thought. 'Tell Miss Delacroix we can't wait to see her.'

I left the old brick building then, sensing an atmosphere of decay and disrepair about the surrounding neighbourhood that I hadn't noted when I'd gone inside. Perhaps it was the proximity to the courtyard where I'd seen Chapin and Savanna that held such unpleasant associations, or perhaps it was simply the way this morning had been going. The carriage ride home had me stewing over events and details sent spinning out of my control. I kicked myself for getting caught in so many seemingly careless mistakes – most of them made by Monique! I just wanted to be left alone in my room.

I had gotten no further than the table in the vestibule, however, when I heard the swish of short skirts and the quick clatter of boots on the parquet flooring. 'Auntie Eve! It's your big day,' she announced. 'The perfect time for –'

I peeled off my gloves without looking at her.

'– your next step into white-hot marital bliss.'

I raised my eyebrow. The fact that 'marital' and 'bliss' came side-by-side in Monique's sentence, and that it involved Chapin Proffit, proved another ironic thorn in my side. Why had I gotten caught in this seduction scheme, the victim of everyone else's imaginations?

'Absolutely not. I'm going upstairs, and I don't want to be disturbed.'

My maid cocked her head, looking like a cocker spaniel whose ears had been hiked up into a white lace ribbon. 'Surely Miss Delacroix wasn't *that* rude, that you –'

'Forget it, Monique.' To drive my point home, I opened the table's centre drawer and fished out the object I'd hidden behind my handkerchiefs and calling cards. 'Chapin presented me with this before I left. He said I should talk to you about leaving your personal effects where others might stumble over them, but he knows damn well it's mine.'

The sight of the dildo, shaped like her beloved T-Jon's cock, made the maid giggle impishly and grab it out of my hand.

'This is good, *oui*?' she exclaimed, wagging the black-and-red leather cock at me. 'Now Chapin not only knows his little wife is not so naive – but he wonders what she *does* with this dildo while he's gone. His curiosity's piqued, like his cock, and he –'

'Monique, did you take this from my drawer and put it outside the service entrance this morning?'

Her eyes snapped black and brown and she turned towards the stairway, gesturing with the dildo for me to follow her. 'You'll never find out, if you don't go along with my plan, Aunt Evil. Hurry now! We have a rendezvous with a handsome man – or two. For lunch.'

12 **Lip Service**

'The Beau Monde Club? You know damn well they'll never let us in there!'

'Have I ever led you astray, *ma tante*?'

'Don't get me started on *that*.' Once again I tried to separate myself from another cockamamie scheme my maid had cooked up, betting she'd eavesdropped on my conversation with Chapin and knew where he'd be in about an hour. 'What on earth does this have to do with my dildo? Or with – with sucking Dewel's cock last night?'

Even as I said these words, in the privacy of my own bedroom, they shocked me. That I had sunk so far below socially acceptable vocabulary and activities – in only a few days – attested to the mental state Monique Picabou had created so effortlessly. That I was watching her slip into trousers and a white shirt she'd snatched from Chapin's closet further proved this young woman was nothing but trouble.

Consider the source, my thoughts warned, and this brought Dewel Proffit's lewd suggestions to mind ... how he'd coaxed me to take his thick shaft into my mouth and then *swallow* after he climaxed! Only a desperate woman would fall so far so fast.

And so I was. Desperate for male affection; for words and gestures to assure me Eve Proffit was a desirable woman, worthy of love and the passion that seemed to be passing her by. Was that too much for a woman of thirty to ask? To have a man hold me, and kiss me, and make love to me as though he enjoyed it so much he lost control?

Monique's chuckle brought me out of my musings. 'You're much happier with Dewel than with his brother, *non*?' she observed in her forthright way. 'But you're trying to be the faithful, loving wife, and I admire that. So, will you follow my plan, Auntie Evil? Or sit home worrying that your man will ask where you got your sex toy?'

'What are you suggesting?' I asked doubtfully. She had something outrageous in mind, for the wily maid had pulled her hair into a tail at her nape and then tucked it down the back of the loose shirt.

She looked for all the world like a boy.

'We'll dress you like this too – skirts are too awkward for slipping you under Mr Chapin's table,' she explained. 'I'll convince the waiter his tip will be much better if *I* serve today. We'll hide you when no one's looking, and *voila*. You'll have all those flies to choose from. All those fine, upstanding men who must sit still while you suck them, as though nothing's happening, while they talk politics over lunch! Too funny, *oui*?'

How could I not grin at this scenario? It would be the ultimate coup, to breach that all-male world of the venerable Beau Monde Club. To make Chapin and his campaign committee squirm in their chairs, trying not to grunt and grimace as they climaxed.

'But what if somebody looks under the table? Or kicks me, and my scream gives me away?' Eyeing Chapin's clothing on my bed, I couldn't believe I would even consider this. It was as though a gremlin had gotten inside me ... daring me to do what the proper Mrs Proffit would consider repugnant and unthinkable.

But Auntie Evil would lap it up. What a lark – to suck my husband in public. To make him squirm in front of men who've invested thousands in his political campaign!

'Nobody'll kick you, *cherie*,' she said, gesticulating in her exasperation. 'You remember how T-Jon loved to be sucked? How Dewel said only special women do that, and do it well? Your big chance comes in about an hour – but only if we stop wishy-washing around here!'

I reached for the trousers she'd laid on my bed, and then drew back. 'But if I'm under the table, and Chapin can't look, how will he know it's me? What will I prove?'

'Must I think of *everything*?' she wailed, and then she grabbed the buttons of my suit. 'Find a way to bring it up, when you talk to him tonight. You do talk to him, *non*?'

I closed my eyes against memories of our recent conversations, for I could already imagine Chapin's reactions when he learned that the hot, willing lips under the table belonged to his own wife. 'But then he'll realise everyone else was wiggling around –'

'So you can tell him Mistress Monique was under there too. I swear, Auntie,' she rasped, tossing aside my green jacket and then tugging my blouse from my skirt. 'We'll make something up, *oui*? For a woman so smart, you've got no brains at all!'

I should have slapped her. I should have ordered her out of my room to oversee whatever our new maids were doing. I should have shut away the mental images of well-dressed men around a table, eating some of the city's finest cuisine while throwing fortunes towards their golden boy, trying not to cry out when they came.

But I couldn't get it out of my mind, that *power* I would have, over Chapin and whichever helpless men I coaxed to a climax they couldn't show.

We were on our way out the pantry door fifteen

minutes later, with Chapin's derbies perched on our heads and his frock coats buttoned over our trousers. Why was I not surprised that Tommy Jon awaited us with a carriage? As he drove us into town, he gave suggestions for passing ourselves off as men once we entered the club.

'Walk slower. Take bigger steps, and don't swing your hips,' he instructed. 'Just nod when the other men address you, so talking won't get you into trouble, and walk directly back to the dining area. If you act like you belong there – a privileged member of long standing – nobody'll question you.'

'That's how it goes with most things, *oui*?' Monique chimed in. She was straightening her clothes and, when we drove along a street where no one else was watching, she smoothed my shirt and coat. 'Pretend you know what you're doing, and most people will believe it! After all, you've been actress enough all these years that Chapin assumes you're happy, *non*?'

The sad truth of that statement dampened my spirits, but by then we were passing the whitewashed brick building that housed the Beau Monde Club. Tommy Jon parked around the block, and then the three of us strolled like the elegantly-attired gents we were to the front door. As he reached for the heavy brass knocker, I thought of another stumbling block.

'How will we get past the doorman? Chapin has mentioned old Iverson as one of the stodgiest –'

The raven-haired Tommy gave me his most debonair smile, gripping his lapels like he had a hold of the world. 'I've been here once, as a guest, Miss Eve,' he whispered. 'I left T-Jon back in the bayou, so Monsieur Beaumont can do the talking. Just follow Monique's lead, and –'

The maroon double doors swung open with a majestic swoosh, to present a wizened old fellow in a tuxedo. He bowed low, to camouflage how closely he was looking us over. 'And how might I help you?' he prompted in a stately voice.

'I've travelled the world, Iverson, but there's only one Beau Monde Club,' our escort replied with a bow of his own.

Iverson stepped aside, smiling. 'Forgive me, sir, but I can't recall your name.'

'Thomas Beaumont,' T-Jon replied with a flourish of his card and a polished French accent. 'My business abroad has kept me from visiting of late. I understand Chapin Proffit will dine here today, and my friends and I wish to contribute to his campaign.'

'He's not yet arrived, sir, but I'll inform him –'

'Oh, I love a surprise,' the devious Tommy said with a wink, and he pressed folded money into the doorman's palm. 'We'll proceed to the dining room – if someone would kindly point out the proper table – and greet him when he gets here.'

Just that easily, we were in! We strolled across the marble floor of the vestibule with our footsteps echoing, as though we toured a grand museum. I tried not to gawk at the high-ceilinged elegance which ensconced the members of this elite organisation. The Beau Monde Club was truly a retreat from the outside world, and its groupings of leather chairs and small tables graced with Tiffany reading lamps encouraged perusal of newspapers from all over the world, or subdued conversations over brandy. Men who were engaged in such things nodded at us, as though we had every right to be there. Others sat in a haze of fine-smelling pipe smoke and silence, poring over chess boards.

As we approached the dining room, where aproned waiters put final touches on their linen-draped tables before the noonday meal, T-Jon distracted the maître de with Continental chitchat. Monique and I merely nodded and passed on to the coat rack, in a back hallway where the toilets were. My maid placed our hats on a table, watching for her lover's signal as he questioned the head waiter.

'It's that little room off to the side,' she whispered, carefully noting that no one else was around. 'Let's go now, before anyone notices us.'

Heart pounding, I followed her at what I hoped was a nonchalant gait, feeling sure things had gone far too well and that we'd be interrogated, or seen entering on the sly. As we passed through the door, Monique gave T-Jon a little nod – and then she whisked me under the table so fast I nearly took the floor-length table cloth with me.

'I thought you were –'

'Too risky, playing server where the waiters have been here forever,' she replied in a breathless whisper. 'Now that we're in position, T-Jon will find a back door out, so Chapin won't spot him. It's up to us – up to *you*,' she added, grinning in the dimness. 'There's no way out. You've got to get it right, Aunt Evil!'

How had I been talked into this? As my eyes adjusted to the shadows under the table, my pulse thundered in my ears. What if we got caught? What if someone peeked beneath the linens, and saw a young man between his knees?

My husband would be *furious*. No doubt in my mind I wouldn't be leaving the house for *days* if I failed at this, and I didn't dare imagine the price I'd pay for humiliating Chapin in front of his most important supporters. I tried desperately to think of a way out of this brazen escapade, but the sound of male voices told me it was already too late.

Monique bussed my cheek and flashed me a thumbs-up. 'What other woman would go to such extremes, to prove how badly she wants her man? How much she loves him, *non*?' she whispered.

This thought would have to sustain me, for as conversations came through the door and chairs were pulled back, my fate as Chapin Proffit's wife was about to be defined by male legs, in boots and trousers.

'So pleased to hear of your support, Senator Searcy!' came a honeyed voice. 'Here, please sit by me so I can become better acquainted with your ideas.'

I swallowed hard: that was Chapin speaking. He would be at the head of the table, so I pointed myself in that direction – yet the ornately tooled boots and pinstriped trousers positioning themselves on the seat did not belong to my husband. Monique grinned, waited for the man to settle, and then ran a teasing finger around his kneecap.

A large hand reached beneath the cloth to clamp hers, and I thought we were already goners. But when she kissed his knuckles, he stroked her face.

Dewell! I had assumed he'd be anywhere but here, yet the appearance of Proffit solidarity would be in both brothers' interests. And now that the bastard heir realised a little game was going on beneath the table, things might get interesting indeed! As the rest of the gentlemen took their seats, I noted a slender set of legs clad in houndstooth at the opposite end, where my husband would preside over this gathering of eight esteemed guests. Guests who were about to receive more than they bargained for, as they pledged their support.

'Gentlemen!' Chapin called out cheerfully. 'I am inspired yet humbled by the enthusiasm of New Orleans's finest, most successful families and businesses, represented here. Today's meeting will clarify our party's goals and platforms, which, as your next mayor, I vow to execute with all the integrity and honour of the Proffit name. For generations my family has helped plot the course of this great city, and I challenge you to join me in this highest of causes, to ensure continued success and prosperity for us all!'

'Hear, hear!' someone chimed in, and glasses clinked above us.

'Time to start on our own high causes, *non*?' my companion murmured. Her eyes sparkled in the shadows, as she pointed to the set of legs on Chapin's left. 'Only fitting to serve a senator first.'

I held my breath as the slender young woman crawled to the overfed calves clad in conservative charcoal trousers, which bulged at thighs that disappeared into the drape of the tablecloth. Monique placed her hands gently on those knees and held them, waiting for the shiver of surprise to ebb. Then she ran a single finger up the inside of each plump leg.

'I commend your choice of meeting places,' came a sonorous voice, as the clatter of china announced soup bowls being set on serving plates. 'I've always heard the service here at the Beau Monde is the finest, and this ... delicious-smelling bisque is only the beginning of a delightful dining experience, I'm sure!'

As the senator patted his napkin over his lap, he spread his legs – and damned if he didn't unfasten his fly! Monique wasted no time fishing out his thick, stubby member, which was rising rapidly between her hands.

Chapin chuckled. 'We can count on the staff's discretion too. It's important that nothing enacted today gets beyond this room, of course.'

Of course, my thoughts echoed. I prayed this would

hold true for my own brazen activities, as I watched my maid take the senator's erection into her mouth.

'Oh ... oh, my lordy-lord,' Searcy groaned, shifting to allow her better access. 'I can see myself coming here, very soon and often, if this ... wine is any indication of the club's other ... refinements.'

I nearly choked on my laughter, aware I was watching an expert at her work – and that I should first practise on someone other than my husband. As the senator's knees began to quiver around Monique's shoulders, I slithered to the opposite end of the table.

Dewel's legs stretched before me, long and muscled and – well, they were the most impressive limbs under that table, possessing the quiet power of an animal that could pounce without warning. The tablecloth had ridden up to his belt – or had he put it there in anticipation of Monique's mouth?

I smiled. He was about to receive something as sinfully delicious as anything my maid could serve up. Just looking at that fly, with the long bulge along one side of its seam, gave me the confidence I needed to go through with this outrageous stunt.

I paused with my hands hovering above his knees. Then I let them rest there, savouring his strength when he parted his legs so I could crouch between them. He reached surreptitiously beneath the table cloth to stroke my face, lingering as though he already knew I wasn't his little maid.

'And what do you think of your brother's being chosen as our candidate?' the man beside him asked. I didn't recognise the voice, but he wore pale grey trousers that should've been a size larger. 'If he scratches the right backs and keeps his nose clean, it could mean a run for the governor's chair down the road.'

Dewel shifted, ostensibly to address this question – but it also opened him to my attentions. His fly was already undone.

'Chapin has always been the quintessential politician,' he replied in a thoughtful drawl. 'Has the looks to attract the ladies – which'll make their men take notice – and the resources and reputation to carry his campaign as far as he cares to. Already talks the talk, and walks with all the right backslappers.'

As I coaxed the hardening shaft from his pants, I detected more resentment or rivalry than endorsement. Sadly enough, he'd described my husband to a tee yet hadn't said anything very flattering. Not that I expected Dewel to kiss anyone's backside on his brother's behalf.

'Will his wife be a problem? They say with her northern upbringing – St. Louis, isn't it? – she doesn't always cotton to the ways of the Southern aristocracy.'

I sucked hard, running my rounded lips down the thick, warm piston poking out of his fly. He chuckled – I could imagine him smiling at his companion in that way that would let the man know nothing about what Dewel Proffit really felt about me.

'Miss Eve should never be given the short end of the stick,' the man in my grasp said with a breathy laugh. 'Personally, I find her much better versed in current issues than most wives, and she's not afraid to try new ... exciting ways of doing things. Much as we good old boys love tradition, we need to recognise more satisfying solutions – more ... mutually beneficial positions – allowing our ladies to ... come with us, into the future.'

Dewel was doing his damnedest not to buck, while I – as a reward for his complimentary remarks – rapidly sucked and licked the engorged head of his cock.

'Are you saying Chapin will promote women's suffrage?' came his companion's reply. 'If his wife doesn't know her place –'

'Oh, Eve Proffit holds her own wherever she is. Positions herself to maximum advantage, and has a strong . . . *grasp* of her husband's political aspirations.'

His voice was wavering, yet he continued with a confidence that made me proud to know him; proud to pleasure a man with such progressive views. 'She'll wait until Chapin's elected before making any radical moves – and by then, who can she hurt? Again, the women who envy her . . . skill and pluck will rally behind Chapin, to keep Miss Eve in the public eye.'

Was he fighting a grimace? Did his companion suspect what was going on in the nether regions beneath his napkin? His hips quivered, and then the first drops shot out, followed by a torrent of buttery honey. I gulped and swallowed, keeping the front of his trousers clean, and then licked all traces of his juice from his cock and the springy hair at its base.

His shaft remained stiff, so I thought it best to move on – to let Dewel get it limp enough to tuck back into his pants. His enthusiastic response to my sucking encouraged me; another caress was thanks enough as I moved from between his fine, long legs. Lord, but he was a sight from the thighs down, compared to those around him! I shifted carefully around all the other boots to my husband's legs, for the waiters were setting down the main course now.

Monique grinned at me in the dimness, wiping her mouth with the back of her hand. The little minx had already serviced the man on the other side of Chapin, who was probably wondering why Senator Searcy and this fellow were both smiling broadly, agreeing with whatever he said! I scooted forward, glad the cool marble floor made easier work of moving around in these close quarters between eight sets of knees and the table's pedestals.

But as I moved in to touch him, Chapin cleared his throat ceremoniously. 'Gentlemen, I'm sure you're aware of the vulnerability of any man holding public office these days – not to mention the time required to maintain his personal investments and properties, while he performs the civic duties he was elected for. With this in mind, I've procured a valet. A man who will assist with my mayoral affairs, and see to my personal safety in public.'

My mouth dropped open. Not a word had my husband uttered about such an employee: in deference to Fanny Frike's feelings, he'd gone years without a valet after her nephew, Will, died in an unfortunate accident. I wondered if these *affairs* included Savanna. Would his new valet serve as his lookout?

'Excellent idea!' a man near Dewel responded.

'You never know what those Republicans might try when your candidacy is announced,' another man agreed.

'Thank you, gentlemen. Your support is heartening.' Chapin straightened in his chair – just as my hands almost landed on the tops of his thighs. 'May I introduce Judd Schuck? You've no doubt noted his burly physique, and the way he's been eyeing all of you as you ate.'

Laughter, followed by light applause, filled the little dining room. Monique's hand went to her mouth when the legs she'd just fondled stood up to be recognised. Hopefully he was holding his coat over his fly, for he hadn't had time to fasten it! Less humorous, however, was the prospect of Chapin having another ally at the house; demanding his own room, no doubt.

'I'm hoping you'll see fit to advance his salary as a party expenditure – which, of course, will come from my own coffers, should I not be elected,' my husband continued. 'His presence should help us all have a more enjoyable time at the parties I've planned – the first being a grand Mardi Gras-style costume ball at the house, a week from this Saturday, to announce my candidacy. You're all invited, of course. Along with your ladies of the evening.'

There was a taut pause and then laughter broke out at Chapin's turn of phrase. I sat seething beneath the table: once again the wife was the last to know, about the valet and now the magnificent social event I was expected to hostess! And now that my husband had charmed these important supporters by invoking that good-old-boy camaraderie – alluding to the courtesans they carried on with, just as he did – the golden Proffit had indeed reached the inner circle. Hosting a costume ball, so their mistresses could attend without being recognised by their wives.

Clever man, my husband.

I was no slacker myself. As soon as he sat back against his chair, I eased my palms over his thighs, stopping to allow his mental adjustment.

Chapin stiffened; not as inspirational as his brother's reaction, given his willowy build. A tentative hand came under the table, bearing his father's signet ring with the Proffit coat of arms. I gripped his fingers, kissing them to get his assent. Did he recognise the press of my lips? Or did he assume Savanna had hidden herself before he arrived?

Feeling bolder – with Monique kneeling beside me to watch – I slowly massaged my way up his legs, to the centre placket of his pants. While I'd always admired the trim figure Chapin Proffit presented in his fine clothes, I had to remind myself why I was going through this tricky ordeal: I wanted this man to want me. I'd had no illusions about why my family agreed to this marriage, yet I still hoped, in my heart of hearts, that it could evolve into a satisfying match.

If it didn't happen now, it never would.

Chapin sat very still as I unbuttoned his fly, then slumped slightly so more of him would be hidden by the linen tablecloth. When I reached in to free his cock, I felt the pulse in his groin; the prick in my fingers shot up to its slim, solid length in seconds. If it was the blonde Savanna in his fantasy, well, she was just missing out!

Into my mouth he went, and I felt more than heard his eager sigh. He moved slightly, rocking to establish a rhythm that would eventually take him over the edge without the senator – or his new bodyguard – noticing. But then, since Judd had already received a sampling of the service here at the Beau Monde Club, he'd probably recommend it as a safe, discreet place for them to come more often. For lunch, of course.

Thoughts of the heavyset valet faded as I closed my eyes to concentrate. I stroked slowly up and down, pursing my lips to squeeze Chapin's warm, corded length, circling the insistent shaft with my fingers to pump him. His downy hair rustled; a light musk enveloped me as I moved faster, driving him to a point that might make his agitation obvious to his tablemates. He deserved some of the same emotional turmoil he'd put *me* through! His subtle shifting told me he was getting close.

He had no way of knowing his wife was under the table; perhaps wondered how his resourceful young 'niece' had gotten here, to service him by surprise. I'd find a way to tell him – would insist I'd done it on a dare, yes, but because the possibility of public exposure seemed minimal, compared to the danger I felt our marriage was in. I was tired of being ignored! I didn't really *care* if these gentlemen found out I was under the table. They'd gotten their share, and they'd be envious of Chapin for having such an adventurous wife.

Wouldn't they?

My husband moaned audibly. He stiffened, about to shoot.

'You all right, Proffit?' the senator asked in a low voice.

'Just a – cramp in my leg, sorry,' Chapin rasped. And then he squirted his thick, salty come, reaching beneath the tablecloth as though to massage that aching thigh, but actually to hold my head in place while he finished.

I licked him, and then tucked his softening cock into his pants. When I was backing out from between his knees, however, he held me fast by clamping his legs together.

'As we enjoy our praline cheesecake, gentlemen,' he intoned in his newly acquired grand manner, 'please accept my thanks once again for your guidance and generosity. Your presence means a great deal to me. I welcome any advice on how to become *your* next mayor!'

'Hear, hear!' someone from the other end piped up. There was a clinking of glasses, and then the eager scraping of forks across dessert plates as the chatter rose to a jovial level.

My heart was pounding, for I assumed Chapin would now peer beneath the table to see who'd sucked him. Instead, he fumbled in his pants pocket – and damned if he didn't shove a wad of folded money at me! I took it, patting his thigh to signal my thanks. *Now* I had proof I'd been the one to bring him off!

I grinned at Monique, stuffing the bills into my shirt pocket. And as we waited, hoping the men we'd serviced would remain the souls of discretion by not lifting the tablecloth, I couldn't help thinking how well this escapade had gone.

Too well perhaps?

Monique and I chattered happily to T-Jon all the way back to the house on Prytania, after making our escape through the Beau Monde's back courtyard and adjoining alley.

'And he *paid* you!' my maid crowed, laughing each time she thought of it. 'Why, I sucked four men to your two – and all I got was the thrill of being the mystery mouth under table. You're *good*, Auntie Evil. Really, really good!'

Chapin, too, was in a buoyant mood when he returned home that evening, wearing a secretive smile only a few of us understood.

'Well, my dear, the luncheon was a huge success,' he said, reaching across the table at dinner to grasp my hand. 'Took in more than forty thousand dollars! The men were all smiles – and by the way, I invited them to a Mardi Gras ball, a week from the coming Saturday. A party befitting the proud Proffit name, to announce your husband's candidacy.'

I widened my eyes, as though his idea was new to me. 'Chapin, that's so *soon*. I –'

'But you have your new maids,' he said, with all the finesse of one who had no idea how to orchestrate such a grand party. 'And it's time I met them, don't you think?'

As he levelled his blue-eyed gaze at me, I saw his usual challenge: *what do you do with all your time, woman? Are you spending it with that bastard Dewel?*

I was about to defend myself when an ominous crash came from the kitchen.

'You clumsy *idiots*. Look what you've done!' Fanny's voice rang out. 'That china's been in the Proffit family for three generations, and now it's in pieces. Don't you dare move! Miss Eve's going to see this for herself – and then we'll see who suffers for it.'

13 **A-Spanking We Will Go**

'Begging your pardon, Mr Chapin – Miss Eve,' the house-keeper said a few moments later. She came to the massive table, drying her hands in her apron as though she'd rather rub the skin off them than say what she had to. 'Seems the new – *girls* have had an accident with some china. I knew you'd wish to *discipline* them yourself.'

Fanny's announcement backed me into a correctional corner, for Chapin was observing how I handled my new staff – and Mrs Frike, by her very tone and the stance of her stout body, expected me to spank them. Monique's method would immediately expose my new maids for the young men they were, so I tried desperately to think of an alternative. I'd had no practice at spanking. Nor did I wish to initiate the nasty fight Chapin would start when he saw cocks and balls popping out of their panties.

How would Monique handle this? I fretted as I folded my napkin on the table. It was another big moment where I proved myself to my exacting husband, and I couldn't bungle it.

'Thank you, Fanny. I'll take care of –'

'Who made this big mess?' a familiar voice cried in the kitchen. 'Someone will confess, or I'll hand out spankings all around!'

I fought a grin, for Monique had arrived in the nick of time! When I walked into the kitchen with my husband behind me, the centre of the floor was covered with shards of pale pink china – a pattern I'd never liked – and along the wall stood Cleopatra, Antoinette and Cinderella. They glanced at me, and then at Chapin, with fearful eyes before addressing my irate maid.

'I had washed these serving bowls, as Fanny asked,' Cinderella whined, 'and I was carrying them back to the shelves when Toinette stuck out her –'

'You tripped over your own feet, Miss Slippery Slippers!' the redhead retorted.

'And how do *you* see it?' I asked Cleopatra, who stood nearest the door.

The queen with the coal-black hair shrugged, looking disgusted with her companions. 'It was an accident waiting to happen. Mrs Frike's been ordering us around, taking swats at our bottoms if we don't move fast enough to suit her. I say we should all –'

'Well, *I* say the three of you will await me in the parlour, on the settee,' I replied, crossing my arms to give each of them a stern look. 'Too bad this unfortunate moment will be Mr Proffit's first impression of you – the servants he expects to perform *to perfection* at our Mardi Gras ball in less than two weeks. Now *go*, before my disappointment gets the best of me!'

I pointed towards the parlour, rather pleased with myself. Had Chapin and Monique not been present, I'd have pooh-poohed the loss of those ugly bowls with just a warning to the new maids and a private word with Mrs Frike.

My husband's expression was impossible to read, as though he couldn't believe domestics would spout off that way. Or else he'd caught their unusual names, and was studying them more closely than I wanted. He remained oddly quiet, crossing his arms.

Monique, too, had her arms crossed beneath the breasts that bulged in her short black dress. Her topknot flopped wildly with each incredulous shake of her head. 'Shall I fetch that new birch rod I made, Miss Eve?' she asked. 'We had just such an occasion in mind for it – panties up this time, but they'll feel the sting of those little knots. And they'll realise that if we have to get it out again, they won't be sitting down any time soon!'

Her gleeful demeanor gave me pause, but I could've kissed her for solving our problem of gender exposure. 'Excellent idea. I'll meet you in the parlour, and we'll proceed.'

I left the kitchen with my heels clacking firmly on the floor, a sound those sissy maids would come to associate with their derrieres' doom. Not that I relished another whipping, for everything within me abhorred corporal punishment. But Monique had opened a door I couldn't close. And consistency was important when dealing with a staff learning the expectations and procedures in a household such as ours.

'Do you always defer to your attendant on such matters?' my husband's voice crept up from behind me. 'Miss Picabou impresses me as –'

'Much firmer and more intimidating than I, don't you agree?' I cut in with a smile. 'Discipline's the best thing, in the short time we have to train these girls. I'm simply allowing my maid – and Mrs Frike – to put their superior expertise to work for us, my dear.'

'And where did you procure these young ladies?'

Was that a warning edge I heard? I paused at the parlour door, deciding the three maids should overhear our conversation. 'Upon several recommendations, I went to Miss Delacroix's School for Domestic Endeavor. She has a reputation for providing only the finest domestics, so –'

'And how did you choose *these* three?' Chapin's eyes

flared with an icy-blue fire I only saw on rare moments, when he was more upset than he was letting on.

Something warned me not to divulge the truth about Monique's acquisition, nor about the backgrounds of the maids themselves. 'If you feel they're unsuitable, this close to the ball, perhaps I should just –'

'Get in there and do the deed,' he said with an impatient wave towards the door. 'No sense in prolonging this nonsense, or letting them think you've changed your mind. We'll discuss this later.'

His tone grated on my nerves, but at least I was off the hook. I straightened my shoulders, and with arched eyebrows I entered the room where the three offenders awaited me. Monique was standing beside the fireplace, silently admiring the bundle of birch switches she'd bound at the bottom with bright red ribbons. Symbolic of the stripes soon to be crossing their backsides, I gathered.

'Mr Proffit, may I present Cleopatra ... Antoinette ... and Cinderella,' I said as each maid stood and curtsied in turn. 'Despite what you must think, I assure you these young ladies will be more careful with the china in the future. *Won't* you, girls?'

'Yes, Miss Eve,' they chanted. They were a demure lot in their ankle-length grey dresses and pinafores – except for Cinderella, who was admiring her reflection in her shiny black shoes.

A loud *tap, tap, tap* of the birch's handle against the mantelpiece brought them to attention. 'Well, ladies, shall we proceed?'

Monique gestured towards a straight-backed chair in the centre of the room, where I sat down as though it were all a part of our plan.

'You realise, of course, that a second offence like this

means a birching with your drawers down around your knees – even if Mr Proffit is present,' my maid continued in her imperious tone. 'Cleopatra, your insolent remarks about Mrs Frike have earned you the dubious honour of going first, *non*? Assume the position. Across my lady's knee!'

Hoping my eyes didn't get as wide as the raven-haired servant's, I sat straighter. What did one *do* with a twenty-year-old male bent over her lap? Neither Cleopatra nor I had much time to ponder this, for Mistress Monique took him by the arm and practically tossed him across my legs. With great ceremony, she then folded the grey uniform and the muslin shift up over the maid's back, to expose a ripe young ass covered only in a layer of ruffled white cotton.

'Four strokes with the birch,' Monique announced, 'and another if you cry out, or try to cover your butt with your hands.'

I held my breath, watching Monique position herself beside me – so Antoinette and Cinderella had to watch – and take a couple of practice aims. The other two offenders sat even straighter when Fanny Frike walked in to stand behind their settee.

Whisss-smack came the first whack, and I thought Cleopatra might jerk right off my lap. Directly in my line of vision, that firm young butt puckered, while his thighs remained tight.

Whisss-smack ... whisss-smack. With great precision, Monique landed her birch bundle so the entire cotton-clad surface felt the sting of her discipline – and hopefully the rest of him felt a humiliation that would encourage his penitence and better deportment.

Whisss-smack came the fourth blow, and the young man in my lap let out a hiss of injury he hadn't acknowledged otherwise. He felt very warm, with his stomach covering one of my legs and his ass bubbled up over the other. His erection prodded the inside of my thigh, enticingly close to my sex. I cleared my throat, determined not to fall prey to such fantasies and ... fascinating scenery, while we were being watched.

'And while you apologise – to both Miss Eve and Mrs Frike,' Monique announced to the maid in my lap, 'Antoinette will take her position. You girls would be finished in the kitchen and doing other work if we weren't punishing your foolishness!'

Cleopatra mumbled a 'So sorry, Miss Eve,' and rose up after discreetly lowering her skirts, appearing feminine again, in every way. Her olive face had two bright pink spots for cheeks, and those defiant dark eyes glistened with tears she refused to shed.

In her place, I could not have remained so poised – which suggested she'd taken a lot of punishment from Honore Delacroix. Yet another point I meant to challenge the headmistress about, when I finally saw her!

'Palms on the floor!' Monique commanded Antoinette. 'Four whacks, for whatever you did to make those dishes fall. Because *you* were the agitator, *non*?'

The russet-haired maid barely had time to roll her defiant eyes and raise her skirts before the first smack landed. She sucked air – and so did I – and then braced her backside, drawing the frilly drawers into her crack.

Again I was taken by surprise at how alluring this view could be; how utterly sensual it felt to have a young man's weight suspended across my legs while he remained at the mercy of Monique's birch – and his own libido. I could feel him growing hard against my thigh.

Whisss-smack and Antoinette flinched with the bite of those little birch teeth.

Then Monique paused, with her bundle poised, a

calculating look on her face. The object of her discipline didn't dare look over his shoulder to see what was going on, but after a few moments of unrealised anticipation, the muscles of that ass relaxed into a rounded cushion that just begged me to caress it. My palm wanted to feel the give of that warmed flesh through those thin, white panties, if only to soothe –

Whisss –

I caught my breath – and my hand! – just as the whack landed, and then the fourth one found its mark on the lowest part of the buttocks. Were those shimmers of heat rising from that quivering skin? Or were my eyes fogged with wanting and concern? The flimsy fabric of those white panties couldn't be much protection, and my own backside ached in sympathy as Toinette made her apologies.

'Your turn, little princess.' Monique stood beside me, lowering her birch bundle so its handle hit the back of my wooden chair. *Tap, tap, tap* came that ominous sound, and Cinderella paled as she approached.

'I – I didn't *mean* to trip and drop those dishes. I'm just a clumsy little fool, and I shouldn't pay attention to Toinette's teasing about my –'

'Shut up and assume the position,' my maid barked. 'We haven't got all night! And remember, sweet Cinderella, you'll get an extra whack – or two! – if you bawl like a baby, or try to cover that naughty little backside!'

The slender blonde beseeched me with huge eyes already brimming with tears, but bent obediently over my lap. With dainty precision she turned back her skirts, steadied herself with her toes, and then gripped the leg of my chair.

Tap, tap, tap went the handle of that birch rod again, which made Cinderella quiver while her two companions felt safe enough on the settee to snicker. They received a simultaneous cuffing from Fanny, who witnessed these goings-on with great interest, and kept her pudgy hands on their shoulders to maintain order. Cinderella, meanwhile, was already shaking like a scared rabbit, and I just wished Monique would be done with this.

'You might be Miss Picabou's aunt, but you can't be *evil*,' came a murmur from around my ankles. 'You have the most exquisite feet I've ever seen.'

Whisss-smack came the first stroke, and then the second followed close behind, covering the rest of the buttocks staring up at me. It shimmied beneath the frilly panties, being softer and less muscled than the other two. The tender skin was turning pink beneath the pale fabric, and Cinderella's stomach lurched with her efforts not to cry out.

The next *whisss-smack* filled the parlour with its hiss, and then with the caterwauling the maid couldn't hold back.

'Please, please! I'm *so* sorry –'

Whisss-smack and then one slender arm jerked back to cover a butt that had to be burning. The only merciful thing to do was hold Cinderella's wayward hand against her side, out of the birch's way.

'One more, because we won't tolerate sissies and crybabies,' my maid crowed.

And with that final, extra whack she turned Cinderella into a sad, hunching bundle that hugged my legs. I released her hand, ready to chide Monique for such a bloodthirsty display – after all, *anyone* could drop dishes! But her dark look and slight shake of the head held a warning I sensed I shouldn't ignore.

And lo and behold, once she stopped whimpering the blonde stood up, straightened her skirts, and faced me with a watery-eyed smile. 'I'm so very sorry about your china, Miss Eve, and I promise to be *much* more careful with your belongings. And thank you, Mistress Monique, for spanking me with such firmness and fairness. I feel ... humbled and penitent. Ready to be a much better domestic now.'

No one expected such a heartfelt remark, and before any of us could react, Cinderella went on. 'Cleopatra and Antoinette might not admit it, but we're all terribly grateful that you've taken us into your home and under your wing, Miss Eve.'

She dismissed herself with a little curtsy, and I reached for her hand. 'And why is that?' I asked – not to torture her more, but because her statement piqued my interest. Anything she said might prove useful, if Honore Delacroix got confrontational during our home visit.

'While Miss Delacroix gave us a home and entirely new lives,' she began, daintily wiping her eyes with a lace hanky, 'the headmistress is so ... possessive. Controlling. We can't have a *thought* to ourselves, and –'

Cinderella's voice rose with her confession, and she became oblivious to the way everyone else in the room hung on her every word. '– and once, when I'd misbehaved, she made me kneel beside her chair, naked. She placed a large pane of glass on my back. I had to act as her *table*, while she served coffee and pastries to – to my mother!'

My gasp was not the only one in the room. When I glanced towards Chapin, who'd watched the whippings from the door, I couldn't miss the horror on his pinched, pale face. 'And your mother *allowed* Miss Delacroix to –'

'She didn't know it was me, for I'd been instructed to face the other way and keep my head tucked between my elbows – as though I couldn't bear to look at her!'

Cinderella rasped. 'How utterly degrading, to be point-ing my bare backside at that woman, while she made her annual donation to the school.'

'And I once spent three days slaving naked,' Antoin-ette joined in with a dramatic rise of her eyebrows. 'Which included sweeping the front sidewalk, where passers-by might see me! And it was quite chancy, helping the cook butcher chickens. It's no easy feat, stretching a squirming bird's neck across the block while someone else wields the hatchet.'

Thank goodness the redhead covered her breasts with her expressive hands, for *my* thoughts had gone to the cock bobbing near that block – an anatomical detail I did *not* want my husband to find out about!

Chapin seemed quite affected by this image: he made a choking sound, and then coughed to cover it. 'It's rude and disrespectful to discuss Miss Delacroix this way, and I'll have no more gossip and tale-telling,' he stated, gazing sternly at the maids. 'You're fortunate to have received your training at such a well-respected school, where you've been prepared to earn an honest living – to serve in the finest homes.'

Silent shame filled the parlour. Even Fanny Frike cowered beneath his glare.

'By the way, my new valet, Judd Schuck, will arrive in a few days,' he announced, his eyes narrowing point-edly at me. 'The servant's quarters seem an inappropri-ate place for him now, so he shall have the spare room adjoining my suite. I trust that your three *girls* – and Mistress Monique, of course – will have it ready for my inspection when I get home tomorrow.'

'Valet, schmalet!' my maid jeered as she fetched my clean underthings the next morning. 'That Judd

Schuck's nothing but a spy, *non*? Why else would Mr Chapin put him in that room between your two suites? *My* room, no less!'

I smiled wryly, for Mr Schuck's presence there certainly wouldn't impede any sexual encounters between husband and wife. 'I wondered if Chapin weren't having illusions of grandeur yesterday, saying he needed a bodyguard. I think he's so damn jealous, after seeing me with Dewel, that he's hired this man to keep track of *me*, rather than anyone who might do him bodily harm.'

'Which might be *me*, Aunt Evil,' my maid replied. The pearl necklace I'd requested clittered in her hand as she shook it. 'Mr Chapin's getting awfully big for his britches. And Judd the Stud – he puts on a big act to cover a little prick. Hardly worth my time yesterday.'

We both chuckled over her turn of phrase as we entered the new valet's quarters, where the three maids were already hard at work. Cleopatra, as the tallest, was running her covered mop around the ceiling to catch cobwebs, while Antoinette and Cinderella rolled up the rug. As they shifted the long, loosely coiled weight between them, Monique placed the rug beater under Toinette's arm.

'Thank you, mistress,' she murmured, and as the two of them passed through the door they gave me a cheery 'Good morning, Miss Eve!'

'Hard at it, bright and early,' I remarked. I noted Monique's gaze lingering on the rug beater, an open paddle-like contraption with a long handle.

'We want Mr Proffit to be *extremely* pleased with our work,' Cinderella said. 'Can't have this Schuck fellow reporting any ... stray cocks.'

'Loose roosters? In my house?' I quipped. 'Why, I haven't seen any such thing, have you, Monique?'

Her lips quirked. 'The only wild cock around here will be the one Mr Chapin aims your way, when he can't keep it to himself,' she said when the maids were out of earshot. 'We're ready for your next lesson. Come with me, *ma tante.*'

As we strolled downstairs, I felt excitement thrumming through the arm she tucked around my waist. We entered the music room – a sunny salon seldom used these days, since no one played the grand piano. Monique playfully swatted my bottom before closing the pocket doors. She was in a feisty mood, judging from the way she pivoted and flipped her short skirt up to expose her bare backside.

'Spank me. With your hand,' she teased.

My hand instead went to my mouth. 'Why do you enjoy whipping the new maids?' I asked quietly. 'And why on earth do they put up with it?'

Monique gave me a look that said I might not understand the answer, if I had to ask such a question. But then she stood straight, removing her short black uniform to tease me.

'Our sissy maids, they like a lashing because that sting across their ass excites them – or because they long for the mama who spanked them as boys. They want a woman to take charge. So they can submit to her.'

My eyes widened. I thought very carefully about this as my maid began to remove my dress. 'But when I got a spanking, I detested it.'

'Because you were the child, and the one with the switch – or the cane, or the hand, or the hair brush – had all the power, *oui?* For me, it's all about the *power* – especially over a man,' she added gleefully. 'We women have so few chances to bring them to their knees, *non?* And when they're *so* grateful for it – like

Cinderella last night – we do them the ultimate favour by teaching them how to *please* us.'

Her smile waxed absolutely wicked as she raised my camisole above my breasts. 'And no matter what a man says, deep down he wants to please his woman. This way, she's more likely to give him what *he* wants, *oui*?'

Comprehension dawned, yet I couldn't miss the mischief on Monique's face as she tossed the silky garment away, leaving me to stand before her wearing only my drawers, the stockings gartered above my knees, and my pumps.

'Pretty, pretty breasts,' she murmured, tweaking one until its nipple hardened. 'But turn around, *cherie*. Show me that sassy ass! Mr Chapin, he got *very* excited last night when the girls were getting birched.'

'That doesn't mean I'll let him strike *me*! Why, if he thinks –'

'You don't know what you're missing,' she whispered, crossing her arms saucily beneath her breasts. Her topknot swayed as she bit back a grin. 'Bare it, *ma tante*. I won't spank you, I promise. Just another love lesson. You want Chapin crazy for you, *non*?'

Little minx. I'd trusted her to sneak me under the table at the Beau Monde Club and get me home, so I could hardly deny her this playful ... perhaps educational request. I slipped my fingers into the waist of my silk bloomers and slowly lowered them, watching her reaction.

'*Oui* – ooh-la-la! It's good, to hold the eyes and make him wait, while you reveal your treasures. You're a natural, Auntie Evil.' She approached with her hand extended, as though to caress my backside. 'Now, what do you think of this?'

Her *smack* startled me so, I had to grab the mantel to steady myself. But then Monique began to rub the spot she'd just affronted, her warm palm making firm, lazy circles around the globe of flesh ... gently pressing while the friction of skin against skin sang an alluring song. My eyelids lowered. My backside extended to fill her hand. I was getting wet between the legs, hoping her fingers would stray to the top of my thighs and then between them.

'Point scored for Monique, *oui*?' she asked as she stepped closer. 'It can be very soothing, but very sexy, this rubbing ... this rhythm that hypnotises with its pleasure. Then I slip my fingers lower, where this pussy's purring so nice ... ooh-la-la, *ma tante*. You're dripping wet.'

When her middle finger entered me, and then was joined by another, wiggling deep into my core, I moaned. I leaned forward, forgetting about valets and irate husbands and the three male maids, as this foxy little female rubbed a knuckle against my –

Smack went Monique's hand on my ass again, only this time she giggled and bolted beyond my reach. I was suddenly chasing after her, following as she ducked around the piano. She waggled her ass at me before sprinting across the carpet – a sight to behold, in her high-heeled boots – before I cornered her at the book-case near the door.

'You little – *you* deserve a spanking!' I laughed, grabbing her around the waist and smacking her back-side. 'This'll teach you to leave *me* hanging, missy!'

Who else could howl and laugh in a French accent? Monique feigned great discomfort and shock – between giggles, anyway – so I continued to spank her, just below her garter belt, with satisfying smacks that rang around the high-ceilinged room. She was wiggling so enthusiastically, her hair came tumbling down in a black velvet curtain.

I made the mistake of nuzzling that soft, wild mane – and then she turned on me. Just that fast, she tucked me under her arm, facing away, and slapped the bottoms of my cheeks. Monique's hand landed daringly close to my slit, which was surely exposed to her inspection from that angle. As my insides began to tingle as much as my butt, I yowled like a feline in heat.

'Please, enough!' I cried out. Yet I was laughing so hard I couldn't stop.

Smack. Smack. 'You've not had enough till Mistress Monique *says* you've had enough. Take this, wicked woman!'

Her fingers slipped between my folds and then dove for my hole. I immediately went hot all over and, with my rear still a-tingle and my slit begging for more, I was totally caught up in the moment's frantic magic.

I didn't hear the door slide open beside us.

'Miss Eve, there's a – Miss *Eve!*' Fanny stepped into the room and quickly slid the pocket door shut, staring at the two of us with an alarm that wilted her usual starch-collared dignity.

'Mrs Proffit,' she whispered urgently, 'I'm sorry to interrupt, but Honore Delacroix is waiting for you in the parlour. She's here for her home visit.'

14 **The Devil's Mistress**

'The nerve of that woman, showing up without an appointment,' I whispered as I hurried into my clothes. Monique was assisting me, but in her wayward Cajun view of things, she found this enormously funny.

'A headmistress who spanks her sissy maids might feel more welcome if we ask her to join us, Auntie Evil.'

'None of that. I've got serious business to – ouch! Stop it!' I slapped her hand away from the clit she'd pinched, hoping my words didn't carry down the hall. 'Round up the girls but keep them working upstairs. In case she wants to see them.'

'Oh, she'll want to see them,' Monique replied slyly. 'Any woman who dresses her young men in white panties does a lot more than *look* at them.'

With a final glance in the mirror – and yes, I looked like I'd been chasing the maid around the piano – I took a deep breath to slow my racing heart. I'd planned to be so competent and collected, with a list of questions for this dubious Delacroix woman. And yet, the disheveled redhead with the bloom in her cheeks, and her breasts rising and falling from having fun, appeared more vibrantly alive than I could ever recall.

Miss Delacroix's opinion be damned! She was about to find out that Eve Proffit wouldn't knuckle under to her as though the sun rose over her illustrious shoulder. This was my home, and these were my maids. I'd been brushed off by her secretary, and I was justifiably incensed at the way I'd been treated.

Straightening to my full height, I let my footsteps echo in the vestibule to announce my arrival. I paused in the parlour doorway, to take full account of my uninvited guest. She was a school marm, after all – merely glorified by her reputation among the city's elite. Knowing how she'd humiliated Cleopatra, Cinderella and Antoinette, I had little respect for –

She was the most stunning woman I had ever met.

When she rose proudly from my couch, her gaze brazenly direct, Honore Delacroix inspired my utmost envy: no amount of coaching or cosmetics would give me her haughty height, or those high cheekbones in that sophisticated face, or that lustrous ebony hair arranged around a decadent red hat with a veil of fringe. Just enough so she could look out without others fully seeing in.

Her gown of shimmering crimson draped her body to perfection, defying decency by skimming her hips without benefit of a bustle, and accentuating ample breasts that rode high and proud. She did *not* look like a headmistress checking on her pupils' progress. She looked like the madam of a very prosperous whorehouse, come from Bourbon Street to lure me into her web of secrecy and sin.

'Mrs Proffit?' she asked, extending a hand sheathed in a scarlet glove. 'Honore Delacroix. I believe you have something that belongs to me, and I've come to take it back.'

The voice was low and smoky, with a soft drawl that slithered like a snake. Such vipers could hypnotise their victims as they fixed them with their slanted eyes, so I reminded myself that looking too long and too closely might be my downfall.

'I believe you're mistaken,' I replied, ignoring her

hand. 'I left a deposit with your Miss Sully when she refused to disclose your fee. I intended to settle this yesterday, so please – sit down while I get you a cheque.'

'You can't pay me for services you're not going to receive. Oh, you *could*,' she corrected with a subtle laugh, 'but I don't think you're *that* stupid.'

I crossed my arms to control my rising temper. 'What are you accusing me of, Miss Delacroix? You run a school for domestics, and I've engaged three of them. They're working out very nicely, I might add.'

'As well they should. But they're not for hire, Mrs Proffit. They are my personal attendants.'

The word *slaves* came to mind, but I set aside this accusation to pursue the matter at hand. 'If that's the case, how was *my* personal attendant able to procure them? And no one prevented her.'

'I run a school, not a prison,' the headmistress replied coolly. Her camouflaged gaze mocked my rumpled skirts. 'My girls come and go as they please, but I believe some underhanded tactics came into play. A large sum of money, perhaps. It will be refunded, of course, when I get to the bottom of this ... unfortunate mistake.'

How I wanted to order this insolent creature out of my home! She was talking in circles that made no sense – a large sum of money? Three young men she discussed as though they were her possessions, bought and paid for? I knew their stories – or at least what they'd shared in brief, unguarded moments – and something inside me welled up in their defence.

'It's not yet public knowledge,' I said in a conspiratorial tone, 'but my husband, Mr Proffit, expects to be elected the next mayor of New Orleans. Surely you understand – and even take pride in – the fact that three of your charges are now serving in his home, preparing us for balls and receptions which –'

'I understand that Annabelle, Chloe and Sylvia are somewhere in this house,' Miss Delacroix whispered tersely, 'and if I have to search room by room, by God I'll find them!'

'No need to trouble yourself,' I retorted. 'My maid has told them you're here. They'll be downstairs momentarily.'

Standing just beyond arm's reach, scowling at each other, we could've engaged in a spitting match. I'd heard such laudatory remarks about this headmistress that her disregard for common courtesy shocked me. Honore Delacroix was clearly from a grittier world, where proper wives like myself didn't venture, yet she was training maids! Supposedly teaching young ladies the finer points of domestic service, in a traditional Southern city where honest, loyal help was hard to come by.

Perhaps her brusque manner and disciplinary measures prepared her pupils for the worst they might find among future employers, but my stomach churned with her nasty accusations – as though I'd stolen something! Or bribed her secretary! She stood as judge and jury, condemning me for the sort of transaction that kept her in business.

As footsteps approached, I studied Honore more closely. Something about her seemed familiar, which was maddening, since she was the kind of woman I tried never to associate with. She enjoyed confrontation, sending poison-arrow insults to anyone who dared cross her. Assumed her reputation would excuse idiosyncrasies her clients found distasteful.

I wished I'd pressed Monique for more details about

procuring the 'girls' in Miss Delacroix's absence. I wished I'd quizzed the three maids more closely about their years at the school, and their relationship to this imposing woman in red. But there was no time for such questions now.

'Shall I bring them in, Miss Eve?' Fanny's voice came from the doorway. My stout housekeeper also appeared to be keeping her temper tightly reined, so I could only guess what she'd endured from this headmistress before fetching me.

'Yes, please,' I replied.

The three maids filed in as though going to their own execution: despite short, pert uniforms like Monique's, their grim expressions and the hands clasped at their waists gave the appearance of a final confession. Last rites.

And why was this? I glanced at Miss Delacroix to gauge her reaction – which she masked by tilting her head so the red fringe veil hid her eyes. Damn siren looked like the devil's own mistress as she assessed their bared legs and shiny black shoes, shaking with her indignation.

'Thank you, ladies. Please be seated,' I said, gesturing toward the settee. 'It seems we have –'

'They shall remain standing. Those indecent dresses will only compromise them further.' Miss Delacroix stepped forward, stabbing me with her glare. 'I can't believe the future mayor's wife would dress her domestics so inappropriately.'

The short black uniforms were a surprise to me too, but I couldn't admit that. My mind searched for a pithy reply – but then in strutted a masked mistress wearing a black corset with an inset of crimson leather lacings. Her bush was exposed above dark stockings gartered mid-thigh, and a pair of knee-high boots that fit like skin. Ebony they were, with insets of red leather in the shape of flames. With each step, she appeared to saunter through the fires of hell.

'You've got questions about these three maids? Ask *me*, lady.' Monique's Cajun singsong sounded as tightly drawn as a drum head and, as she flicked a riding crop across her gloved hand, she stared boldly at our visitor. 'Mr Lincoln freed the slaves decades ago, Miss Delacroix. Yet you *bought* Cleopatra from his mama, way back when –'

'I don't know who you are, or where you got your information,' the headmistress said in a coiled voice, 'but the circumstances of these young ladies coming to –'

'Let's call a spade a spade,' I interrupted. 'These servants are young *men*, who – mostly because of *you* – now live as women. That alone would cause quite a stir, were I to tell my friends – or the authorities! – about the deceit being carried out at the School for Domestic Endeavor! I find it quite interesting that you came here, without an appointment, to reclaim them as though they were your ... *possessions*.'

Honore Delacroix's face hardened with her anger. 'This is none of your business, Mrs Proffit. It is between the girls and me, how I –'

'Shall we stop talking about them as though they're not here?'

Monique turned to the maids, who stood apprehensively before the settee, watching the volley of remarks. 'Antoinette, Cleopatra, Cinderella,' she continued in a friendlier tone, 'let's sit down, to have a civil, productive discussion. So Miss Delacroix understands you're not going back with her.'

'Why do you put words in people's mouths?' the headmistress snapped at the minx in black. 'And speak up, you three! Since when do you go by Antoinette, and Cleopatra, and Cinderella, for God's sake?'

The redhead in the centre smiled bravely. 'Since we've been declared queens.'

'And a princess!' Cinderella piped up.

Disbelief dawned on Miss Delacroix's face. 'You've allowed them to rename you? After a queen who was beheaded, and another who died of a snakebite? And a fairy tale maid?'

'Marie Antoinette was a victim of her times and circumstances,' Toinette replied more boldly. 'Not unlike a certain young boy wanted by the law, for setting a fire of questionable origin. Moulded and controlled by those in power. Made to behave as they wanted her to.'

'And Cleopatra *asked* for that snake,' our raven-haired namesake declared. 'Rather than live as a slave, she chose a cobra – which, according to Egyptian beliefs, granted her immortality. She was a brave, adventurous queen who chose her own destiny even after she no longer ruled her world.'

The headmistress shook her head, as though three stupid sheep had gotten loose from their pen. 'And of course you'd go along with whatever the other two did, Sylvia. How quickly you forget the advantages I've given you! The freedom from working as common maids –'

'Cinderella was despised by her family. Made to perform menial labour,' the slender blonde responded. She was twitching like a mouse cornered by cats, yet she spoke with conviction. 'But thanks to a fairy godmother, she went to the ball. She won her prince because she wore the prettiest shoes. *And she lived happily ever after*. It's a life I couldn't even dream of, until I came here!'

Cinderella's retort touched me, just as her bright smile bespoke more gratitude than I deserved. All the more reason to send Miss Delacroix packing.

'These maids intend to stay,' I stated, calmly watching the vixen in red. 'You've received your initial deposit, so tell me what I owe to clear my account, and the matter's settled.'

'Not by a long shot.'

Honore stepped in front of each maid, to tip up his chin and scowl as though they'd betrayed a sacred pledge. 'I never dreamed you'd betray me, after the *devotion* I've shown, and the *love* I've lavished upon you – as though you were my own *children*. I can't understand –'

Cleopatra smirked. 'You'd teach your sons to fondle each other?'

'So you could watch?' Antoinette added – and then her head snapped back with the force of Miss Delacroix's slap.

Monique went to one side of the headmistress and I stepped to the other, before the fight could escalate further.

'I've seen all I need to!' I said as I ushered the headmistress to the door. 'When Mr Proffit hears of these grossly inappropriate behaviours, he'll have your school shut down. I'll see to it!'

The woman in red shook me off with surprising strength, brushing her crimson sleeve as though I'd contaminated it with my touch. 'A noble sentiment, but extremely naive,' she muttered. 'How would it look if Mr Proffit's political contributors learn your maids are actually men in skirts? Consider the stir *that* will cause – because I'll see that it does!'

With all the dignity of a European monarch, Miss Delacroix straightened her spine and stepped out the door Fanny was holding. She hailed her driver, and then turned to me with an acidic grin. 'You're going to be sorry we ever met, Mrs Proffit.'

'I already am,' I whispered as she swayed down the walk.

Inside, however, I was immediately crushed in a hug by Cinderella and her two cohorts. 'You did it! You and Mistress Monique set us free,' she sang out.

'You did the right thing, missus,' Fanny Frike chimed in. 'Didn't like that bitch from the minute she walked past me, like she owned the place. Said she was going to march through every room of the house, looking for these three – starting in the music room!'

Images of frisking around the piano naked, and Monique slapping my ass, made my bravado slip a notch. Thank God Miss Delacroix didn't have *that* for ammunition! Or had she heard our girlish giggles, punctuated by the rowdy sounds of hands spanking bare backsides?

The young woman beside us, looking triumphantly feline in her black and red leather, smiled as though she knew a lot she'd never tell me.

'It's the boots,' she murmured, directing our gazes along their slick, flame-kissed length. 'Best diversion T-Jon's ever made me. When I wear them, I *always* get my way.'

I now had more questions about our maid situation than before, but I admired Monique for her flair – and for flying in the face of a headmistress who made Aunt Evil seem like a preacher's wife by comparison. I sensed I'd see that nasty woman again, soon. And I vowed to have my rebuttals ready if she caused trouble during Chapin's campaign.

'Well, ladies,' I said, 'we have a new valet to prepare

for – and a masked ball that will astound everyone who attends it. Why are we standing here congratulating ourselves?'

As the three maids started for the stairway, Cinderella gave me another dazzling smile. 'It's the boots,' she agreed with a breathy sigh, gazing at Monique's feet. 'Nothing says "fuck me" like a great pair of shoes!'

I watched their backsides ascend the staircase, again in awe of shapely legs and swinging skirts and shiny black pumps that gave the uncanny impression of being totally female. Until they stepped on to the first landing.

'My God, Monique, how *could* you let them come down here without – they're not wearing panties!'

The sly maid grinned. 'It's a man's world, Auntie Evil. We girls must use everything – every *thing* – at our disposal, to win our way. And we've just begun to fight, *oui*?'

15 Schuck's Come-Uppance

'So, this is the illustrious Mr Schuck,' I murmured. Monique and I stood on the landing of the stairs, looking down into the vestibule as Chapin ushered in his new valet. 'I liked him better from under the table.'

'*Everything* about him's short and stubby, *non*?' My maid let out an unladylike snort. 'Little prick! Not fair that he gets my room. If he sticks that thing in my mouth again, he'll find out Mistress Monique has teeth!'

He glanced up to find us watching him. A knowing smile flickered on his thick lips: he assumed we were deciding who got him first. His curling, mouse-brown hair fell about his head in no particular style, nor did his black frock coat complement his brown plaid trousers. Why my husband chose this pug-ugly creature as his valet was a question I knew better than to ask. For now, I had to play the gracious hostess.

'And here's my little lady,' Chapin announced, smiling brightly as I came down the last few stairs. 'Miss Eve, may I present Judd Schuck, my new valet? Judd, this is my beloved – and her maid, Monique, who will show you to your room. This is your home now. We want you to feel comfortable and accommodated in every way.'

I almost laughed, for as Judd wetly kissed my hand he was eyeing Monique, unaware she'd already accommodated him. Blissfully ignorant of how she would put him in his place if he ever put anything up her skirt.

'How very nice to meet you,' he said. 'Mr Proffit has told me so much about you.'

This used up Mr Schuck's entire repertoire of social niceties, for then the conversation fell into a lull. Had Rémy not come in with a large trunk, I would've felt compelled to comment upon the sultry weather, or to ask if he had family here in New Orleans. Any *pertinent* questions would earn a frown from my husband.

'Well then!' Chapin exclaimed. 'I'm sure you'd like to settle in, so while Monique takes you to your new quarters –'

'We're on our way to the kitchen,' I replied pointedly, 'to inform Mrs Frike we'll be ready for dinner soon. You two gentlemen have many things to discuss, so we'll not intrude.'

I started towards the back of the house, knowing I'd set myself up for a lecture later. Monique kept quiet until we'd entered the dining room.

'Well done, Auntie! You're getting more like *moi* every day, *oui*?'

'Schuck is *not* a member of this big, happy family. He'll be of no more use than breasts on a bullfrog,' I said with a caustic snicker. 'And if he finds out about *these* girls, those toady little eyes will bulge, for sure!'

Monique's laughter brought the new maids out of their huddle, where Fanny was demonstrating the finer points of working with fresh bread dough. 'Come give it a squeeze,' Cinderella said, waggling her flour-coated fingers at us. 'It's warm and soft and springy –'

'Like your ass,' Cleopatra breathed.

'That's quite enough,' the housekeeper snapped. 'Mr Proffit will soon be home, with his new manservant. A valet's main function is to inform his employer about what goes on in the household, you know.'

'Spying, yes. And dressing him, and getting him places on time. Rather like a nanny,' Antoinette remarked. She was kneading her ball of dough with the weight of her body and her powerful hands, which blew puffs of flour at her black uniform. 'But we'll soon show the new boy how things are done around here!'

'I'm not showing him anything.' Cinderella looked at me, her eyes tight with conviction. 'After the way Mr Proffit watched our spankings the other day, I'm keeping my butt covered! If you'll pardon my saying so, ma'am.'

Had Chapin shown such predatory interest in the whipping? I'd had my lap – and line of vision – so full of these young men and their pantied backsides, I hadn't noticed.

'That's perfectly acceptable, Cinderella. And since Mr Schuck has just arrived, you'll be meeting him at dinner this evening.' I watched their arms flex as they worked the bread dough, inhaling the aroma of the warm yeast ... imagining how those six hands would feel on my body. 'And thank you for shifting your beds, so Monique can share your quarters. Things are different for us all, with the staff up to full capacity.'

Different indeed, I mused as I ambled back through the dining room. Never had I envisioned three male maids, nor a brazen young lady in flame-licked boots, inhabiting the staid, stuffy Proffit home, so the addition of Judd Schuck shouldn't have made a ripple. After all, he was my husband's bodyguard – which meant his time would be spent with Chapin rather than spying on us as we prepared for the Mardi Gras gala.

Yet knowing that uncouth man would sleep in the room beside mine set me on edge. While Monique assisted in the kitchen, I slipped upstairs to dress for dinner – and discovered the adjoining door had been left ajar while Chapin showed his valet the house. The two men were in Judd's room now, engrossed in talk.

'...and these French doors open to the gallery overlooking the garden,' Chapin was saying. 'A convenient escape route, should you or a *guest* need to come and go unseen.'

Their conspiratorial laughter widened my eyes, for I'd never known my husband to consider such a thing. Nor had I ever suspected he'd sneak somebody past my own French doors on the way to the garden stairs.

This is the man who screwed his 'niece' in someone else's courtyard, remember?

Rather than slide the bolt on my side of the door, I stood stealthily against the wall, where I could peek through its crack for a better view. Chapin was opening the massive walnut armoire, his smile expansive.

'This is for your use now,' he was saying as he gestured at its drawers and spacious interior, 'and this door beside it connects to my suite, although it now opens into my closet – one of the few changes I made after my parents' deaths. Seemed a more efficient use of this alcove area, because now the entry to the attic – this door you see in the wall – is tucked out of sight. It's seldom used anyway.'

How *interesting*, that he'd mention this attic to his valet, but never to me during the seven years we'd been married! I made a mental note to further investigate his quarters, tomorrow when he left for the Cotton Exchange. Then I chose one of my new dresses, a flowing silk print of green, gold and maroon. It buttoned primly up to my neck and disguised almost everything about me. Perfect for a first dinner with the new valet, who already had me seething.

But it was Chapin to blame for my seeing red and

feeling green: Chapin who'd brought this disreputable-looking man into the house and shared confidences with him; Chapin who was engaged in a longer, friendlier conversation with Schuck than he'd shared with me in years.

And it was Chapin I had to convince of my devotion – because I still wanted his affection, despite Monique and Dewel's distractions while training me towards this end.

Things were getting more difficult, however: not only did we have a staff member sleeping between us, but any extra efforts to coax Chapin to my bed would appear contrived. I should've attempted this years ago, before my husband was thrust into the political limelight ... before my beliefs about true love and the sexualities of the two genders had been shattered – or at least radically altered.

I would do my best, however. And it had to start tonight, to set the tone for the valet my instincts warned me against liking. Or trusting.

As I put on my jewellery and smoothed my hair, I wished for Monique's assistance – she knew how to attract a man's attention far better than I. She was up to her own devices, however, or she would've been standing beside me at that wall, absorbing the men's conversation and its ramifications for us all.

In the hallway, I heard Chapin's voice. 'Until dinner then,' he said in a jovial tone. 'If you find anything in the drawers or under the mattress, it's Monique's. Bears watching, that woman.'

'So I've noticed,' came Judd's reply.

'It won't be long before my wife realises Miss Picabou wasn't a wise choice as a lady's maid. But then, you can't tell a woman anything! Dinner's at seven.'

I slapped my hairbrush against my hand. My husband was acting chummier than I'd ever seen him, as though talking with a good friend from the Beau Monde Club – as though no one else, namely his wife, would overhear his derogatory remarks.

In the vanity mirror, I practised the calm, gracious smile I would paste on my face throughout dinner: the expression of a wife who believes she's the centre of her man's universe. That's how Judd Schuck had to see me, so that's how I would act – and Chapin would have no choice but to respond lovingly in front of the help. Schuck had surely noticed we didn't share the same bed, so it was my mission to refute whatever nonsense Chapin had told him about *that*.

I arrived in the dining room, and there among the massive carved table and sideboards, beneath chandeliers of Austrian crystal which had graced this home since Virgilia Proffit designed it, I composed myself. I still had moments when I felt like an outsider, as though I were one of the newer fixtures Chapin had installed, just as he'd converted that alcove to a closet. And while Monique had improved my outlook immeasurably, I realised that only Evelyn Marie Proffit could alter her sense of not belonging here. I had every right to rule this roost. And rule it I would!

'Begging your pardon, Miss Eve. May I have a moment?'

Judd Schuck observed me from the doorway, twitching in an ill-fitted suit of blue serge. I caught a hint of fresh cologne, slapped on with a heavy hand; his reptilian grin suggested a motive I didn't want to know about.

Ever the gracious hostess Chapin expected me to be, I smiled and stepped towards him. 'Of course, Mr Schuck. I hope you've found your room comfortable and –'

'Actually, I've found *this*,' he said, reaching inside his coat, 'and I was wondering if it belongs to Monique. Or maybe you ladies share it.'

The blood rushed from my face. He pulled out a dildo – a far more extravagant style than mine – and brandished it in front of my face. It had *two* black cocks, long and thick and angled away from each other, and it looked positively lewd, laced together in the centre with ridged red leather thongs that glimmered beneath the chandelier.

'You, sir, are the rudest, most –' I gasped, grabbing for the toy.

Judd snatched it away, back over his shoulder. 'Is it yours, Miss Eve? Despite your unfavourable impression of me, I *can* keep a secret and –'

I tried to take hold of it without touching him, but he slipped his arm tightly around me, laughing. 'Is this one of those things Chapin told you so much about?' I rasped. 'If you think for one minute he'll allow –'

'What's going on here?' came a siren of a voice. Monique let a heavy bowl of something thump to the table, and then tried to squeeze between Judd and the door jamb to rescue the dildo. 'Thief! First you steal my toy, and then you accuse Miss Eve –'

'Unhand them!' came the cry from the kitchen door.

'Grab his damn leg, Toinette, while I take hold of his –'

'Mr Schuck, you skunk,' came Cinderella's shriller outcry, and then she slapped his face soundly. 'In *this* household, we respect Miss Eve, and there's no messing around with other people's *things*! So you can just take your hands off –'

Judd cussed as two sissy maids grabbed his feet and then set him down with an unceremonious *whump*. Monique snatched the dildo, and then the four of them

169

stood with their hands planted on their hips, scowling at him as I stepped away.

He leered, thinking his chances for gratification had quadrupled in the last few seconds – for the maids made an enticing sight with their shiny black shoes and stockinged legs beneath their short French skirts. His expression corrected itself, however, when my husband's footsteps came down the hallway.

'And what have we here?' Chapin demanded. He shot a disgusted glance at the four girls before offering his valet a hand. 'Surely you maids have something better to do than accost my –'

'Does defending your wife's honour count?' Cleopatra blurted. 'We heard her holler, and when we came from the kitchen, this nasty man had snatched something away from her, and had her in his clutches.'

'And what was so important that warranted his landing on the floor?' He was brushing off Judd's backside with an indignance that boded ill for the rest of our dinner.

'It was mine, and I recovered it, thank you,' Monique muttered, wisely concealing the lurid tool behind the fullness of her skirt. 'I walked in just as Mr Schuck lured Miss Eve into a very ... unflattering position. *Disgusting*, the things he asked her!'

'*You* are the hired help, and *I* am the man of this house.' Chapin's crystalline eyes glittered with malice for my circle of girls. 'Don't you *ever* take it upon yourselves to manhandle my valet again. Understand me?'

With a stiff nod, Monique came to check on me, and the other maids beelined towards the kitchen. Before I could ask any questions, she rolled her dark eyes. 'I'll explain later,' she breathed, and then more audibly she asked, 'You are all right, Miss Eve? If I stepped out of line, I'm sorry, but when I saw him –'

'You caught him in the nick of time. How can I ever thank you?' I asked as she walked me towards the kitchen door. Once inside, she cupped a hand to my ear.

'We'll get Stud Fuck – I mean Judd Schuck – on our side by hinting at what we'll do later tonight in your room –'

I almost choked on that thought.

'– because then he'll either keep it a secret – not tattle to Chapin about you and me and this toy I left in his armoire drawer,' she gushed, 'or, he'll *tell* your husband, and Chapin'll get so hot he'll have to see for himself. Or just have *you*, Aunt Evil! You're ready for him now. I've been working both sides the best I can, *non?*'

My head was spinning at the speed of her Cajun chatter, but I suspected I'd once again been framed by my feisty maid. How could I not love Monique for her loyalty? For her efforts on behalf of a marriage that might have died long ago without my even knowing it.

'Thank you,' I murmured, for I truly appreciated her creative ways of handling things. 'But how can I face that awful man now? What can I possibly talk about after his lewd advances?'

'Talk about lewd advances.' Her eyes sparkled like coffee splashed with champagne. 'You're not alone in there, *ma tante*. I've been training the girls for the big party – tonight's a trial run, with several courses. Several chances for something to get dumped in Stud Fuck's lap if he doesn't treat you with respect, Auntie.'

About ten minutes later, Fanny announced dinner. My husband seated me to his right, while he sat at the head of the table with Judd at his left. I'd always felt odd eating in this huge room at such a monstrous table – its remaining length was so long and so glossy, I could've skated on it. But it was a monument to the grandeur of the Proffit past – and in less than two weeks it would once again serve dozens of guests, celebrating Chapin's new political aspirations.

This evening, however, I was forced to face Judd Schuck. He was observing me with a suggestive smirk, which my husband didn't seem to notice.

'I hear Fanny has outdone herself this evening,' I said to fill the awkward silence. 'Several dishes she plans to serve at the Mardi Gras ball.'

'And here we are with the first one! A delectable she-crab soup,' came a voice from the doorway.

As Antoinette set our bowls before us, I inhaled the seasoned steam rising from the rich, cream-based chowder.

'What's in this?' Schuck demanded. He stirred the soup with a doubtful frown, and then jabbed at a chunk of the crab meat with his spoon.

'Fresh crab, with butter and cream,' the redhead replied in a pleasantly modulated voice, 'with a splash of sherry –'

'Take it away. I don't eat fish.'

Without batting an eye, Toinette removed the offending food. 'I'll return momentarily with another offering,' she said, dismissing herself with a curtsy.

Judd urged us to begin without him – a situation my husband found more intolerable by the second. Schuck didn't seem to notice. He was too busy watching me eat, as though he'd like to be licking my food off my lips.

'It's improper for a guest not to have a plate in front of him at all times,' Chapin lectured. 'At the ball, I must insist –'

'And here we are!' Monique chirped, expertly balancing her tray atop her raised arm. 'A lovely array of fresh asparagus with artichoke hearts, marinated in a red wine vinaigrette –'

'You expect me to eat this?' Schuck blurted. 'What ever happened to a good steak and potatoes? Or fried chicken with biscuits? Or ham with –'

'The ham is in your chair, Mr Schuck,' my maid muttered as she snatched up his salad plate. She set our salads where our soup bowls had been, and awaited our reactions.

I shifted nervously, for I hadn't expected such an outburst from anyone my husband would hire. Chapin's table etiquette was exemplary, to the point he rarely spilled a drop and had never slurped his soup. Yet he was cutting his asparagus spears as though his new man had done nothing unseemly.

'At the ball, of course, Mrs Frike will offer a wide assortment of foods on a buffet,' Monique said, filling in the heavy silence with a patter devoid of her usual Cajun sing-song. 'But for now, aren't we delighted she's giving us a preview of these mouthwatering attractions?'

Mr Schuck raised an eyebrow, looking directly at her bosom. 'All your fancy talk's not filling my plate, now is it, honey? Just bring me something to eat, dammit, and be quick about it!'

Monique's nostrils flared. 'Certainly, sir. Right away, Your Highness.'

My husband glared at Monique's retreating backside, where the swishing of her uniform announced her wrath as surely as the harsh tattoo of her boots. 'Miss Eve, you must speak with your maids – once again – about proper deportment,' he said in a deceptively quiet voice. 'They *cannot* offend the people who are funding the very future of this family!'

Heat prickled in my cheeks, and I stuffed an artichoke heart in my mouth to keep from saying something I'd regret. It was obvious to *me* who needed a lesson in deportment! And it was just as apparent that my husband had given Judd Schuck permission to run amok in a household that had run so smoothly before his arrival.

This time it was Cinderella approaching the table, bearing a silver tray between her dainty hands as she *click-clack-clicked* across the dining room in her high-heeled shoes. She paused to give the valet her prettiest smile before lowering the tray so he could see it. The gaze he fixed on her bosom left nothing to the imagination, concerning what he would really like to devour.

'Perhaps Mr Schuck will enjoy being the first to sample our desserts,' she cooed, leaning towards him with a flirtatious shimmy. 'We have a four-layer bourbon praline torte, French bread pudding with brandy sauce, an eclair filled with raspberry creme, a –'

'How about a slice of cherry pie, served up with a little of your pussy sauce, darlin'?' the valet asked in a husky voice.

Cinderella's face went from white to red, and in her agitation – or was it on purpose? – she dropped the tray of gooey, sauced sweets against the edge of the table. It bounced, to tilt the food into Judd's lap – which sent him scooting back from the table with a roar of obscenities. This brought Monique scurrying from the kitchen, followed by a foul-faced Mrs Frike wielding a wooden spoon.

'You clumsy ... What have I told you about setting the tray *on* the table before speaking?' Monique raged. 'Across my knee this instant, young lady. You deserve a spanking, and you know it!'

To everyone's amazement, Monique grabbed Cinderella's sleeve and wheeled her around, while the house-keeper pulled a chair from the table. The blonde was howling, of course, blubbering about how sorry she was. But she was no match for her determined mistress.

'Here – face your superiors, so they can see what a miserable excuse you make for a maid!' Monique positioned her squawking charge across her lap and then yanked down her panties. 'And after I tan your back-side, you'll stand in the corner to ponder your sins – with your red cheeks displayed for all to see!'

My heart rose into my throat. Surely Monique realised she'd be exposing Cinderella's secrets, to two men who would use that stunning surprise to humiliate – or fire – our male princess. Yet as the smacks rang out, punctuated by the penitent's cries, I suspected this whole scenario had been staged. Cinderella appeared more frantic with each whack, but the sound of skin smacking skin was far more sensational than the actual colouration of her behind.

'Look at those cheeks jiggling!' Judd stood beside Chapin, with the forgotten desserts drifting down his pant legs. Glee animated his whole face. 'You do have a mighty attractive staff, Mr Proffit.'

With a final whack, Monique glared at the valet. As she marched her charge towards the far corner, white panties bunched directly beneath her swollen pink behind, Mrs Frike moved in Judd Schuck's direction.

'Is it my imagination, Mr Schuck, or do you have extraordinarily bad manners?'

The housekeeper swatted her palm with the rounded end of her wooden spoon, eyeing the valet with a disdain that made her tight curls tremble. 'You've been brought here as staff yourself, rather than as a guest, and you'll be treated accordingly. You think it's amus-ing that a well-meaning maid just got a spanking, don't you, little man? Well, in this house, what's sauce for the goose gets poured on the gander as well!'

Judd laughed. He was the boss's protected pet, after all. 'You can't touch me, you old windbag! I'll just –'

'Watch me, fool.' Mrs Frike grabbed his lapel and hauled him up until his face was in hers. 'If you learn nothing else here, you'll know better than to taunt a woman who's smarter – and larger – than you! Now drop your pants, and don't give me any sass about it!'

Judd's face paled and his Adam's apple bobbed with a hard swallow. He was teetering on his toes, glancing frantically towards Chapin but, when the housekeeper led him to the chair, he realised he was bested. He turned towards the wall and, with quivering hands, lowered his pants past his bubble-shaped behind.

The room was silent: the two maids peering around the kitchen door – and the two in the corner – were too delighted by this spectacle to make a peep. Chapin could only stare as the housekeeper he'd grown up with flipped his new valet across her broad lap. She took her time positioning him, so the gravity of his predicament could sink in as part of his punishment.

'Palms to the floor,' she ordered. 'And by God if you kick me or wiggle around, I'll have the girls hold your feet. Understand me?'

'Y-yes, Mrs Frike.'

'Fine.' For effect, she paused again, pulling his shirt-tail up over his back, and then fingering his buttocks to determine the best point of attack. 'Mr Schuck, you have such a fat ass, this spoon will have no effect at all. I'll have to use my hand.'

Her first smack landed before Judd could protest, and her second one made him arch like a beached fish.

'Talk about jiggling,' Fanny said with a tight laugh.

'It's just as well you didn't eat any of that dessert. You certainly don't need it, do you?' *Smack!*

'Hey! You've got no call to –'

Smack! 'What say, Mr Schuck?' Fanny asked calmly. 'Who's calling the shots here?'

'You are, but –'

'Yes, *butt*,' she replied, bringing her broad hand down upon his juddering flesh again. 'You're still forgetting your place. And your manners. Now what do you say to Fanny for correcting you, before you embarrassed Mr Chapin at his party, in front of important guests?'

'Thank you –'

Smack! 'Thank you, *what*?'

'Thank you, my *dear* Mrs Frike, for showing me the error of my ways.' The stocky little frog was panting now, his backside ablaze from Fanny's hand. 'I promise to never again complain about your food, or make improper remarks about the maids, or insult Miss Eve. I'm a better man for this.'

'Don't overdo it, Schuck.'

The housekeeper's final swat was almost playful; she was fighting a smile she didn't want Judd to see. 'Go to your room without your supper. We'll all pray that when you come downstairs tomorrow, you'll be a model of proper behaviour.'

I bit my lip to keep from chuckling, for Mrs Frike had enjoyed this immensely. And when Schuck stood to cover himself, he couldn't hide his blunt, jutting erection – nor could he fasten it into his pants without the rest of us seeing it.

This rallied Chapin from the dazed state in which he'd witnessed his valet's shame. 'In the future, Mrs Frike, you will leave the discipline of my personal staff to *me*. Understood?'

The housekeeper rose from her chair with the stout dignity of one who truly knew her place, no matter what this particular Proffit had to say about it.

'I understand quite well, sir,' she replied with a smile. 'If you'd like to host your Mardi Gras ball without me, that'll be just fine. I've not tolerated such rudeness – towards your family, or the help – in all my years of service, and I won't start now! *Understood?*'

The blond waves around Chapin's face trembled; his nose pinched into a slender beak like an eagle's. He couldn't find words as Fanny returned to the kitchen, except, 'I'm going to my study, and I don't wish to be disturbed.'

'Before you go, sir –'

Monique's strident tone had the rest of us turning to hear what she would say. For weren't we all looking to ease the tension that throbbed like a cock rubbed raw, after so many surprises in such a short time?

'– I feel I should mention a broken keyhole cover, on Miss Eve's side of the door adjoining Mr Schuck's room,' she continued.

Her features shone with sincerity, and for once her tone showed no flippancy towards my husband. In fact, she had returned to that elegant turn of phrase which surprised me earlier. 'It was of no concern when I stayed there, of course. But since your valet has insulted a maid and made advances towards your wife, I suggest repairing this as soon as possible. Miss Eve's privacy is my utmost concern, of course.'

Chapin's face registered the repeated shocks of an evening gone awry. 'Of course,' he muttered. And off to his study he went.

16 **Double Dipping**

I would've enjoyed standing at the gallery rail overlooking the garden that evening, with the fragrance of magnolia blossoms wafting on the breeze – except Judd Schuck would join me. I could hear him on the other side of our common wall, squatting for a peek through that damn keyhole. I didn't want to envision him awkwardly balancing against the door while he fondled that fat erection, so I thought back over events of these past few hours.

What was going on here? My Cajun maid had set me up as Schuck's target, presumably to attract Chapin's attention, and in the meantime we'd seen Cinderella take a spanking towards the same end. The biggest surprise of all, however, was the gleam in Fanny's eye as she'd hauled that little toad over her knee to smack his backside. Like a mama correcting an errant son, but with a decidedly unmaternal glee all over her face.

And to think some people actually *enjoyed* corporal punishment! I could understand the power element Monique had mentioned, from the perspective of the one doing the spanking. But Schuck had loved it too. His cock wasn't large, but it had stuck straight out.

And when Cinderella had bent over my knee for that birching, she'd gushed her appreciation, as though I'd granted her a new life. She'd apparently volunteered to drop those desserts down Judd's front, so she could get her bottom swatted again.

Interesting, as well, was Chapin's reaction. While

he'd been quick to help Judd up from the floor and chide *my* attendants for their misbehaviour, he hadn't come to his valet's defence when Fanny took him over her knee. He'd watched with a fascination I hadn't expected, gripping the table, barely breathing, as his bright blue eyes followed every stroke of the housekeeper's broad hand ... every jiggle and flush of Schuck's fleshy buttocks.

Personally, I felt Fanny deserved a raise in pay for standing up to Judd's inexcusable behaviour – and for standing her ground with Chapin too. Where I'd worried before that she'd have Monique dismissed, I now had another ally. A very important ally, as my husband's campaign escalated.

All this because Monique had brought in those sissy maids, and administered the discipline they craved. Inexplicable, the ways of this new world. And it was spinning out of my control, right here in my own home.

A quiet knock made me scowl. Damn that Schuck, thinking I'd want *his* company! Far as I was concerned, he could stick that dick in the keyhole. When I looked up, however, it was a lithe, familiar figure slipping through my door. Even in the evening's shadows, her impish grin lit up her face.

'Good thing I removed that keyhole cover, *oui*?' she whispered with a mischievous wink. 'I figured he'd fall into our trap – and keep quiet about what he sees here tonight. He thinks you or I, or both of us together, will fuck him because he's such a stud.'

Her rolling eyes made me chuckle. 'He's watching us, yes – that rubbing on the other side of the wall has stopped now. But Monique,' I said in a more serious voice, 'I'm concerned about the turn things have taken. I can't believe Chapin will be more in the mood –'

'*Mood?* What do you think he's doing in his study?'

She giggled, slinging an arm around my shoulder. 'He's drinking brandy, *oui*? He's licking his wounds, after Fanny defied him, *oui*? But he's stroking himself, Aunt Evil! He left the dining room with a shaft so hard, it could've knocked Schuck down.'

My eyes flew open, for I'd never imagined my husband taking himself in hand. Nor had I noticed the placket of his pants. I'd been too engrossed in his facial expression; too naive to believe the evening's surprises might excite him.

'Do you think he wants Judd?'

She shrugged, and then slipped out of her uniform. 'Cinderella's my guess. He paid closer attention to her and Toinette at that first birching. Which is why I had *them* serving dinner tonight. Let me serve *you* now, *ma tante*. You've got a man downstairs who wants it pretty bad, but he'll have to wait his turn, *non*?'

With the moonlight falling over her half-bare body, my maid looked heartbreakingly beautiful. And when she leaned over to fumble in her skirt pocket, she gave me quite a shot of her marvellous backside, bisected by her black garter belt and the straps holding up her stockings. As she flashed that double dildo at me, her breasts rippled deliciously, tipped in nipples that dipped and swayed with her every move.

Someone sucked air in the other room.

Or was that my own sigh? While the contraption in her hand intrigued me, as a way to prepare myself for taking Chapin, I felt a tingling attraction for my tutor in this fine art of ... fucking. Of all the surprises revealed to me of late, this quivering in my belly – the heightened sense of excitement and forbidden pleasure – far outstripped my expectations.

Had someone told me I would ever want a woman, I couldn't have believed them. Not before Monique.

As though she read my thoughts, the zany maid unfastened her topknot and shook her hair with the abandon of a dog after a bath. She reached for me then, her joy contagious, and I laughed as she plucked the pins from my own hair and tossed them against the wall.

This time it was a groan we heard, followed by a low laugh. Young Schuck thought he was keeping secrets, but we knew exactly what he was doing over there – and my maid's face told me she'd get him even deeper into this game, at his own expense.

'Step over by the doors,' she whispered, guiding me to where the moonlight washed over us. 'Make yourself naked. Touch your body, like Chapin was watching you. Wanting you.'

Was it me, or had the sultry Louisiana evening entered my room with Monique, to infuse everything with its erotic heat? I smelled her sex. I peeled away the layers of clothing proper ladies wore: the dress that covered me to the neck and wrists and ankles ... the shift that shimmered to the floor like a dying ghost ... the corset cover and drawers – which Monique delighted in tugging over my hips, so she could caress my thighs as I stepped out of them.

'Why do you wear this nasty thing?' she asked as she unlaced my stays. 'Let your breasts and curves flow, *ma tante*. A woman who feels free and breathes easy, she moves like a panther in heat. Like a pussy always hot for a cock, *oui*?'

I did feel wonderful as she tossed my corset aside, yet I rolled my eyes. 'And what woman has time to think about such things, except before bed –'

'Every woman! *You*, Auntie Evil,' came her sibilant whisper.

She turned me to face her, both of us bare except for

our stockings and shoes, silhouetted in the moonlight pouring through the French doors. 'If sex is a game you always want to play, think how happy you'll be! Like Monique with her Tommy Jon. And I promise, *ma tante*, your husband won't stay in his room if he thinks you always want it. If he knows you sleep naked. If he believes Miss Eve's got a wet little cunt that wants fucking.'

She ran her hand down my front, rustling my curls with her fingers before slipping them inside me. My legs parted of their own accord, and I couldn't hold back a moan.

'See there?' she crowed softly, rubbing my own honey into my lips. 'You're soaking wet, *cherie*. It'll be a wild night, even if Chapin never takes his turn. I'm going to show you our new toy now, *oui*? You're going to love it.'

She held the oddly shaped contraption between us, so the moonlight fell on the dark leather, making it glimmer seductively. 'Same thick shafts, same wide, rounded heads like the other ones T-Jon's made,' she explained, running her fingertip along each feature. 'He moulds them on his own cock, you know. Then he laces the leather skin over a wooden shaft, so it stays hard all the time. We'll never find a *man* this good, *non*?'

I laughed, touching the dildo to feel its bump-studded centre, where the two cocks came together at differing angles. 'It looks very ... filling here in the middle,' I murmured. 'And these ridges –'

'Designed to excite both clits, while the cunts get stuffed full. Its curves and length are just right for rubbing that sweet spot way up inside,' she breathed, as though her own were already tingling. 'So when both pussies are pushing and pulling, going out of control, things will get wet and wild, Aunt Evil. Very wet ... and wild like only your Monique's imagination can make them. Are you ready?'

I nodded. Schuck was drinking all this in as well, and his rhythmic rubbing against the wall was having its effect on me. 'You first.'

'No, you! Get down on the floor and I'll warm you up.'

As though the night wasn't already hot. As though my body wasn't already quivering with inner heat as it obeyed her siren call. The rug chafed my bottom as I sat on it, and then scooted back against the armoire. 'I want to watch you ...'

She grinned. 'Watch me fuck you with it? Watch this big black cock slip inside –'

I moaned, opening my legs further as she inserted it; kneeling before me like a slave, to sate the desires of my night. Something told me Monique had arranged everything to the last detail, so our nasty valet got a profile view of our nude bodies through that keyhole.

'– and then tickle you with its ridges ... and rub you in all the right ways, and places, *oui*?' she continued her hypnotic chant. 'In and out, so slow and solid ... getting my auntie so hot and bothered, before I *prod* her –'

I gasped when the tip of that dildo found the sweet spot she'd alluded to, high and forward, and so very, very sensitive. I couldn't sit still. My ass danced, rubbing against the rug with a suggestive whisper that told of my secret hunger, my need for more release than I'd realised. 'Please – I – Monique –'

'Raise up and thrust against it, *ma belle*,' she coaxed. 'Think of Dewel, sinking himself into you like he's got all night. Like he wants to make you come and come and come, so your poor little puss can't stand any more – but can't say no to it either. You are desperate, *non*?'

The mention of that bourbon-skinned scoundrel shot my pulse to a gallop, and I rose to Monique's challenge. Faster she pumped it into me, driving me towards those spirals that started like a fire down deep, and suddenly flared to a point of no return.

'My turn, you.' She yanked the leather cock out of me, her sly laugh saying my need was no secret. 'Here. Make me beg too – and then we'll ride together.'

Monique's hair swayed in alluring disarray as she positioned herself between my spread knees, with her feet on either side of my hips and her elbows on the floor. Her high-heeled boots gave her leverage, and as I slipped the dildo inside her, her garters stretched over her flexing legs. As dark as her stockings, her bush parted with her sex lips, giving the toy full access ... allowing me to twist and turn it, so the ridges and leather lacings titillated her channel in all the best places.

On impulse, I shoved it all the way up, so the wide, ridged centre held her fully open as it pressed into her clit.

She muttered French obscenities, all the more intense because she was trying not to be heard. Her hips gyrated; she pulsed forward and up, thrusting shamelessly to attain the level of pleasure where she'd left me hanging. Her eyes closed, the long lashes casting shadows on her smooth, moonlit cheeks, and when her head fell back she made the most erotic sight I'd ever seen. Her breasts were jiggling, pricking the air with distended nipples I so badly wanted to suck.

So I rolled forward, to let my mouth go where my mind had led it. Monique's eyes flew open, and then, hooded with her passion, they fixed upon my lips as I suckled.

'Climb on,' she breathed. 'Straddle me, like a man. And then fuck me, like a woman.'

The groan from the other room overrode my own and, as I positioned my slit at the tip of the dildo, I felt a surge of power. I had it within me to bring us both to a mind-boggling climax, if I settled just right ... if I pushed just right and got into her rhythm.

I impaled myself, allowing a moment for my sheath to adjust to the thickness. The angle felt more advantageous than I'd imagined, deep and curving to fit my channel. I braced my arms alongside Monique's shoulders, and began my brazen attempt to drive her until she cried out for mercy.

Where had this desire come from? My slit instinctively found the pressure points it yearned for, while my maid shifted beneath me. She thrust upward, grinning lasciviously, and the control I'd thought was mine got snatched away.

'You like it, *oui*?' she whispered. 'Auntie Evil looks wicked and wonderful, her breasts dangling in my face, spreading my legs with her hips. Now rub me, *cherie*! Grind against the centre, and I will too.'

The rustling of our curls ... the incense of our combined sex ... the heaviness of my breasts as they slapped my ribcage – faster now, as the wily woman beneath me began writhing in earnest. Our breathing came in duelling bursts, filling the room with a song only vixens could sing. I felt unbelievably full, yet greedy. My spasms began, deep and leisurely, but as I settled lower to scratch that intense inner itch, Monique arched up.

She nipped my nipple, and I shot forward like a horse from the starting gate. I lost track of everything save the fine, frenzied heat between us and the wetness splattering my thighs – and then Schuck's bumping against the wall drove us home. Monique curled around me, groaning her encouragements, commanding me not to stop. Then she convulsed like a crazed puppet whose strings were being pulled very tightly from behind me.

We collapsed with a gasp. The room rang with sudden silence. My mind was trying to wrap itself around yet another sexual adventure made so stunning by this Cajun maid: could it be I preferred girls? That I'd never known this, and had sent some unwitting signal to Chapin, which made me undesirable to him?

Monique's chuckle brought me out of these distressing thoughts. 'Stud Fuck got his too. And how nice that we didn't have to touch him!'

I dismounted, leaving the dildo between her gaping legs like a huge, lewd erection. It took several moments for my boneless limbs to recover as I stretched out beside her. 'I'd like to step outside, to cool off on the gallery,' I breathed, 'but I don't want Judd coming out.'

My maid sat up. The leather toy made a loud slurping sound as she pulled it out. Then she cocked her head towards the wall that adjoined Schuck's room. 'He's snoring. Come on, *ma tante*.'

The breeze was barely there on this hot New Orleans night, but as it caressed my body, the scent of the magnolia trees and gardenias drifted around us too. I leaned over the railing – very brazen indeed, for I'd never stood naked outside my room. Had never experienced many simple pleasures that were second nature to Monique.

'Thank you,' I breathed.

Her dark eyes sparkled in the moonlight as she lit a cheroot. 'For letting you be on top?'

'For setting me free. For breaking the rules. For ... proving men aren't the only ones who possess power.' I smiled when she patted my arm in her childlike way. 'That's a lot to learn in a very short time.'

'Oh, there's more, Auntie Evil,' she replied. She drew deeply on her little cigar, letting its smoke surround her in its mystical haze. Then she playfully slapped my ass. 'But enough for tonight, *oui*? We must set those three sissy maids to cleaning the ballroom tomorrow! Sleep well, *ma tante.*'

Through the open doors I heard her gathering her clothes, and then quietly slipping out of my room. I spent a few more moments gazing over the gardens, so cloaked in ethereal beauty at this hour; so much more symmetrical and planned-out than my life seemed to be. Chapin had *his* plans, but what about mine?

Was I ready to approach him? To seduce him, now that my sensual awakening made me aware of what we'd never shared?

Or would I only learn things I didn't want to know?

I slipped into bed naked, but couldn't sleep. I was too aware of my own skin, so boldly on display without benefit of even a sheet – although no one else would see me, or slip through my open French doors like the subtle sounds of the night. I felt alive and on edge – saw scenes in my mind, of bare asses across my lap, juddering beneath the smack of a hand ... of a wicked little woman returning thrust for thrust, moaning in breathy French ... Dewel, peeling away his silk shirt, taking control of me with that molasses drawl and the deceptive power behind his languid ways.

I stiffened. Was that a footstep on the gallery? Looking towards my doors, I wished I'd closed them like any proper wife whose suite now adjoined the valet's.

I heard the noise again – furtive footfalls, indeed. And then a figure hurried past, towards the steps at the end of the gallery! Recalling Chapin's remark to his valet, I rushed to the gallery to look out, but all I saw was the predawn retreat of someone in swirling skirts and a shawl that shone an unearthly white in the thickening mist.

A woman! Far too sophisticated to be Monique sneaking off to see Tommy Jon, so who *was* she? The snoring that drifted through Judd's open window gave me an answer – a conclusion no wife wants to reach, for it rips her heart out and fills in the hole with suspicions, which coil and hiss like a nest of snakes.

The only other room with access to the gallery was Chapin's.

17 **A Closet Rendezvous**

He had already gone to the Cotton Exchange when I went downstairs for breakfast. Or was Mrs Frike covering for him, out of the loyalty that spanned her years of service to his philandering father as well?

As she set down my plate of stewed fruits and pecan sticky buns, I almost asked her if Chapin had entertained a guest last night, while supposedly sequestered in his study. But did I really want to know? What else did I need to see, after watching him hump that blonde in the courtyard a few weeks ago?

'Fanny, I've been thinking about our Mardi Gras ball,' I ventured, deciding another avenue of exploration might yield tastier fruit. 'And I'm wondering if we'll find things in the attic – decorations, and perhaps even costumes – we could use? Surely Chapin's parents hosted such parties.'

The housekeeper's grey eyes lit up. 'Why, yes! Virgilia Proffit prided herself on being the hostess to be out-done. Spared no expense, that woman – and Chapin loved those balls too.'

'So why hasn't he entertained more often, these past seven years?'

Mrs Frike's wrinkles tightened as she decided whether to divulge such information. 'I'm not sure,' she admitted, 'but I think once his mother died, your husband lost his enthusiasm for such pageantry and dancing. And when his daddy's will split the Proffit properties between him and that Creole courtesan's son, Chapin became a shell of his former self.'

Eaten away by jealousy, even more than greed, my heart whispered.

I nodded, proceeding cautiously along a path I hadn't planned in advance. Perhaps my husband's absence was inspiring me, after watching that woman flee his suite: I felt compelled to explore this rambling family mansion, hoping I'd find answers without having to ask any nasty questions.

'Well, I think we should look up there,' I announced with my best smile. 'I'm guessing we'll find all sorts of finery that deserves another fling. If you want to come with me –'

'Mr Chapin has the key.'

The finality of this pronouncement sounded a warning. Might I find things besides the usual cast-away clothing and furniture, and the costumes I was hoping for? Things a husband didn't want his wife to see?

I smiled sweetly. 'Now, Fanny, you've run this household since before I was born. If you feel I'd be trespassing on old family secrets by –'

'I'm sorry, Miss Eve. When he did some remodelling in his suite – which was Virgilia's, when she was alive – he put a lock on that attic door.' She shrugged, making her pillowy breasts rise behind her starched apron. 'I use it as my excuse not to clean up there. I would never compromise Mr Chapin's privacy, you see.'

Not the answer I wanted. And when she asked what I'd like the three maids to do today, the subject got locked up as tight as that door in the alcove – a door I was determined to open!

Opportunity knocked within the hour. I made an appearance on the third floor – where the unaired ballroom was so stuffy, Monique allowed the maids to work naked – and then slipped away. I was the lady of this house, after all. I saw no reason to avoid my husband's chambers.

I removed my shoes and glanced around his small sitting room; checked the drawer of his secretary, but found it locked. What was he so afraid someone else might find? This only prompted me to pass through his bedroom, past the half-tester and other furnishings of cherry wood that belonged to his mother. Such sentiment touched me, yet keeping this room as a sort of shrine to Virgilia Proffit seemed incongruous to Chapin's current relationships with ... Other Women.

I paused at the arched entryway to the alcove he'd remodelled as a closet. There I saw the frock coats, trousers, silk shirts and shoes of a gentleman with excellent taste; a man who chose the tobacco browns, creams and pale blues that complemented his golden complexion and eye colour, over the darker, more staid hues currently in fashion.

But I was drawn to the two wooden doors – the one in the alcove, which led to the attic, and the identical one in his room that gave access to the gallery. Both bore conspicuous padlocks, as though Chapin needed *safety* – from outside intruders and the household staff, I presumed, since I'd never spent enough time here to threaten his sense of security.

I smiled and pulled a pin from my hair. Apparently men assumed their women too stupid – or too obedient – to finesse a locked door! But I'd gotten some practice as a little sister who'd raided her brother's gun cabinet, where he kept his stash of ribald magazines until he married and moved away.

In went the rounded end of the slender hairpin. As I held the lock in one hand, I gently felt for the place I could push to snap it open.

'Allow me, Mrs Proffit.'

I gasped and dropped the padlock, my pulse pounding. Behind me, wearing only his maid's apron, stood Antoinette. With a sly smile, he showed me a slender metal rod, and then reached around me to grasp the padlock.

'Thieves and the police find these extremely useful,' he said, standing so close his breath dampened the back of my neck. 'I overheard you at breakfast. I thought I'd find you here.'

'But I –' The surreptitious *snick* of the lock didn't distract me from his surprise appearance. 'The others must think –'

'That I had to use the toilet. So I haven't much time.'

How odd it felt to have a man's voice coming from lips that had been rouged, accentuating a smile that brightened his slender face. Odd, and – improper!

'Toinette, I must remind you that the help –'

'My name's Russell. Let's go on in, before Mrs Frike comes hunting us. She was in a real dither after you asked about the attic.'

I couldn't argue with that logic, but I couldn't assume his intentions were entirely honourable either. 'And why are *you* here? Has Chapin told Judd Schuck what he's hiding?'

His smile made my stomach shimmer. '*You're* here, aren't you?'

He steered me up the short flight of wooden stairs into what appeared to be another spacious closet – far roomier than where my own gowns were hung, and lit by skylights.

'I don't understand.' I was trying to block out the array of female finery I saw, by concentrating on this male maid's interest in me. 'You're telling me your real name – touching me like – like a –'

'Man?'

'Yes! Yet you wear your hair in an upsweep, and look so fetching in your uniform –'

'We play the roles we're assigned, until a better one comes along.'

He glanced around, but when his gaze returned to my face, Russell slipped an arm around my waist. 'You learned during that first spanking that I'm very much a man. But unlike Cleopatra and Cinderella, I consent to wearing maid's clothing only as a ruse. Appeasing Honore Delacroix is most important, you see.'

He had a pleasing natural voice, smooth and low, now that he wasn't altering it to appear female. Still, I stepped away from a touch that felt far too familiar – which put me closer to those clothes. Gorgeous gowns and accessories of jewel-toned fabrics told me Chapin's lady friend – or were there several? – commanded a pretty penny from the Proffit coffers.

'And *I* have noticed, Miss Eve, that while you don't protest those spankings, you don't participate either,' he went on, sounding urgent to express several ideas in a short amount of time. 'Pardon my saying so, but your husband's far more interested in watching us get our asses whacked than –'

'Does he know? That you're not a woman?' My concern for the maids' privacy suddenly overrode my discomfort. I could imagine Chapin's reaction, if he learned the seedy little secrets of the maids Monique had secured on my behalf.

'I don't think so.' Russell lifted my chin, so I had no choice but to look up into his eyes – gentle tawny-green eyes that were strikingly similar to my own. 'And pardon my saying so, but it's a crying shame that a splendid woman like you doesn't get what she needs. From a man, anyway.'

The implications of these last words sent my hand flying towards his face, but Russell was faster than I. The grip around my wrist startled me, even though he was by no means abusing his superior strength. No, he'd taken me by such surprise I was easy to subdue. All I could do was return his steady gaze ... wondering what other secrets it hid.

He relaxed then, grinning. 'All right, so I've spied on you. I hope you'll forgive me, but watching you and Monique last night ... and when you frolicked in the fountain, is much more fun than cavorting with Cleo and Cindy. I'm entrusting you with these secrets, hoping you'll allow me the same sort of trust. I can't tell you how good it feels to be out from under Honore's thumb! Thank you for allowing me – all of us – to stay when she came to claim us.'

I swallowed, unsure of what to do next. Russell, however, was lowering his face towards mine, his expression softening. 'I want to help you, Miss Eve. I'm merely a maid on the lowest rung of the household ladder, but I crave affection, and I think you do too. May I kiss you? I was just a kid when Miss Delacroix took –'

His lips touched mine, tentatively. The attic's dry, stifling heat enclosed us in a cocoon of forbidden sensations, and while my body went hot, the skin of our lips felt soothing and cool. He was curious rather than possessive. He dipped again, tasting more firmly, slanting his mouth for fuller contact that had to feel even more rewarding to him than to me, a woman ten years his senior.

I pulled away, my eyes still closed with pleasure. 'Russell, what do you see here? In this little anteroom to the attic?'

He held me against his chest, and then I heard a

sudden intake of breath, along with the deep beating of his heart. '*Dresses*. Hat boxes. A – a jewellery chest in the corner.'

I nodded, opening my eyes. 'This is Mr Proffit's closet. And since I've recently seen him in some rather ... compromising situations, I must ask you *never* to tell the others about this. If I catch one hint that anyone else knows, it's back to Miss Delacroix you go, young man.'

He cleared his throat, comprehension dawning as he stared at the beautiful gowns. 'Can't have such indiscretions getting out during a political campaign.'

'Exactly.'

'But what about you, Miss Eve? Are you going to keep this information buttoned up like the dress you're wearing – which is much too conservative, by the way,' he added with a grin. 'A woman with your marvellous skin –'

'Will handle these matters as she sees fit,' I cut in firmly. The time was passing faster than I wanted, despite the lift Russell's remarks had given my spirits. 'Actually, I wanted to see about any Mardi Gras costumes or decorations I might find for the ball.'

'You can't take anything downstairs. Mrs Frike will know you sneaked up here.'

'True.' I continued up the wooden stairs, into a large, open room that served as the actual attic. 'But since we've picked the lock and risked discovery with every minute you're away, we might as well indulge ourselves. It's better than tearing my hair out, wondering who those beautiful clothes belong to. My God, it's been going on so long, she keeps a wardrobe here! And right under my nose.'

Curiosity compelled me to open musty trunks, and riffle through boxes of old letters and records. An armoire in the corner caught my eye then, a behemoth of a piece with angel faces and wings carved into its corners and along the front edges. When the tall doors creaked open, we sucked in the dusty sweetness of sachets made many, many years ago. My wildest dreams had come true!

'They're beautiful!' I breathed, fingering the folds of gaudy gowns and exquisite veils. 'Harem suits, and a medieval queen's attire, and –'

'Masks. Hanging here on the side. And wigs.'

My heart was beating so hard I nearly fainted. I could envision myself descending the main stairway on the night of the Mardi Gras ball, arrayed in this finery of a bygone time. Perhaps for a moment I'd even steal the limelight from my husband; could assume my rightful place among the other society wives, as a woman to be recognized. Respected.

Perhaps, if he saw me in a costume that brought back happier childhood times, Chapin would see me in a more desirable light too. What did I have to lose?

'Help me carry these,' I said in an urgent whisper. 'We really must be going, before anyone sees that door is open – or, God forbid, shuts us in!'

Russell held out his arms as I took down a taffeta gown that shimmered from periwinkle to sky blue, with huge sleeves that puffed like iridescent white balloons. I snatched up the petticoats too, and oversized patent leather shoes that matched the dress. Instinct had me grabbing a shepherd's crook, along with the most striking of the masks: the traditional shiny-white face of Mardi Gras had a beaded headpiece, which attached it to an outrageous blonde wig that resembled a beehive.

We stole down the steps. Russell walked ahead, so I could keep the colourful lengths of fabric from dragging on the dusty floor. I quickly replaced the padlock, while the maid hurried on to my suite.

'I'd best get back,' he said, heading out my door as I was entering. Then he glanced around, and gave me a thoroughly rakish kiss. 'Can't wait for the party, Miss Eve. Can't wait to see you decked out in such splendour, like the queen you are.'

It was odd, watching the maid's bare backside retreat down the hall with his apron flapping on both sides, while its bow bounced saucily above his butt with each step. My fingers went to my lips, reliving the feel of his kiss as though it had led to something more illicit.

And yet, hadn't I already learned the most intimate secrets about Antoinette? As I quickly hid the costume in the back of my armoire, I wondered where today's revelations might lead – and what would come of the pact I'd made, with the maid I now knew as Russell.

18 My Best-Laid Plans

'Ooh-la-la!' Monique's eyes filled half her face when she saw the glorious periwinkle sheen of the costume I'd stashed behind my other clothes. I'd let three days go by before showing it to her, so she wouldn't associate it with Antoinette's absence – or my own – while the maids had been polishing the ballroom.

'I found it in the attic,' I whispered, hoping Mrs Frike wasn't eavesdropping from the hall. 'It must've belonged to Chapin's mother. Fanny told me how much he enjoyed those lavish parties, so I'm going to surprise him with it at the ball.'

'You'll be the belle, Auntie! The pièce de résistance among ladies who think they're so superior, *non*?' She gave me a speculative look, perhaps gauging the dress's curves against my own. 'But I really must see you in our outfit to drive Chapin wild. Today's the day!'

'But why now? I'm not sure I'm –'

'Ready?' Monique tossed her head, nearly toppling her topknot. 'We're ready *not* to see more strange ladies stealing away at dawn – or cavorting in a courtyard, *non*? Chapin should know you won't tolerate his sneaking around. A bad habit for a man soon to be mayor.'

She had instructed the sissy maids to wash windows and launder table linens today, so with Mrs Frike in charge of these activities, Monique wanted to play – to groom her student for the command performance she'd come here to orchestrate.

She fetched the large white box from Madame

LaRue's and opened it on my bed. With a feline grin, she lifted the black lace, delighting in its seductive softness as she unfolded it. 'Not naked yet?'

Electricity passed between us as she arched her eyebrow. Was she recalling our first rendezvous in the dressmaker's fitting room, as I was? I set aside those memories, hoping this day would mark another momentous occasion: the seduction of the husband who should've been my lover all along. I had to wonder if I'd feel this attraction for Monique, had Chapin come to my bed over these past seven years.

Not that it mattered to my maid: her fires flared at every opportunity, and she didn't let her conscience prevent her pleasure. Didn't let everyone else's moral code affect her needs and desires.

And maybe that was her secret to finding the joy and affection she craved: she assumed her right to take it wherever – and with whomever – she found it. I envied her that. It flew in the face of the good-girl, dutiful-wife image ingrained since my childhood, yet it felt so *right*.

'You're thinking too much,' she murmured, slipping her warm fingers beneath my dress.

'Let your body move towards its target, like an arrow going for the mark. Chapin doesn't stand a chance, *non*? Who could resist a woman like you, Auntie Eve?'

Who, indeed? I tried not to think about him as Monique peeled away my clothes with much more ardour than befitted a maid.

Rather than caress my bare body, however, she began to dress me – wrapping the film of ebony lace around me before draping the final folds over my shoulder from a deep cowl in the front. With a grin, she arranged the daring fabric so that a black rose clung to each of my bobbing breasts.

'We'll find you a clasp,' she said, leading me to the jewellery box. 'Elegant, but sturdy ... ah, *oui*. This pearl brooch is perfect, *non*?'

With agile hands she fastened the clasp at my shoulder. Then she stood back to admire her ingenuity. 'Stunning,' she said with a decisive nod. 'The pearls are pale and flawless, like your skin. And when it comes to seduction, a black dress is a woman's best friend, eh, *cherie*?'

As I turned in front of the glass to watch the barely-there lace follow my bared curves, I felt more wanton – more decidedly decadent – than ever in my life. 'For my hair, I should –'

Monique plucked out my hairpins, tossing them aside with impish abandon. 'Men want their women's hair *loose*,' she exclaimed. 'Looking slept-in, like she spent a wild night with him. So he can run his fingers through it ... imagine it fanned across his pillow as he mounts her.'

Her talk was having the desired effect, for that woman in the mirror – that auburn-haired hoyden I didn't know nearly well enough – looked flushed and ready for rampant sex. My eyes were shining and the smile I saw did wonders for my confidence. Not only did the lace's texture tease at my skin, rasping my nipples into peaks, but it made a subtle sound every time I moved, like satin sheets being rumpled by lovers.

'It's awfully early to –'

'Who says love only happens in the dark?' Monique ran her fingernails down the centre of my belly to make the lace sing. 'Mr Chapin's going to the Club for lunch, so you can catch him early. Have the whole afternoon *and* all night to be his wicked woman, *oui*?'

His wicked woman. I'd never done anything even approaching wicked – until I met Monique. Maybe it was a femme fatale Chapin wanted, rather than a mate of such prudent predictability. I let my smile overtake my face.

'Much better!' Monique moved behind my shoulder to gaze into the glass. 'Now touch yourself, Aunt Evil. Starting high – in your hair. Caress every inch of your body.'

I stiffened. But then, my modesty had gotten me *nowhere* in the last seven years, had it? I placed my palms on my head, noting the way my breasts lifted beneath the filmy lace, making it ripple with my distended nipples.

'You can do better, *ma tante*,' she whispered. 'Ravage yourself. You want to look and smell and taste like a woman of insatiable ways. A woman no man can resist.'

Insatiable ways. My Lord, did it get any more brazen than that? With a laugh that sounded like a hussy's, I speared my fingers through my russet waves, tossing my head as though I could shake all my old-fashioned inhibitions from my mind.

Monique's grin spurred me on, until I was stroking my shoulders and then kneading my breasts. I watched, fascinated, as the ebony roses cast their shadows over my ivory skin. Lower I went, pressing both sides of my rib cage as I stuck out my chest. Grinning lasciviously at the way I bulged and bobbed.

'Lower,' my maid whispered, caught up in the bawdy reflection I made. 'Rub your slit with the fabric, so your perfume clings to it. Part your legs. Watch them flex while you excite yourself. It makes quite a sight, *non*?'

The breath I'd been holding came out like a desperate pant. My hands obeyed Monique's command, slithering over the filmy fabric to rub it against my ... cunt, for that's what she would call it. A warm wetness told me I was extremely aroused. Propping one foot on the vanity stool, I continued to ply my folds and watch the effect in the mirror, for even beneath the sheer curtain of lace, I could see my sex lips unfurling like little wings, to reveal the moist, pink tissue beneath them ... that little nub thrusting out to receive some attention.

'Oh, my,' I moaned, captivated by the sight of my fingers strumming faster, around that place I'd been forbidden to touch since my mother had slapped my hands away.

'Ah, *oui*,' Monique breathed. And when she placed her palms on my hips, massaging in firm, sensual circles, I closed my eyes with the utter sensuality of it.

'*Non, non, non!* You watch! Spread your legs and catch that trickle ... push yourself over the edge, and see a beautiful rose in bloom, *ma tante*,' she rasped.

The inner spirals curling lazily below my belly intensified: I began to gasp and thrust and strain against my fingers. I watched in awe as those secret folds deepened to a dusky blush, right before the spasms overtook me. I was shaking so hard, crying out with my climax, that I'd have lost my balance had Monique not caught me from behind.

I was still catching my breath, gathering the scattered fragments of my mind, when the maid reached around me. Quickly she slipped her hand between the folds of the black lace and up my pussy. Rubbing herself against my backside, she wiggled two fingers deep inside me to create a frothy, wet sound, panting with her own climax as she brought me to another one. Together we convulsed in front of the mirror, watching wide-eyed as we stifled our cries. Juice was dribbling down my thighs, and Monique mopped it up with the filmy black fabric.

'*Now* you're ready to meet your man, *cherie*,' she breathed. 'I'll have Rémy bring the carriage around.'

The ride into town from the Garden District was too long, yet too short. Would things go according to Monique's script? Would my husband come out of the Beau Monde Club, peer into the shadowy carriage, and be unable to resist the wanton woman within? As the passing scenery told me we were near that whitewashed brick building, my blood pumped with a raw edginess. The next few minutes would either be heaven or hell.

As Monique had instructed, my driver pulled up in front of the club's doors and went inside to speak with the doorman. He, in turn, was to inform Mr Proffit that a carriage awaited him, and hopefully my husband would excuse himself from whomever was bending his ear about cotton prices or his political views.

Facing the carriage door, I bent one knee against the back of the seat and arranged my lace to fall open around my decadently bare legs and feet, so I'd be fully displayed when Chapin looked inside. Never had I felt so boldly improper. I sat back, telling myself this ploy would work ... waiting ... wondering why Rémy was taking so long.

Had Monique misunderstood my husband's plans? Had all my heart-pounding preparations been made on the false assumption that he'd want –

The carriage door flew open. I bolted upright when I saw the raven hair, the bourbon skin, and that unmistakably rakish grin. 'Dewel! You can't let Chapin find you here!'

'So there *is* a house afire.' He slammed the door behind him, undressing me with eyes that glowed like a demon's in the dimness. 'I can smell the smoke, and something much more provocative, clear over here. Good afternoon, Miss Eve.'

Had ever a man been so exasperatingly dense? Or had old Iverson summoned the wrong Proffit? 'I'm telling you, you can't stay here! I've come to fetch Chapin—'

'And isn't this just my lucky day? My God, but you're gorgeous, darlin'.'

'—so I can — can—' I stopped my verbal flailing to scoot to the edge of my seat, knees together, when he sat down across from me.

With utmost arrogance, Dewel relaxed against the leather upholstery. Then he stretched a long leg over to tap my bare toe with his boot.

'Stop it!' I snapped. 'Every woman in this world does *not* play mouse to your Pied Piper, Mr Proffit! Monique's been preparing me for this — because *you* sent her to! Now *leave*!'

His face lost its wolfish angularity. 'I see,' he said quietly. 'So it's not only my mistake, thinking you'd prepare yourself for such a rendezvous with me, but also my misfortune to bear some ... unfortunate tidings. Chapin's not here.'

My mouth fell, along with all my shining expectations. 'But Monique heard him say—'

'Oh, he was at the Club earlier. But he left.'

'But where—'

'You don't want to know, sugah.'

I shivered, and then flushed with the truth he was trying not to tell me. 'He left with *her*?'

'Had I known of your seduction today, I'd have talked him into—'

'You're not my husband's watchdog, dammit! Of all the filthy, low-down—'

'Cheating, dastardly, *bastardly* things to do,' Dewel muttered in agreement.

But my shattered hopes rose up into my throat, until I had to sob for breath. 'Shut up, Dewel! Get out of here!' I shrieked. 'I want to go home. Rémy, please –'

My brother-in-law crossed the carriage in one fluid move, to cover my mouth. 'I'm sorry, Eve,' he murmured against my ear. 'I didn't intend to make light of your efforts, or this unforgivable situation. You have every right to be upset.'

Upset? Was that why my entire body quaked while I tried not to wail like a baby deprived of its most basic needs? Like a woman denied her rightful place beside her husband? Like a widow ... mourning her marriage?

Hot tears rushed down my face. I turned away from the man who tried to comfort me, for comfort was the last thing I could accept. It was humiliating to learn Chapin was off with that floozy Savanna again, but even more degrading to have his smug half-brother witness my disgrace. My failure to entice my man.

Yet when Dewel slipped an arm around my shoulders, I railed against this injustice – the hopes nurtured like flowers, now evaporated like the dew. Driven by a shame rapidly turning to anger, I sobbed against his shoulder. How could I feel so weak and defeated when only moments ago I'd been flying like a kite?

How, indeed.

I sniffled. Pulled myself together by thinking how Monique would handle this unanticipated detour, on my road to becoming Chapin Proffit's undeniable wife. Or had I come to a crossroads? A realisation that I might never reach the destination I'd set out for ... and that perhaps I needed a whole new travel plan.

I sat up, blinking away my tears. 'Please excuse me for acting so –'

'Loyal? Lovin'?' Dewel thumbed a tear from my cheek, lifting my chin. 'Any man should consider himself damn lucky to have a woman like you waitin' for him in this carriage, Miss Eve. *I* certainly would.'

Even in consolation, his words were edged with egotism: he'd probably had dozens of women awaiting him over the years, for his animal magnetism drew them like moths to the proverbial flame. Yet, as he focused those blue eyes on me, studying my face and my rumpled hair and the dress that now seemed extremely inappropriate, I felt a compassion I hadn't anticipated.

'So here we are again. Brought together by Chapin's cheatin'.'

It was such an opportunistic observation, I wondered if Dewel had lied. What if he'd simply seized the moment to beat Chapin to the punch – enrage him again – after Monique had hinted I'd be coming for my husband?

Yet his hands remained chastely on my forearms. And he wasn't kissing me, or making lewd suggestions, or unbuttoning his fly – although I couldn't miss the ridge that had risen there, and the way his breathing filled the quiet carriage.

'So we are.' I sighed, deflating like a balloon. I wasn't looking forward to facing my maid, to report the failure of our mission. We'd both worked so hard, for so long.

'What happens now, Eve?' he whispered. 'What would you have me do?'

Again it struck me as extreme arrogance, his linking those two thoughts as though they naturally belonged together. When I looked at him, however, I couldn't miss the longing in those fiery blue eyes, the heat that would scorch me if I got too close – if I allowed myself to bask in his warmth for these few moments of my recovery. Dewel Proffit was the *last* man to whom I should entrust my feelings, or confess my fears about what did happen now.

Is he really so wrong? my heart retorted. *Seven years of your life you've given to Chapin, and he repays you by slipping off with Savanna, and sneaking another woman into his suite. Damned heartless of him. And careless. Very, very careless.*

As my thoughts shifted, so did the expression on Dewel's dusky face. I caught the brandy on his breath now, and that subtle, musky scent of a man who flaunted himself and his taste for loose women. Preferably bored society wives who only wanted a skilful, willing cock in exchange for keeping their marriages and reputations intact.

That was Dewel, down to his diamond-studded cuff links and his cold, calculating heart.

'You haven't answered me, Eve. I can leave, and let you go home.'

Or? coiled around me, like the tight spirals that preceded an earth-shattering climax. My heart thudded. To fill the silence that was giving me far too many ideas, I blurted, 'Do you find me attractive, Dewel? Monique swears I could excite any man, but –'

'Oh, you excite the livin' daylights out of *me*, sugah,' he drawled, his chuckle rumbling like thunder. 'Unfortunately, that leaves only my darkness to find your way in. And who knows what evil lurks in this black sheep's heart? Knock on *my* door and you might never make it home again.'

A blinding streak of awareness – of *wanting* – shot through me. And while my proper mind wondered if

I'd married the wrong Proffit, my body reached its own wayward, damning conclusion. I'd resisted this dangerous train of thought before, but now it raced along its track, like the fear and adrenaline in my veins, never to return to its proper station.

'Take me, Dewel,' I whispered. 'High time I found out what I've been missing with a man.'

He was on me, his mouth burning into mine as he pulled me roughly against his body. The buttons of his coat bit my breasts as his hands found my hips, holding me captive for a kiss that left nothing to assumption. Shoving his tongue between my teeth, he slanted his face to give his passion full reign, stealing my breath with the sheer force of his arousal.

Then he pulled away, leaving me dazed. 'We're going to do this right,' he muttered.

He disengaged himself to open the carriage door – to give our driver instructions brusque with urgency. The carriage lurched, clattering down the cobblestones so loudly I thought all the world must surely know that Chapin Proffit's wife was now racing towards perdition, falling from grace into the arms of the man who'd ruin her.

Yet I was smiling. Welcoming Dewel with open arms and a body barely covered by lace I hoped he'd rip right off me.

But no, Dewel was ever the Southern gentleman, in his rakish way. 'You look good enough to eat,' he breathed, loosening his cravat. 'But for now we'll just nibble and suck and lick at each other. When I get you home, I'm gonna swallow you whole.'

So this was how it felt to be devoured by a man's eyes, while he delivered delicious, intoxicating promises. The lace dress, insubstantial as it was, suddenly felt too confining. But he was right: better to be shut away from prying eyes. Better to be off the gossiping streets and in the safe haven – if any place with Dewel Proffit was safe – of Bayou Belle.

He lifted me into his lap, making me so very aware of his size, his power, his . . . rigid erection. As he cradled me in one arm, his fingers took their sweet time caressing my breast, watching the play of the unfettered flesh beneath the filmy black fabric.

'I knew you were an eyeful, Eve, but Lord have mercy! There's just *nothin'* to this dress, but it does everything right.' He caught my nipple between his thumb and forefinger, grinning when I twitched. 'Ripe as a cherry, beggin' to be plucked.'

'No, *fucked*,' I corrected, feeling brazen beyond belief. 'I didn't dress like this to go to church, after all.'

'Good. 'Cause the way I want you to play my organ, nobody's gonna be singin' hymns anyway.'

With a flick of his wrist, he parted the flimsy lace to run his fingernail up the inside of my thigh. I held my breath, knowing where that finger would go – gasping when it slid into my wet slit, and was then joined by a second, and a third. My eyes closed with this incredible fullness, and as my head fell back over his elbow, I could feel his wicked grin.

'You don't yet know the meanin' of surrender, Miss Eve,' he promised in a sultry baritone, 'but you're gonna find out.'

19 **Perdition**

A lady should never detail her adventures in the bed of a devil like Dewel, but then, by the time I got there, I was no lady. Once he carried me up the oak stairway, burning away my clothes and my best intentions with a gaze like a blue gas flame, my seat in hell was guaranteed. So I decided to enjoy every inch of the trip.

'There's worse places than hell,' Dewel remarked when I mentioned this. 'I'll do my best to see you never visit them, but who can say? The next few weeks'll take you a lot of places you never thought you'd go.'

Was that a promise or a threat? His look of raw passion filled me with an anticipation I could barely stand, yet his words had an ominous ring. 'If Chapin finds out –'

He shushed me with his finger. 'He won't hear about it from me, Eve. No matter what incriminatin' things he's told you over the years, I'm the soul of discretion. Which means I know a lot of things I've never told anybody – and for your own protection, that includes *you*, sugah.'

I opened my mouth, but he stifled my protest with another mind-altering kiss.

'But never mind that,' he breathed, running the tip of his tongue along my neck. 'From this point on, while you're with me, Chapin doesn't exist. I don't want to hear his name, or anything about him. I only want to hear you hollerin' out with a pleasure so extreme, you'll never leave me – and then hear what you want me to do next.'

And I did shriek, with the sheer exhilaration of being tossed on to his four-poster bed! Chapin could never have managed such a feat – but I put my husband out of my thoughts. He'd had his chance, and I was tired of trying to entice him. His half-brother stood at the foot of the bed, stripping off his silk shirt with the determined grace of a man who intended to ravish me so completely, I might not get all my pieces back afterwards.

A frightening, provocative thought. As decidedly indecent as the way Dewel's cock jumped free of his fly to sway like a divining rod pointing him towards water. My sex, completely open to his inspection as I sprawled on his bed, was already so wet his rod couldn't possibly miss. And as he stepped from his pants, I once again marvelled at this man's masculine beauty, at the strong symmetry of corded arms and muscled thighs and the solid body in between.

'Yours for the askin',' he suggested, taking himself in hand.

'Oh, God – *please*. I want it *now*.'

His rich laughter wrapped around us as he stepped closer, teasing me. 'Gotta sound more desperate than that, Eve. Don't you know I won't leave you one shred of pride, woman?'

I fumbled with the pearl clasp at my shoulder, already writhing beneath his relentless gaze. Did I really *have* any pride? All I could think about was his body lowering over mine, watching that cock as it plunged inside my aching hole.

'Leave it on.'

His breathy command stilled my fingers, while his smile gave me goose bumps. 'You went to a lot of trouble to look this trashy, Miss Eve. Let's enjoy it for awhile, before I rip that dress clean off you. I intend to spend all day fuckin' you. And all night.'

Dewel took hold of my legs, to lift and spread them so the lace slithered to my waist. I couldn't stop watching him watch my pussy while he toyed with me; his cock's eye beaded with a drop of honey. When his thumb found the centre of my sole, I sighed with the exquisite pressure there – and then jerked with the sensation of having my toes sucked.

'That's not fair! I can't reach you to –'

'Who said I'd play fair, darlin'? It's my game and the rules'll change from one minute to the next.'

He kissed his way down my inner thigh, his eyes on the prize as he coaxed my legs closer to my shoulders. There was no modesty in my position, nor mercy in his face, as he wagged his pointed tongue at me – and then drew a teasing circle around my open hole with it. I was squirming with such torment, already thrusting as though he were inside me.

'Dewel,' I murmured, 'oh please, Dewel, I want it hard and fast. I want it *now*.'

His chuckle infuriated me. 'I'm not always gonna give you what you want, Miss Eve. Certainly not because *you* say I should.'

Damn his control! His arrogant way of putting me in my place even as he held me hostage. With blithe disregard for my quivering need, he kissed his way up the other thigh, leaving a wet trail that tickled when the air hit it … a trail punctuated by little nips that only intensified my predicament.

'You bastard, give me –'

'That I am, and I'm damn proud of it.'

'– what I came here for!'

He leaned between my legs, his cock prodding just

below the hole that so badly wanted to swallow it. 'Sorry, sugah. You don't get to come till I decide it's your time. And to make my *point* –'

Dewel slid his shaft over my slit and then back again, spreading my wetness with a furtive slurping sound that drove me further to distraction. For a man so enraptured by my assets, he was doing his damnedest to avoid penetration. His slippery friction was just enough to rekindle my itch. Thinking to get around his tricks, I flexed my hips downward to catch his next thrust.

Again he laughed, levering himself on the backs of my thighs. Now he was looking down into my face, his raven hair mussed and the faintest sheen of sweat on his upper lip. I fixed my gaze on that lush fullness, and the soft mauve contrast to the shadow of his clean-shaven face. I reminded myself that patience was a virtue, even with a silver-tongued devil to whom virtue seemed a foreign concept. I held very still, hypnotised by the flare of his nostrils as he breathed, and the corresponding movement of his chest. If I dared look into those sparkling blue eyes, I was lost.

'Eve,' he whispered.

Just that easily I fell. When I saw myself mirrored in those huge black pupils, framed in cerulean rings that glowed with frightening desire, the air left my lungs with a wanton hiss.

He entered me then, moving only his hips, pressing me into the mattress with the slightest effort, letting those eyes take me captive ... his willing, wayward prisoner in this battle he'd already won. Oh, so slowly he rocked, in and out. Filling me with his rigid cock, and then slipping it out. Waiting just a second too long, so my jaw would drop further with my need, before shoving it up me again.

Then, when I thought I couldn't stand any more, he thrust all the way in, grinding his root high and hard against my bone – knowing he'd caught my clit, and knowing when my spasms began, even before I did. With a satisfied smile, Dewel held himself hard against me, his minimal movements making the wildfire leap until I shook uncontrollably.

'Give it to me,' he rasped, so close to my ear the dampness gathered in its shell. 'Writhe with it, Eve. Yield yourself so completely that no other man can ever have you. And then call out the name of the demon that just stole your soul.'

I gritted my teeth, determined he wouldn't dictate my body's response. But Dewel was still rocking, showing no sign of letting up. His body was curled completely around mine, suspended just enough that I wouldn't be crushed while holding me helpless. His victim. The woman who'd begun her day in search of her husband's love, and would end it in the arms of his lifelong rival.

I heard a keening sound, and realised it came from my own throat. My head jerked back and my hips surged forward. The friction of his body hair against my lace rose to a sibilant hiss that drove me over the precipice. I arched, racked by spasms that claimed me from my pussy outward and didn't let go.

'*Dewel!* Oh, Dewel, my God –'

His hips kicked into a frenzy then, and he slapped against my wetness, grunting with each stroke. Between my slitted eyelids I saw his grimace grow tight, and when his body went stiff, I instinctively curled upward with one last seizure. He shot into me, grabbing me hard to squeeze out the last of it.

We collapsed. For several seconds we could only pant desperately. As the fragments of my rational mind returned, I realised the magnitude of what I'd just done: I had now sunk as low as the husband I'd set out to seduce. I had broken vows I considered sacred, even under the sad circumstances of a marriage arranged for my family's financial benefit.

But I had also become a woman who gave herself over to desire, and I'd taken a man into oblivion with me.

This observation struck like a storm as my lover rolled to his side, taking me with him. Dewel still quivered with the force of our climax, and as he held me against his chest I felt the beating of a powerful heart. My epiphany seemed far too important not to share, in his rare moment of vulnerability.

'Dewel,' I whispered. 'How can I ever thank you for –'

'Don't jump the gun, thinkin' I've done you any favours, sugah,' he sighed. Then, to soften the emotional blow, he kissed me so sweetly I wanted to cry. 'And don't start talkin'. I'm not nearly finished yet.'

20 **Over the Edge**

I awoke from a doze to find Dewel grinning lasciviously as he sat on the edge of the bed, studying my nude body. Unaccustomed to being so closely observed, I scrambled for the length of black lace now rumpled among the covers, but he grabbed my hands.

'No need for modesty on my account,' he said with a low laugh. 'You're the most gorgeous creature I've ever seen, and my brother doesn't deserve you. Should've kept you for myself, Miss Eve. Should've approached your daddy before Chapin had the chance.'

How different might the past seven years have been, had that happened?

'Why didn't you?' I asked softly. 'I know very little about that arrangement. I suspect my parents were deeper in debt than they let on, but when I asked Chapin for details, I was told not to worry my pretty little head over it.'

'His answers don't satisfy you any more, do they?'

Dewel slid alongside me, making the sheets rustle seductively as his warm skin tantalised mine. For a man who worked a plantation, he had a luxurious sensuality – just enough feathering of dark hair on his chest to render his whisky skin more mysterious, coupled with a softness I never expected. His midnight hair fell loosely around his ears, and as he smiled, with his Creole face directly over mine, I was overwhelmed by him all over again.

'Kiss me,' I whispered.

'Glutton.' He bussed my lips to tease me. 'You think I can pleasure you again and again? Just because you can't get enough?'

'Yes.'

His laughter made my heart dance, and as he knelt between my legs, his eyes took on a feral glow, like a wolf's at dusk. A wolf who'd found a willing mate and intended to chase the full moon into the dawn with her. Another erection prodded my bottom. Dewel was eager to do my bidding, even if he pretended to have other things on his mind.

'After Daddy died – when my half-brother learned the plantation was goin' to the bastard heir – Chapin felt the Proffit name and bloodline might be compromised, unless he became a family man,' Dewel explained quietly. 'Some legal affairs in St. Louis required both our signatures. While we were there, he caught wind of a stock market deal gone sour, involving your daddy. Mr Wheeler bemoaned havin' a daughter he couldn't marry off in the style local folks figured on.'

I rolled my eyes. 'It wasn't as though potential husbands were beating down my door. I was twenty-two, already written off as an old maid. The few men whose company I'd enjoyed were intimidated by Daddy's high-falutin expectations.'

'So my half-brother caught him with his defences down. And Chapin asked *me* to look you over.'

'Why?'

Dewel chortled. 'Because I enjoyed the challenge of sneakin' a peek at you while he kept your daddy distracted. And because I had a way with the ladies – which was why, at the time, I didn't snap you up myself. Didn't see the need, cocky as I was at that age.'

He propped my hips against his thighs, splaying my

legs over his upper arms. Was that a shadow of sadness beneath his blue eyes, as his gaze raked my body? Lying at a slant, with my head at the edge of the bed, I knew better than to assume Dewel Proffit would ever relinquish total control or confess to any regrets ... although I thrummed with the anticipation of driving him to a wild, frenzied distraction, once he revealed all he was going to.

'Your daddy was no fool. Said it was all or nothin' – that Chapin would pay his promissory note, and take you sight unseen. But once I got you to the window by throwin' some gravel at it, I assured him, durin' our trip to the bank, that he'd never be sorry.

'And when I saw you at the 'wedding, lookin' so pretty and innocent,' Dewel went on in a softer drawl, 'I swore I'd never do that son of a bitch another favour as long as I lived. I hoped, for both your sakes, you could turn him around, but ...'

'But what?' After all of Chapin's warnings not to trust his half-brother, I was finally getting some straight talk. Not the most flattering information, yet I'd guessed long ago that romantic flights of fantasy hadn't prompted the golden-haired Proffit to offer for my hand.

'You've suffered more than your share of humiliation over the past seven years, and for that I'm sincerely sorry, Eve. No sense rubbin' your nose in it now.'

'Ah. His chasing after the others.'

'Yeah. That.' His fingertips skimmed my sides as he watched me closely. There was more he wasn't telling, unless he heard certain cues from my response.

But what could I say? Even now, all I knew was that I knew very little about my husband, Chapin Proffit.

'The wife's always the last to find out,' I offered,

shivering when he brushed my nipples with his palms. 'I didn't have a hint about his ... extramarital activities, until that day a few weeks ago, in the courtyard.'

'And then you got into trouble for bein' seen with *me*.' His grin turned wicked again, and with the flats of his palms he coaxed my breasts into peaks of need. 'So we might as well live up to his accusations! Nothin' like a steamy little affair to highlight his campaign. We'd all suffocate, if it weren't for society types waggin' their tongues to create some breeze.'

Had ever a man sounded as downright unrepentant as Dewel Proffit? While part of me could laugh at his cavalier attitude, I might already be in trouble when I got home. 'I should probably be going –'

'*Nowhere.*' His command sent shivers up my spine as he riveted me with those defiant eyes. 'My illustrious brother didn't tell you about tonight's meetin' to finalise the party's platform? Damn thoughtless of him.'

Effortlessly, Dewel lifted me further up his spread thighs, opening my slit to his full view as he braced himself. 'Wrap your legs around me. Take hold of my cock,' he breathed. 'You know where it wants to be, sugah. High inside your hot little pussy, makin' you melt all over me again. Makin' the bed so wet we can bathe in it.'

Like a dog trained to its master's voice, my body was already anticipating that divine fullness when he shoved his shaft inside me. Its head slipped between my sex lips like a sausage filling a buttered bun, to leer at me, red-faced, above my coarse curls. I could feel the strength of Dewel's bent legs; could watch his chest muscles flex beneath that swirl of black hair ... could feel my honey pooling at the rim of my hole. I smelled shamelessly ready to fuck him again.

He sucked air when I wrapped my hand around his hardness, pressing it into my silky-wet folds. 'Tell me what to do, Dewel. Tell me what you want.'

'Keep your hand there, darlin' ... rub it a couple of times, and then don't keep your man waitin'. My Lord, but you're pushin' all the right buttons – again –'

His last word came out as a gasp and then he thrust downward, stopping with just his tip inside my entry, holding me with that blue flame of a gaze. I enveloped him slowly, savouring the tightness, the sense of being filled as never before while I used my legs for leverage. Ah, the luxury of loving a man whose overall size let me revel in his strength!

Dewel Proffit made me feel small and enticing and desirable. For the first time in my life I didn't wonder what was wrong with me: my lover was as hungry for this intimate play as I, encouraging me with his smiles and quiet moans, and hands that cupped my ass with the promise of a passion like no other.

'Up and down on it,' he murmured. As I complied, I listened to the friction of our bodies and then the wet, sucking sound when he pulled out to tease me.

'That's disgusting.' I laughed, and felt him shaking beneath me – with mirth and the building of his next climax.

'No, Eve, it's the sound of a woman who wants me. It's the hot slickness of her pussy, beggin' me to fuck her senseless. Communication in its finest form.' Dewel buried himself to the hilt then, so thick and rigid I lay impaled at an angle that left me totally at his mercy.

My eyes closed as the pressure inside me mounted. The sensations danced like maidens around a Maypole, coy at first but more adventurous as they circled closer to the centre ... to a completion that promised to be as cataclysmic as all the earlier ones combined. He was so deep his balls rubbed my butt; so still I began shaking with my need.

My head rocked back – over the edge of the bed! – and then adrenaline shot through me as my body slipped with the loose sheets. Dewel gripped my wrists, grinding against my mound until my clit rubbed his cock with each shove. I gasped, glazing over with pleasure as he rode me, giddy with the sense that at any second I might slip to the floor and be crushed beneath his weight.

A bloodless breathlessness overtook me. My legs parted further, despite my instinct to hold on with them, and then I hung suspended, almost upside down, connected only by his cock and the fingers around my wrists. His ruddy face emanated a power so elemental I couldn't fully comprehend it, while those hot blue eyes held my gaze until lightning passed between us. I knew then that destiny had led us down its irrevocable path.

'Take us home, sugah,' he panted. 'Got you right where I want you, and there'll be no gettin' into this bed any more with anybody else, little witch. Squeeze me, now! Clamp that snatch around me and make me surrender. I wanna shoot like a damn cannon. I want –'

My moan drowned out his provocative patter, for his root plied my clit with a steady pressure that would make me explode if release didn't come soon. Once again my body clutched for meaning, in this reclamation of the woman who'd never sampled such delight in the marriage bed. I now intended to claim it as my right all the time.

Dewel dove deep, hard against my sweet spot, and I cried out his name. Bucking like a cowgirl on a bronc, I hung on by wrapping my ankles around his neck. Driving my hips up to meet his every thrust, I sought that blinding moment when I lost myself and soared out of this world and into the next.

I had to leave Dewel's world that evening, of course, but I lingered, taking in the furnishings of pecan and cypress wood, and the whitewashed walls and beamed ceilings that graced Bayou Belle. It was the home of a man who was comfortable with himself; who chose decor that pleased him, rather than following current fashions.

Once downstairs in the main parlour, I fastened the clasp more securely on my makeshift lace dress. From above the mantel, a provocative portrait dominated this room, and I had no trouble guessing who she was.

'Your mother,' I murmured, walking closer for a better view. Her raven hair tumbled loose about her shoulders, which were bared above a peasant-style blouse. Large gold hoops dangled from her ears. Her blue eyes sparkled with a mischievous passion, and her smile looked every bit as mysterious as the Mona Lisa's. 'She was beautiful. Free, like a gypsy.'

'Which was why Robert E. Lee Proffit loved her and kept her here. Maria Castalantez was everything Virgilia was not, and I've never felt an ounce of shame about bein' her son.' As Dewel stepped behind me, his hands found my loose breasts beneath the filmy lace.

'Is that why Chapin strays?' I asked in a subdued voice. 'Because I'm not the kind of woman he –'

'I've never understood Chapin's tastes, so I won't explain them,' he said, turning me in his arms to emphasise his point with those probing blue eyes ... eyes so like my husband's, yet they focused on *me* whenever he spoke. As though I mattered. As though he couldn't look at anything else. 'But we are who we are, Eve. I'm a man with few regrets, but I'm sorry you're not mine. And I'm doin' my damnedest to change that.'

I could only stare as his words washed over me: Dewel Proffit intended to take me away from my husband. It wasn't a question, and he didn't ask how I felt about it.

This revelation rocked the foundations of all I'd been raised to expect as a woman, a wife. It made hope fly within me like a wild bird trying to escape an aviary. My breath left me in a rush, and I had to drop my eyes. What he implied defied decency, for if I became his mistress I'd be no better off than Maria had been: much loved, but socially unacceptable. Still held captive, but in a different sort of cage.

My lover lifted my chin, the lines of his bourbon-coloured face softening with a smile. 'That's not a threat, sugah. It's a promise. Chapin's had his chance to make you happy, and we both know he's failed miserably.'

With a last glance at the intriguing mistress of Bayou Belle, we turned towards the door. My emotions warred within me: I had to go yet I yearned to stay, despite the consequences of a night away from home. With every step, the clinging lace reminded me that I'd started out as a hoyden with an honourable mission and was returning as a hussy – a fallen angel who'd made a mockery of her marriage vows. I was no better than the husband for whom I'd lost all respect.

On the small table in his foyer, a tabloid caught my eye among the other mail. An artfully drawn sketch of Honore Delacroix highlighted an article headlined, 'Headmistress Seeks Students for School of Domestic Endeavor.'

'Well, well,' I murmured, lifting the folded paper on my way out. 'Look who's making news. Probably because three of her favourite pupils now live under *my* roof, and she's not a bit happy about it.'

The brief article outlined requirements for potential applicants, stressing the School's reputation for only the highest calibre of servants. At the end, it gave the time for a reception and open house, inviting the public to visit her facility in the Vieux Carré.

'That's tonight,' I mused as we stepped into Dewel's carriage. 'Too bad we've had other things to occupy our time.'

'Other things, to be sure.' Before the horses were even on their way, the darker Proffit lifted me into his lap and parted my legs with his inquisitive hand. 'And this little *thing* is gonna occupy my thoughts day and night, until I can claim it again.'

Did he never tire of sex? This brazen man took every opportunity to touch my body, to incite that inner riot – revelling in my responses even when I didn't repay his favours. Tipping me backwards over his lap, so my head hung suspended lower than his knees, Dewel proceeded to drive me insane with his probing fingers. He fixed those eyes on me, found my vulnerable spots – all of them on edge from such constant attention these past several hours – and watched my face as I clutched him with another orgasm.

The climax rolled over me, and rolled me over, as though I'd been caught in the undertow of a tidal wave and then scooped up, to be tossed towards the halcyon shore I'd discovered only today. How many times had I landed there? And how many times would I dare return? By the time we reached the house in town, I'd once again slipped into that boneless state that followed extreme release: I could easily have curled up on the carriage seat and slept the night.

Yet when the tall windows came into view from

Prytania, lit by the table lamps, I sensed I'd better have my story ready.

'What if Chapin's already home?' Desperately I rewrapped the black lace, which was redolent with the scent of fresh sex. 'What if he wonders –'

'He's been pursuin' a new level of power, Eve,' Dewel replied in his soothing baritone. 'When Monique realised you were still out – if Chapin returned without you – she gave him some plausible excuse for your absence. She's creative that way.'

I nipped my lip, praying he was right. Hoping whoever was inside didn't peer out to see Dewel's carriage pulling up under the covered entrance. With a quick, nervous kiss I bade him goodnight – but Dewel would have none of that. He placed his hands on either side of my face and pressed his fine, full lips into mine as though he had every right to my passionate farewell.

'Take care of yourself, sugah – until I can. If he gives you any trouble, you come to me, understand?'

Was that a promise, or a prediction of disaster? I slipped into the house and padded barefoot towards the staircase, hoping to avoid Mrs Frike. Anyone who saw my breasts and hips jiggling beneath the translucent pattern of roses and ivy would know I'd been up to no good.

I reached the bottom stair, thankful that the solid construction of the staircase and its carpet runner would prevent any creaking. But I'd rejoiced too soon.

'Ah, Miss Eve!' a courtly voice rang out from the study. 'A timely arrival, indeed! We need to discuss a matter of utmost importance, regarding the dismissal of your lady's maid.'

My mouth fell open. Not only had Chapin made it home ahead of me, but he'd caught Monique in some sort of mischief ... perhaps cornered her in a lie about my whereabouts. There was no way to escape my duties as mistress of this house; no way to avoid my husband's censure of an appearance that looked every bit as tawdry as my situation.

When I turned towards the perfectly groomed blond, the black lace fell open around the knee bent on the bottom step, revealing an expanse of bare leg that would've done a prostitute proud. My hair was askew from hanging upside down in the carriage, and my embarrassment intensified the musk of Dewel's most recent teasing. Yet somehow I faced my husband without bursting into tears or prostrating myself to beg forgiveness.

Chapin's expression hardened. 'We'll discuss this later,' he growled, pivoting to precede me into his study. 'The goings-on in this house have reached a level not even the most indulgent man would tolerate. Even if I weren't in the political spotlight, I would nip this inexcusable situation in the bud.'

As I entered the study behind him, Monique's face registered her relief at my return. But her expression quickly switched to a thin-lipped mask of anger – warning me that things had been said, and my story would have to match hers. Judd Schuck stood smugly by the window, looking like a pinstriped pork barrel as he clasped his hands behind his back. The sissy maids huddled in the opposite corner, near Fanny Frike, wearing expressions that foretold my doom.

Chapin snatched something from his desk. 'My valet informs me that you and your maid have engaged in things no normal, decent wife would consider, much less know about. What do you say to *that*, Mrs Proffit?'

He nailed me with his gaze as he held up Monique's double dildo – the toy his dutiful new manservant had snatched from my vanity in my absence.

A few weeks ago, I would've melted into the Persian rug from extreme humiliation – but no, I would've been dumbfounded by a device resembling two long, hard cocks curving away from a textured red centre. Exasperation overruled my fear, however. Then it was sheer wrath that made my answer strike like a snake.

'If you already know the details, Mister Proffit, why do you ask?'

21 **A Proffit of Doom**

I regretted my retort immediately. But there was no right answer for a man who'd discovered his wife had a lady playmate – no matter how he found his evidence.

'I'm telling you, Mr Proffit,' Monique cut in, 'it's Judd Schuck who needs dismissing! How can you trust a man who watches your wife through her keyhole? Then he sneaked into Miss Eve's room and took that toy from her vanity drawer. How do we know he didn't also steal her jewellery?'

Chapin's colour rose with each remark. 'Enough out of you, slut! My wife never had such – *ideas*, until you came here!' he blustered. 'I knew you were one of those damned Cajuns living downriver from Dewel's plantation, and I should've sent you packing long ago. Now get *out*.'

Silence rang around us, until the old housekeeper could keep still no longer. 'Will you *please* reconsider, Mr Chapin?' Fanny pleaded. 'Your Mr Schuck has compromised his own integrity – not to mention your wife's. And with the Mardi Gras ball only a week away, I need Monique's help with the preparations. She's been invaluable –'

'She's been the downfall of this entire household if she's bamboozled you too,' he snapped, shaking the double-hung toy at her. 'And from here on out, you'll keep your opinions to yourself, Fanny Frike, or those three worthless maids will be the next to go! And maybe *you* will be considering retirement sooner than you anticipated.'

Cleopatra, Antoinette and Cinderella stiffened, glancing at each other with their lips pressed into thin lines. Mrs Frike's shelflike bosom shook against her apron with her effort to remain quiet. And Schuck, the toad, was practically rocking on his heels with the crisis he'd caused, as though he'd been promised a bonus for each irregularity he reported.

I had my own axe to grind with this ill-kempt troublemaker, but I'd brought on some of these problems myself. Had I not been chasing around in see-through lace, asking Chapin's lifelong rival for advice on seduction, none of this would've happened. But then, it all circled back to that day I saw my husband in a public courtyard humping his *niece*, didn't it?

This image bolstered my resolve. It wasn't the time to mention his duplicity – his own glaring infidelity of late – but I did have an ace to play. A long shot, but sometimes a pellet of hard-packed truth is more useful after it rolls down the mountainside to gather snow. If I could diffuse this dire situation, it was worth being further humiliated by my husband in front of the staff.

'I have a confession,' I began quietly – hoping to bring Chapin's breathing under control, for his colour looked high. I smelled perfume on him too, but that was another issue entirely.

He shot me a sour look. 'I told you we'll discuss your *affairs* at a later –'

'My *affairs* are not what they seem,' I hedged, stepping towards him. 'I'll admit this is not the attire of a proper wife, but when I set out wearing it, the idea was to attract *your* attention, Chapin. I was going to whisk you away in the carriage after your lunch at the Beau

Monde Club. A surprise designed to pique your interest in me, as a woman who *wants* you –'

'If you think I'll believe that –'

'– but you'd already left,' I pressed on. 'And during that earlier meeting with your financial backers? Again at your gentlemen's club? That sucking you got was my doing too!'

Chapin's face went pale. 'Not only have you become a habitual liar, but you've lost your mind, woman. Females are *never* allowed inside –'

'I've got your tip, folded and shaped by the heat of your hand, as proof.'

I stood only a few feet in front of him, crossing my arms beneath my breasts. 'Yes, this is an indelicate matter to mention before the staff, but a desperate woman takes desperate measures. Better to expose myself as a shameless hussy trying to win her man's affection than to expose other matters that have come to *my* attention. *Isn't* it?'

Once again, my tongue had jumped ahead of my strategy, dammit. Chapin's pale-blue eyes hardened into marbles, in a face turned to stone. Worse yet, when Judd started snickering, my husband assumed I'd sucked his valet's cock under the table too.

'Don't go popping any fly buttons, thinking Miss Eve did you the same favour, Mr Schuck,' Monique chided. She stood taller, holding her head so her unruly topknot looked balanced. 'That whole escapade – and today's black lace caper – were my idea, Mr Proffit. Like she said, Miss Eve just wanted her man. And I just wanted Miss Eve to be happy. If this doesn't please you, I will leave after I –'

'You're already gone, bitch. Mrs Frike will send your belongings when she finds time –'

In the blink of her scalding-coffee eyes, the maid sprang forward to snatch the dildo from Chapin's hand. The tattoo of her high-heeled boots in the hall, and then the slam of the front door, marked her departure. Without a backward glance, Monique Picabou was gone.

'If any of you have any similar *ridiculous* notions about relations between my wife and me, you may collect your pay and leave.'

The small study reverberated with silence, and the fidgeting of the three maids wearing short, sassy uniforms like Monique's. They kept their panties pulled up these days, but if Chapin or his new watchdog caught a whiff of their equipment, I didn't want to think about the fit my husband would throw!

After a full minute of lording over us with his pointed glare and flaring nostrils, Chapin dismissed us. 'Except for you, Miss Eve. We'll continue our discussion after the others leave.'

I stood aside to let them pass, noting the maids' beleaguered looks and the apology etched on the housekeeper's face. Schuck smirked, falling in at the end of the subdued parade.

'I suppose you're going to spank me for this,' he jeered.

'Bastard,' came Fanny's reply, 'you'll get yours, for telling tales on Miss Eve. Not worth the trouble of heating up my hand on your fat ass, that's for sure.'

My husband let these remarks pass, and then closed the door. He brushed the lapels of his natty double-breasted suit, and was still gripping them when he confronted me. 'Where have you been, Mrs Proffit? Don't bother lying! Everyone in the room smelled the reek of your sex.'

I widened my eyes at him, thinking quickly. 'I have a toy of my own, you know. Who's to say –'

'Where did you go, after you supposedly stopped by the club for me?'

'And where were *you*?' There was no point in mincing words, for what did I have to lose? 'Just couldn't wait to be with your niece, Savanna? Or did you visit that woman I saw leaving your room the other morning?'

Chapin's face paled until his eyebrows and lashes looked painted on. 'I don't have to answer to –'

'Why not? For seven years you've treated me as though I'm no more enticing than a piece of your mother's furniture!' I blurted, grinding my fists into my hips. 'I'm tired of feeling like –'

'Oh, for God's sake, *cover* yourself!' He gestured at my poorly wrapped lace dress, scowling. 'Any man would be upset to learn his wife is messing with her maid, but I have a campaign to manage! If it gets out that you're one of *those* kind – or running around with that bastard Dewel –'

'You won't be the next mayor of New Orleans? Wouldn't *that* be a shame?'

I stalked towards the door without bothering to rewrap my dress, for I'd revealed far more than my breasts and my bush today. Chapin knew what I knew: he hadn't refuted his dalliance with young Savanna, or the presence of that other woman in his suite. Like most men, he felt himself exempt from the social strictures binding a wife's behaviour – and now, no amount of coaxing or cajoling would get him into my bed.

Not that I wanted him any more. When I got to my room I locked my door, and then shoved my vanity in front of that open keyhole. His damn valet wouldn't be privy to anything else I said or did either!

* * *

Schuck would've had little to witness as the night wore on, however. I couldn't sleep: I was reliving my terror when Chapin hailed me from his study, and the anger that welled up as his insidious inquisition continued. Why had everything Dewel and Monique arranged for me, with the best intentions, gone sour? My husband always ruined it by appearing at just the wrong moment.

I was partly to blame, of course: I had allowed the illegitimate Proffit and his Cajun protégée to take charge of my private life. It was no wonder Chapin railed about my deteriorating morals, for I'd undergone an amazing transformation these past few weeks – just at the time his reputation depended on an obedient wife.

Well, that was too damn bad! And there was no turning back, nor reverting to the previous Miss Eve, who followed the rules of a society and a husband who didn't give a *whit* about my happiness.

It grieved me, too, that Monique had left without so much as a furtive wink – anything to show that our friendship didn't end with her position here. But she'd had no more choice about it than I had. Chapin perceived my maid as a threat to his almighty position in this household – in the entire city – so she got sacrificed on the altar of his gratification.

A thumping above my head made me blink, and listen. Mrs Frike had a small suite behind the kitchen, but the main servants' quarters were on the third floor. The sissy maids had made so little noise before this, it hadn't occurred to me they might be right above my own room.

Was that the bumping of a bed against a wall? I didn't want to consider which of those effete young men was doing what to whom, yet the attraction was there. They had urges, just like I did. And now that Monique had established the intrigue of same-sex relations, I could hardly act repulsed about how my hired help behaved in their off hours.

I heard a raised voice – Cinderella's it was. 'I don't *care* what you say! Chapin Proffit is a horrid, manipulative bully who –'

She got shushed, and as I glanced towards the corner of the ceiling, I saw a circular grate. It had once housed a furnace pipe, but since steam radiators had been installed on that top floor it served only as a vent for air circulation.

I smiled, realising I had access to their conversations. But then, those three could listen in on my activities as well – and I suspected they already had.

On impulse, I grabbed my fireplace poker, stood on the vanity bench, and tapped at the metal grate. The squabbling – which sounded suspiciously like part of a three-way sex session – came to an abrupt halt. I tapped again, in a pattern that couldn't be taken as coincidence.

An eye and a dark eyebrow appeared in the centre hole. 'Yes, Miss Eve?' Cleopatra said in a stage whisper. 'If we're being too noisy –'

'No, I . . . just wanted someone to talk to.' I was again aware of the impropriety of sharing my thoughts with the help, but Monique's departure had left a void I was already feeling. 'I'll come up the back stairs. If that's all right.'

'That would be lovely!' It was Cinderella's face partially framed in the round opening now, peering down with an eye that appeared red from crying. 'We must stick together, you know. It simply isn't fair –'

'See you in a moment,' came the brunette's calmer voice. 'The *princess* is beside herself tonight.'

I wrapped a robe around my nightgown and slipped

down the hallway, wondering if Judd Schuck monitored this activity. Or perhaps, as the Golden Boy's new pet, he was downstairs indulging in his master's fine brandy and imported cigars, basking in the light of privilege and favour. Fine by me if those two kept each other company. They deserved each other.

As I entered the large, dormered servants' quarters, I felt as though I'd joined a pyjama party where young girls twittered the night away in gossip. But, of course, these 'young ladies' had cocks and balls clearly visible through their nighties. Their flat chests seemed incongruous, after I'd grown used to seeing them with stuffed uniforms. The room smelled of male musk, with overtones of perfume.

Cinderella, draped in a lacy confection of translucent blue, greeted me with a hug. 'I am *so* sorry about tonight, Miss Eve,' she gushed. 'We tried to persuade Mr Chapin that you were taking care of details for the Mardi Gras ball, but he wouldn't believe us.'

I hugged her, touched by her concern. 'I was a fool to say as much as I did – especially about Mr Proffit's own activities. But at least it's all on the table now.'

'We knew you were with Dewel, of course,' Cleopatra said with a suggestive wink. She plucked at the strap of her beaded red peignoir, which flickered like embers each time she moved.

'But it's easy to see that you and the other Proffit are so perfectly matched – if you'll pardon my saying so.' Antoinette looked directly at me, with a speculative expression. Wrapped in a dressing gown of a pale green floral pattern, she was the most discreet of the three. 'We saw you cavorting in the fountain with Tommy Jon and Monique, you see. And after that, we watched that handsome Creole take control of you, until you were crying out with –'

My appalled expression made the redhead grin.

'We couldn't resist watching,' she said with a coy shrug. 'It inspired a night of our own sort of ... cavorting.'

I swallowed hard, slipping free of Cinderella's embrace. I hadn't realised just how visible my trysting had been ... how much evidence my husband could've gathered by stepping out to the gallery. 'Do you think Chapin saw us?'

'No. He was out that evening, remember?' Cleo replied. 'With Schuck trotting along behind him like a damn bulldog, kissing his butt.'

'And I, for one, refuse to let it pass!' Cinderella stiffened with renewed resolve. With two pink cheeks aglow on her porcelain face, and her blonde hair flowing past her behind, she looked like Rapunzel pitching a fit. 'We have our ways of getting back at those two –'

'Don't get noticed. Get revenge.' Even with her exotic cosmetics washed off, Cleopatra had a regal bearing as she sat against her propped-up pillow, demurely arranging her red peignoir over her outstretched legs.

'Be careful. We're the next to go,' Antoinette agreed. 'And what choice would we have, but to crawl back to the School, to grovel at Miss Delacroix's feet? I say we construct a plan that will not only benefit Miss Eve, but cover our own asses as well.'

I studied the redhead with a new respect, for she spoke with a voice of calm in this storm; her loyalty was clear, yet she had no illusions about its consequences. I wished I had more of Antoinette's allure and Russell's practicality.

'I hope you can remain until the ball next week,' I said. 'You're excellent help, and Fanny and I need –'

'A masked ball is just the place to wreak a little

revenge – if we have your permission to wear costumes.'

Toinette had obviously given some thought to this subject before tonight's confrontation with my husband. 'I see no reason why you can't,' I replied after a moment's thought. Then I had to smile, sensing these maids craved the dressing-up as much as paying Chapin back.

'Shall we choose something from that ... other woman's wardrobe? The clothes locked away in the attic?'

My eyes widened further. 'Oh, my, yes! Won't *that* be a shock – and with me in that Bo Peep outfit his dear mama probably wore!'

'Exactly.' The redhead waxed foxlike. 'He'll be too busy hosting his influential friends to raise any sort of ruckus at the ball, since he needs us to keep the tables filled.'

'And he wouldn't question *where* those costumes came from either – at least not until afterwards,' Cleopatra remarked. 'I like it! It's time we put his uppity ass in a sling, and hang Judd Schuck's beside it! They have no right to mistreat you this way, Miss Eve.'

Cinderella was dabbing her eyes with an eyelet handkerchief, looking brighter by the moment. 'Is there something in a pretty blue for me? With shoes fit for a princess?'

'I think you'd all look stunning dressed as the royalty Monique named you for,' I said with a chuckle. 'That way, I can keep track of you. The house will be awash in a sea of outrageous Mardi Gras costumes, you know. Glorious to behold, but we'll have no idea who's behind those elaborate masks.'

The furtive allure of this plan was making my pulse thrum, with only one regret. 'I don't suppose Monique will get here though. And she'd be in her element on such a night.'

The three maids glanced at each other. Then Antoinette smiled, with that same intimate bravado she'd shown in the attic. 'Have you ever known Mistress Monique *not* to have her way?'

22 **A Dual Proffit, Revealed**

With every waking moment of the following week occupied by preparations for the party, I had no time to stew over my personal predicament – and no chance to further incriminate myself, for I saw nothing of Dewel or Monique. It was as though my life had returned to its previous balance, before those two conspirators turned my world upside down with passionate possibilities I'd never dreamed existed.

This tranquility was an illusion, however. Beneath the glasslike smoothness of that oasis pond, the muddy bottom waited to be churned up once again by the strained emotions and revelations of the past week. Chapin and his valet were gone late into the evenings, pandering to political supporters – or so they said. The maids and Mrs Frike laboured like souls possessed, staying out of Chapin's sight when he was home. I had but one purpose, and that was to hostess the grandest masked ball New Orleans had ever seen – hoping that after the election, my husband would return to his more regulated life of cotton commerce and the Beau Monde Club, and possibly playing mayor, so I could return to my own routine as well.

Things would never be the same, of course. But after this party and the election, I could escape the public eye. I could ponder and pursue a life that fulfilled my emotional and sexual needs – an unheard-of luxury for most Southern ladies, which had become an absolute necessity for me.

So, on the morning before the ball, as I was on a last shopping excursion in the Vieux Carré, I didn't anticipate seeing Honore Delacroix – and certainly not with Tommy Jon Beaumont! I paused in the doorway of a little bakery, and then ducked into the nearest alley to remain unseen. The headmistress of the School for Domestic Endeavor was plying her wiles as only an experienced demigoddess could do: arrayed in shimmering shades of purple silk, with a matching, peacock-feathered, veiled hat angled coquettishly over her coal-black hair, she was *flirting* with him! Teasing T-Jon with the bending of her gloved finger in a come-hither, which I could only assume was for a kiss.

It was too delicious a scene to miss. I stood against the brick building, in the shade of an ancient magnolia tree, and took note of Miss Delacroix's technique: how she cajoled him with a low patter I wished I could hear. How she batted those lashes and smiled her artful smile, enticing T-Jon into her web like the spider she was.

While I realised Monique and her man probably saw other lovers, I felt a flush of anger at this public seduction by the virago I'd butted horns with. Was she still soliciting for students? Trying to replace the slaves I'd taken from her?

I wanted to holler a hello to T-Jon, if only to distract him back into the real world, but instinct stopped me. He towered over the headmistress, with his broad shoulders straining at his blue cotton shirt and legs flexing with a superior strength. A mere woman was no match for this fine fellow! Who was I to step in, even though my loyalty to Monique prodded my conscience?

I couldn't distinguish what was being said, but their voices lowered to a seductive hum. Honore was slowly backing towards a gated courtyard – probably belonging to the apartment in that building's upper stories. The iron gate swung silently with the pressure of her back, while her smile grew more coaxing. Was she inviting Tommy Jon upstairs for a quick romp? He knew who she was, of course – who didn't? Sketches of her appeared in all the papers, touting her exemplary training for domestics and her panache for hostessing the most whispered-about receptions in the Vieux Carré.

I held my breath as the pair slipped past the lush oleander foliage, and then the tall Cajun swooped down for a ravenous kiss. Honore's arms twined around his neck, coaxing him lower to accommodate her lesser height, insinuating her body against his. My pulse was pounding, and my nipples rasped against my corset. Thank God there were no passers-by to notice my arousal – or block my view.

As though Honore felt this deserted area was now her private playground, she spoke in low, urgent tones, gesturing towards the ground ... lifting her purple skirts over the tops of her pumps. Tommy Jon knelt, running his hands down her front as she leaned against the brick building. My Lord, she was raising her skirt higher. That hussy wanted a tonguing, right here in broad daylight!

I bit back a moan. My slit quivered with the audacity of it ... the delicious sensations I recalled from having Dewel's tongue lapping at my folds. T-Jon's response was just as cocky as the proposition he'd received: with practised speed, he ducked under her skirts for a taste of her pussy.

The headmistress was at least modest enough to cover her lover's head with her clothes, so I had to imagine what was going on between those long, stockinged legs. My knees were knocking with the need this scenario brought on, for I'd gone too long without any attention from Dewel or Monique. I thought it odd that Honore pressed her hands against the sides of his head, but perhaps in her extreme excitement she feared losing her balance, or –

She cried out, but the sound was a startling mixture of smug laughter and vengeance. I stepped forward to watch more closely, sensing that all was not fun and frolic across the street – that Miss Delacroix had lured Monique's man into a nasty trap hidden beneath her fashionable gown. He began to struggle, but she held him as though intending to – to *suffocate* him?

It was none of my business what these trysters did, but T-Jon's grunts and struggles convinced me to cross the street. After all, this vile woman had stormed out of my house vowing revenge. She'd be just as angry at Monique for stealing away her maids as she was at me for keeping them. If Miss Delacroix was ambushing a man too polite to fight a woman, I wouldn't stand for such an unfair advantage! Whatever awaited Beaumont under those gorgeous skirts –

But suddenly the headmistress toppled sideways, screaming as she lost her hold on T-Jon's head. His French obscenities matched the volume of her appalled outcries ... in a voice suddenly lacking its cultured, dulcet overtones. Miss Delacroix landed so hard on the sidewalk, she could've been seriously hurt.

She sprang up like a panther, however, and ran at Tommy Jon before he could right himself. Her broad, peacock-plumed hat sat askew and her legendary looks had given way to a beastly grimace. It was now a match of wits and physical strategy, for what the headmistress lacked in size and strength, she made up for with her wrath.

Whatever T-Jon found beneath Honore's gown had

enraged him to the point where he considered her no lady: he grabbed her shoulders and *shook*, making her head bob like a rag doll's. And then he let go.

The vixen in purple flew backwards again, this time losing her hat – which loosened the dense, dark curls it was pinned to. My eyes widened as that perfectly coifed hair left her head completely – a wig, it was! Tommy Jon stood poised above her, as though to punch her in the face – but he stopped with his fist suspended in midair. Sheer amazement, and then horror, crossed his face as he looked at the woman sprawling on the sidewalk, with her pale blonde hair crushed untidily around her head.

'*Sacré bleu.*' He backed away as though a monster lay leering at him. Then he bolted, blindly racing in front of an oncoming carriage. Only the driver's skill prevented the horses from knocking him to the street and crushing him, before they raced off in a noisy fit of skittishness.

During this commotion, the fallen headmistress collected her hat and wig, doing her damnedest to get out of sight. Crushing the feathered hat to her breast, she glanced around to see if anyone had witnessed her incident. I was clutching a lamp-post, still dismayed by Tommy-Jon's close call and what had preceded it, when her eyes found mine.

Her dark eyebrows and artfully painted face camouflaged a truth I wasn't prepared to see: blue eyes paired with that wavy, golden hair, which delivered a punch to my gut that nearly felled me.

Honore Delacroix, the city's most talked-about headmistress and femme fatale, was none other than Chapin Proffit. My husband.

23 Dire Straits

The carriage ride home was a blur. Thank God Rémy had been parked nearby, and if he'd seen Miss Delacroix's true identity – or had known it all along – he carried on with his usual dignity. I simply couldn't have dealt with his questions or consolations.

My thoughts raced back, through seven years of living with this unbelievable secret. While it seemed incredible – the ultimate humiliation – that I hadn't had the vaguest idea about Chapin's other life, things were suddenly falling into place. The whiffs of perfume ... the times he'd not been where he said he'd be ... the ways he'd found to avoid having sex with me, except in total darkness, and usually on occasions of rage or disgust rather than desire.

My husband was not seeing another woman. He *was* the other woman.

And he was far more beautiful than I, or most ladies, could ever hope to be. He had elevated Southern femininity to an art form and lived it to perfection.

How did I explain these things when I got home? Or did I simply swallow my shock – my revulsion – and pretend I didn't know?

I slumped against the carriage seat, feeling like a hollow, very fragile shell of myself: the wife of the city's next mayor, if he and his political backers had their way. None of those good old boys from the Beau Monde Club knew of his other identity, of course. Old Money was good at looking the other way, but the city fathers weren't *that* tolerant!

My immediate impulse was to rush to the *Times-Democrat* office and spill my incredible story. But whom would they believe? Not the distraught woman seeking to dispute Miss Delacroix's gender and ruin her reputation, checkered though it was. Word would get around town, back to Chapin, and I would quickly be secreted in some asylum, far from New Orleans, to live out the rest of my days in madness and mayhem. No, such a scheme for revenge would only backfire, badly.

But what about the three maids from the School for Domestic Endeavor? Honore had taken them in as young boys, and they'd described themselves as her slaves in a sexual way. Had they recognised Chapin Proffit in his male role and clothing, as head of one of the city's most respected families?

I thought not. That coal-black wig and those kohled eyebrows made a distracting camouflage. During Miss Delacroix's home visit, it was their own hides they'd been concerned about, not the hidden identity of the headmistress they'd come to loathe. Had they known Honore was anyone other than a man who lived as a woman – albeit more stunningly than they did – it would've come out in our chats. Cinderella couldn't keep such a secret while living under Chapin's roof.

But it certainly explained my husband's silent animosity in their presence, didn't it? He *had* his favourite pets back, but in his own home where he couldn't reveal himself to them. Or control them. If the whole situation didn't betray some of my most basic beliefs about the man I'd married, I could've laughed at the anguish Chapin must've felt when Monique birched his best boys and he couldn't do a thing about it – or do it himself!

It also explained Antoinette's sharp intake of breath when we speculated about the Other Woman's clothing in the attic ... clothing the redhead must've recognised as Honore's, while realising that a bizarre twist of fate had landed the three of them in Chapin Proffit's Garden District household. The Russell beneath the flirtatious maid uniform was a cool character indeed, to know such a secret and keep it from his two closest friends – to realise he'd been beholden for half his life to a man with a more dubious secret than his own! No wonder Toinette was so set on getting her revenge at the Mardi Gras ball tomorrow night.

Concern about the consequences of the maid's plan almost choked me. But events were out of my hands, weren't they? I was betting that 'niece', Savanna, was also a young man, too pretty to be accepted by his family. Long before I'd peered through that courtyard gate – before I'd ever heard the Proffit name – forces had been at work, aiming Chapin towards the reckoning he'd eventually face. It wasn't my fault: he'd brought it all on himself.

So, of course, Dewel knew. Living at the plantation, away from his older half-brother, had protected him from the truth while they were growing up. But Chapin's feminine tendencies had been obvious enough to Robert E. Lee Proffit that he'd bequeathed the sugar plantation to his truly *male* heir, hadn't he? It explained Chapin's complaining that things would be so different had his mama outlived their father, for he'd been Virgilia's pride and joy despite – or perhaps because of – his empathy for the fairer sex. Nothing was stronger than a mother's love for her only child.

And nothing drove my husband like the opportunity for profit ... which had motivated Honore Delacroix to create herself and her school in the first place: other families had sons well-suited to service careers, or simply too prissy to be tolerated at home. Had the city's most illustrious headmistress not turned out to be *my* husband, I could have applauded her sense of mission and entrepreneurial spirit – providing career training and friends of like kind for a segment of humanity I'd never dreamed existed.

Now that these details were assuming the neat precision of the formal gardens in back of the mansion, I recalled Dewel's other allusions over these last few weeks: his assertions that I should've been *his* bride. His innate knowledge that I was, for all practical purposes, a sexual novice until he claimed me. He'd alluded to things he knew but couldn't share, for my own protection ... knowing it was only a matter of time before I found out.

Which was the very reason he'd teased that I needed a niece, and sent Monique to hasten his half-brother's fall. And he wouldn't have allowed his flirtatious Cajun maid to assist me in the ways of women and men without telling her about Chapin's talent for living on both sides of the sexual fence.

Being the plucky sort, Monique Picabou went to the School when she knew Honore was out of town, and snatched her personal servants to get this snowball rolling down the mountainside a little faster. While she'd had her fun spanking those sissy maids, she'd gotten far more enjoyment whipping up Chapin's frustration by making him watch, knowing he couldn't respond as he wanted to – or quiz her about how much she knew.

Oh, yes, it all added up. But as the carriage turned off Prytania to enter the Proffit driveway, my heart felt leaden. I had been grievously betrayed by the two people I'd come to love most, and they hadn't shared the one secret I had every right to know.

And now I had to face the consequences of their plotting, alone.

I thanked Rémy as he helped me from the carriage, still not detecting anything different in his demeanour – but then, if he'd always known Chapin doubled as Honore, nothing would feel out-of-balance for him today, would it? He owed me no allegiance, so why would he divulge the shocking knowledge my two dearest friends had kept from me?

I felt so hollow – so incredibly *stupid* – for not figuring out my husband's double life, that I hurried up to my room with my packages. I couldn't face Fanny or the other three yet. I needed time alone, to ponder the most disturbing, bewildering, *degrading* discovery of my entire life. My sense of femininity and competence – my very soul – dangled by a fraying thread.

I stepped out to the gallery overlooking the garden, now tranquil in afternoon's shadow of the massive house. Monique's cheroots seemed like a very practical prop right now. Something for nervous fingers to clutch when no straws were left.

But I couldn't bear to think about all the times my seductive Cajun maid had enlightened me with her wiles – and lightened my life with her zany ways. She and Tommy Jon could go on as they had before: they had nothing to lose, now that she'd played her part so well for Dewel. The three of them were probably cavorting at this very moment, knowing I had to face Chapin alone. They'd done a fine job of awakening my passions – making me feel like a desirable woman at last, only to *leave* me when my sexy, sensual dreams got me caught in this nightmare.

What was wrong with me, that Chapin didn't want my body? That he'd duped me for seven years, never intending to reveal his dual nature?

And why hadn't I figured this out? Now it made sense, Dewel's asking why I hadn't left my husband years ago. He figured I'd notice the telltale signs, if only in Chapin's lack of interest in sex. The rogue must've had many a laugh at my expense, plotting how he'd bring Chapin Proffit's double life into the public eye and then steal his wife as well.

A pity the symmetry of the garden's hedges and ornamental plantings no longer soothed me: every time I looked at the fountain, and the bench near the old magnolia, I recalled my frolic with Monique and Tommy Jon, followed by Dewel's seductive play in the shadows. I saw his blue eyes when I looked at Chapin's. His touch − just the memory of it − sent shivers of gooseflesh all over my body because he was such a master of my senses, my emotions.

A pity I couldn't out and out despise him, but his lovemaking and molasses drawl would haunt me forever; the tender perfection every woman wanted, which I could never have.

I drew my thoughts back to the present, wondering how to go about my life now that I knew what I knew. Wondering how I could ever face Chapin without exploding in his face. He had to come home eventually: his big party was tomorrow night. And, meanwhile, the maids and I had to have everything in perfect readiness as though I was the blissfully naive Eve Proffit I'd been when I left for town this morning.

Did Mrs Frike know of his double life?

I thought back over things she'd said, and how she'd acted in his presence − and then recalled Honore's unannounced home visit. Fanny was appalled to find me chasing Monique around the music room nearly naked, of course – but she'd kept the headmistress from discovering us. And she was clearly offended by Miss Delacroix's lack of manners, and her attitude towards the three maids. Whereas, she'd always considered Chapin the perfect gentleman and head of the Proffit household, never letting on about any misgivings – although every housekeeper had her opinions of those she served.

No, if Fanny had thought it odd that this Mr Proffit didn't share a bed with his wife, well, Robert and Virgilia had occupied separate suites too. Even if she found some of Chapin's tastes a bit effete, I doubted the housekeeper had recognized him in Honore's scarlet gown. She, like I, had probably assumed the presence of an extramarital woman or two. And she, having served in a Southern household most of her life – for a Proffit who was proud of his illegitimate son – had accepted it as The Way Things Were.

I could not.

But neither could I walk away, for where would I go? Dewel's plantation would be the first place Chapin looked – and now that the scheming Creole had used me to bring his brother down, I wanted no part of his pretty lies about making me his own woman.

My best strategy, it seemed, was to go along with whatever Antoinette had planned for the ball tomorrow night. She had a level head, and a head start on all these secrets; Cleopatra and Cinderella would play along with whatever she dictated as the party progressed. If I let on about discovering Miss Delacroix's true identity, my Egyptian queen would be set on her own retribution and my fairy tale princess would dissolve in tears and be useless. Indeed, my silence was golden. But it left me feeling horribly, vulnerably alone.

My role as hostess would keep me occupied greeting guests, while the spotlight would be on Chapin: playing politics would keep us from clashing – although his mama's Bo Peep costume would surely have its effect! He would know I'd entered the forbidden attic, to choose a costume that would upset him the most when he could do nothing about it.

I opened my armoire and took out the glorious confection of periwinkle taffeta, with those puffy white sleeves that glowed with a light all their own. The shepherdess costume suited the occasion perfectly – for Chapin was a very black sheep indeed! Not only would I be completely disguised to his guests and supporters, but once I made my entrance, Chapin couldn't order me to change clothes.

As I held the elaborate mask to my face and looked in the mirror, I felt a wave of hope: the shiny-white caricature of a little girl's face, with its apple cheeks and dimpled, pink-lipped grin, hid *everything*: my identity, my disgust, my ... fears for the future. I could never compete with Honore Delacroix, nor did I want to live with her. And we both knew it.

So this mask symbolised my own secret: it hid the Eve Proffit who was scheming her escape. She would appear as the perfect wife and supporter of the party's golden boy – the hostess who gave the season's most lavish and talked-about party.

And then she would be gone.

24 I Get My Licks In

'You can't do this to – let me *go*, dammit!'

I struggled as Judd Schuck tied my wrists to my bedposts, but the little toad was more efficient than he looked. He was loving it, that this task brought him into full contact with my naked body, and that I couldn't do a damn thing about it. Chapin stood with his arms crossed and an expression of serene control while his valet did his dirty work.

'You were the perfect wife while you remained ignorant and knew your place,' he remarked with a sarcastic grin. 'But like that temptress Eve in the Garden, you'll be forever cursed for knowing too much. And you'll be out of my life without a penny to your name, for taking up with that bastard Dewel.'

'You'll never get away with this,' I tried to reason. 'The guests will *know* something's amiss when you have no hostess at your party!'

'Ah, but I will, my dear,' he crooned. 'Antoinette has consented to be your double for the evening. Costumed as the French queen you named her for, with her auburn hair and similar figure, she'll easily pass as the wife my guests expect to see. A lover who's received my affection for *years* now, you know.'

I ignored yet another emotional gut-punch from my husband – and another apparent betrayal by the maid who'd inspired my dream of revenge and freedom. 'And how will your – *slave* carry on appropriate conversations with –'

'Such illusions of grandeur you have, Miss Eve,' he clucked, testing my leather ties. 'As Annabelle, she's long been overseeing Miss Delacroix's soirees. And now that she understands my double identity, and the importance of keeping it a secret, she – and Judd here – look forward to elevated positions when I'm elected mayor.'

Chapin focused those blue Proffit eyes on me with such arrogance I nearly choked.

'Gag her as well, Judd. Can't have her screaming to attract attention.'

His sycophant forced one of my own silk scarves between my teeth, chuckling gleefully as he tied it.

'Too bad you never took an interest in my political activities, dear wife,' Chapin continued smugly. 'And too bad Mistress Monique isn't here to pay the piper for *her* part in this little escapade. I'll get her, though. Meanwhile, you'll have the evening to think about your ... mysterious disappearance. If Annabelle plays her part well tonight, no one will even realise you're gone. Ever.'

My eyes widened and I chomped furiously at the gag that cocked my jaws open. But with my ankles and wrists bound to the bedpost and my voice silenced, I was truly this insidious man's prisoner. He had the gall to act as though he'd planned to replace me all along, with his ... boyfriend!

'Shall we go, Judd? By the time we're in costume, Annabelle should be ready for her instructions –'

The door closed on Chapin's sentence. I cried out my hatred at the top of my lungs, but of course he didn't hear me. The snick of the lock was louder than any noise I could make.

The room's silence magnified the thoughts rushing through my head. I had spent the day planning the buffet layout with Fanny, and giving the three sissy maids their final instructions – complimenting their wonderful costumes. Once again I'd been oblivious to a traitor playing along.

Or had Antoinette known of Chapin's plans? I wanted to rail against her – against the hope she'd given me for getting out of this marriage with a scrap of personal pride and dignity. She was a smart one: she understood my husband's dual personality, and was bright enough to secure her future with it.

Yet I suspected that this morning, Toinette hadn't known she'd replace me. Chapin was probably bluffing about that part to further intimidate me, and he was now informing the redheaded maid about her evening's role as hostess. I had to believe this, for being betrayed by yet another person I'd come to love and trust – the young Russell who'd revealed his affection in the attic – was more than I could bear.

I heard musicians ascending the stairs ... then tuning their instruments in the third-floor ballroom. The maids' quarters above me were empty, and by now Cinderella and Cleopatra were too busy with last-minute preparations to slip away – if indeed they would. Perhaps Miss Delacroix-turned-Chapin was making *them* some wonderful offers in exchange for their silence too. There was so much I couldn't find out while held hostage in my room!

In vain I rolled the leather ties up and down the bedpost to loosen them, but I only rubbed my wrists raw. My mouth felt parched from being propped open, and my jaw throbbed from the tightness of the gag. Tied higher than my head, my arms had already gone numb and were prickling from lack of circulation, while the rest of my body was growing stiff from its position along the post. And I had to pee. Badly.

I could discern the arrival of the first guests ... female voices exclaiming over the lavish decorations and each other's costumes. The periwinkle gown I'd intended to surprise Chapin with was of no use to me now. Male voices conversed over the genteel clatter of silver on china plates ... someone called for a toast, and there was a loud cheer, followed by applause. From what I could apprise in my darkening room, everyone was having a splendid time without me – not even aware of my absence.

Soon came the tread of guests going upstairs to dance, walking within sight of my suite without knowing it was my prison! The music began, and in my mind I saw ladies whirling gracefully, showing off their magnificent costumes as their partners led them in a waltz.

I rested my head against my bloodless arms, tears trickling down my cheeks. We'd entertained so seldom. I'd truly looked forward to this evening's splendour, not just as the place to stage Chapin's fall from grace, but as a tonic for a soul that had languished in my barren marriage. I realised now that even before I'd met Dewel and Monique, I wasn't happy. I wished I'd had the grit to act sooner. And the foresight to use the bathroom when I'd had the chance.

A furtive click made me look towards the door, where a stout little clown with a white face and a long nose was slipping inside. Even in the shadows, I could see Judd Schuck's other prominent point tenting the front of his costume.

'Just making sure you're all right, Miss Eve,' he said in his reedy voice. 'Chapin's put me in charge of you now, since I requested permission to, uh, *fill in* for him.'

Since I could move nothing but my head, I turned it away from him. Yet this left me completely vulnerable to the valet's nastiness – which began with his hand insinuating itself between my bare thighs.

'Such soft skin,' he sighed, his body pressing mine against the wooden bedpost. 'It was more than I could hope for when I took this job, but my dreams are coming true! Not only am I to be the mayor's right-hand man, but I can *handle* his pretty wife as well!'

He laughed at his own joke, making my stomach roil with revulsion. He brought his hand higher, against my bare slit – which forced my thighs apart and made me fall against the bed.

'That's what I like to see, total cooperation,' Schuck said with a laugh. 'Play your cards right and perhaps – *perhaps* – I'll keep you in a little hideaway somewhere, when this is all over. Such a shame, to dispose of you the way Chapin wants to.'

My eyes widened, yet my mind told me this, too, was another attempt at intimidation. I moaned against my gag, feigning arousal. Maybe if I played along with his clumsy fumblings, I'd have a better chance at being untied. I was tall enough that Judd would have trouble taking what he wanted, from this position.

He shifted quickly, and then my backside suddenly stung from the hard whack of his free hand. The surprise attack made me dribble against his fingers.

'Is the lady losing control?' he said with a chuckle, rubbing the wetness against my folds. 'What would she give me in exchange for her chamber pot?'

He brought his wet hand up over my mound, and suddenly pressed it against my bloated abdomen. I grunted into the gag when he spanked me again.

'Not as much fun to be on the receiving end, is it? But then, Fanny Frike is much more accomplished at spanking,' he added dryly. 'She sends her regards, by the way. But she knows better than to help you.'

Another whack, and more liquid escaped – both from my pussy and the corners of my eyes. Only a cur like Judd Schuck could devise such a degrading game, knowing the party's gaiety would cover any noise I made.

'I'll get that potty now,' he breathed, his mask chafing my ear, 'and then I'm going to loosen one foot so you can piss while I watch – holding your leg so you won't do anything stupid, of course.'

Desperate as I was, such a concession seemed a godsend. He roughly removed his hand, causing more warm water to trickle down my thighs and into my Aubusson rug. Damn him, he took his sweet time fetching my commode from beside the vanity, knowing that this initial release only made me more anxious to go.

'Not another drop,' he warned, placing the porcelain pot on the floor in front of me. 'Once I untie this left leg, you'll wait for my permission to relieve yourself, understand me? If you can't be a lady about it, I'll smack your ass and have you pissing all over the floor – and your bed! Then I'll hold your nose in the wet spot while I fuck you from behind.'

I closed my eyes against those ideas, coming from such a lurid mind. Schuck took his time loosening the leather binding, running little nips and kisses inside my thigh. I was squeezing myself tightly, thinking of what I might do with my free leg, while the valet's breathing deepened: he was sniffing my crotch like a dog, panting for it now.

Suddenly he knelt, to thrust the cool porcelain bowl between my knees. 'Do it!' he ordered. 'And whatever you splash on my hand, you'll have to lick off!'

With my wrists still bound above my head and one leg tied, squatting was impossible. I let loose with a splash, trying not to empty too fast, thinking of ways to waylay this bastard. Schuck, however, was so caught up in watching me pee, he didn't notice the door opening. Seeing the iridescent sheen of Cinderella's gown in the dimness, and the obsidian hair falling around Cleopatra's shoulders, I almost laughed aloud.

Wisely they waited, observing Judd's fixation and noting the ties around the bedpost. As though by silent agreement, Cinderella went around the other side of the bed while her cohort slipped silently behind Judd Schuck.

'Come on, Miss Eve – let him have it,' came Cleopatra's sultry voice. 'Wet him down!'

'He's got his nerve, treating you this way!' Cinderella chimed in.

Schuck was so startled that he prodded me with that damn clown's nose. Cleopatra had grabbed him by the backside, while I felt the slight dips of her partner crawling across the bed behind me.

'You should see his face, not to mention his cock,' the Egyptian queen muttered. 'He wants it bad.'

When that nose poked me again, I did the unthinkable: with what I had left, I sprayed him full-force, delighting in the strangled cry he made. His grip on my ankle made me whimper and shift, which dumped the chamber pot on him too, but I was beyond worrying about stains on my rug. A jewelled dagger passed beside my head, and Cinderella took it to cut my wrists free.

Schuck sputtered. 'If you think I'm turning her loose –'

'I think you're so damn horny, it doesn't matter what happens to Miss Eve. *Does* it, Stud Boy?' the maid behind him challenged. 'Cut us some openings in this clown suit, Princess. We'll keep Schuck busy, so Miss Eve can be the belle of her ball.'

Cinderella nimbly hopped off the bed; I heard fabric

giving way to that dagger, while the valet squealed as though his manhood felt threatened. The circulation returned to my arms with such stabbing sensations, the slender blonde might have been using the weapon on me – but then she reached down my other leg to free it.

'You don't want to go back to the ball anyway,' she teased the valet in her girlish voice. 'Dewel and Monique would make *short* work of you, little man. Just as I intend to. Here – you've always wanted to peek beneath my panties. *Haven't* you?'

As I shook off the last leather binding, Cleopatra wrestled Judd's arms behind him. He was indeed distracted by Cinderella raising her skirts ... the display of those frilly white panties that glowed in the dimness of my room. But he was *not* ready for the long, hard cock he saw when she tugged them down – nor expecting her to stifle his outcry with it.

'Bite me and it's all over,' the princess growled in her natural male voice. With her dagger poised in plain sight, she rocked in and out of his mouth while Cleopatra clutched him from behind. 'Suck me nice, and you'll get a little reward from the Queen of Egypt.'

I laughed for the first time in days, but there was no time to watch the two maids manhandling Chapin's valet. I quickly donned the Bo Peep costume and then pinned my hair to my head. On went the wig with its beehive of yellow curls, and then I attached the jewelled headband to the shiny white mask. Instinct told me to wear kid slippers rather than those awkward oversized shoes, and then I took the shepherd's crook from my armoire.

'I think he could be doing a better, more convincing job on you, Cindy,' Cleopatra was saying as I headed for the door. And with that, the dark queen raised her tunic to reveal another impressive erection, which she placed at the crack of Schuck's ass.

I allowed myself the pleasure of watching him get skewered from behind while Cinderella held his head to pump into his mouth. 'Come on, you,' she muttered. 'Suck this candy cane like you *mean* it – like you *love* it, little man! You're not finished until we've both shot all over you – and you don't want Mr Proffit to come looking for us and find you this way. *Do* you?'

Out into the hallway I stepped, and then I headed upstairs to the ballroom. The orchestra was playing a merry quickstep, which had the revellers clapping in time to the music. This party I'd planned was going well, even though things were not as they seemed . . .

But I couldn't lose my focus: this was my moment to avenge the deceit I'd lived with for seven years. Now, with all his political friends resplendent in their costumes, imbibing wine while feasting from sideboards covered with fine food, I could strike without fearing his reprisal.

Yet, if Cleopatra and Cinderella weren't here to assist me . . . with Antoinette acting as myself, and her loyalties uncertain . . . and if Dewel and Monique – those traitors! – had also appeared . . .

But I couldn't stop now. Unless I acted without hesitation, my plan would fall flat, leaving me even more vulnerable to Chapin's wrath than before. I paused in the arched doorway to peruse the crowd, to get my nerve up while everyone was still unaware of my presence.

Chapin and his redheaded companion were the centre of attention, stepping with heart-stopping precision around the dance floor as the music quickened. As Louis the Sixteenth and Marie Antoinette, they made a stunning couple, resplendent in flowing silks and velvets of regal purples and greens, adorned with gold braid and brilliant detail. It didn't escape me that hours – years – of practice made them such expert partners, for I'd never seen my husband dance as though his feet were guided by nimble spirits. And the way he was gazing at his partner with those intense blue eyes, the audience assumed he was desperately in love with his wife. The devoted husband, the successful businessman from an old-money family; the perfect man to be the next mayor of New Orleans.

It was time to set them all straight. *My* moment, after seven years spent with a total stranger who'd made me live his lie.

The music rose to a giddy pitch, and I scanned the crowd for Dewel and Monique – the friends who'd caught me up in their seductive instruction without telling me Chapin's secret. I spotted a tall, handsome gypsy king near the punch table, imperially fit in his sleek black pants and a poet's shirt open to the centre of his chest. With a mysterious wisp of a black mask above a pencil-thin moustache, the heir to the Proffit plantation could have stolen the show. But it was the lady beside Dewel who made me gape.

She was the very image of Maria Castalantez, as though she'd stepped from that painting above the mantel at Bayou Belle.

Her dark hair fell lushly around shoulders bared by a peasant blouse, and gold hoops glimmered in her ears. In fact, the entire effect was rendered so perfectly, Monique had to be wearing the clothes in which Dewel's mother posed for her portrait. The couple's proud stance made me wonder if Robert E. Lee Proffit had appeared at a ball in this roguish guise with Maria beside him. And wouldn't it be too sweet if Chapin's mother Virgilia had dressed as Bo Peep and discovered those two black sheep among her flock of socialite admirers?

As though my thoughts had travelled across the noisy, crowded ballroom, Dewel and Monique both focused on me as I paused in the doorway. He had the nerve to lightly blow me a kiss, while the minx beside him flashed a wicked grin – as though nothing had come between us. As though they, too, planned to beat Chapin at his own game.

Well, they could do as they wished! This colossal joke had been on me, and it was my turn to shine! I stepped aside as someone stopped beside me with a large tureen of spicy gumbo, and then heard a gasp.

Fanny Frike – the poor housekeeper now tending the buffet tables alone – was staring at me as though she'd seen a ghost.

I smiled, more confident now, as the orchestra brought the folk dance to a close. 'Thank you, Fanny,' I murmured. 'It's the moment we've all been waiting for.'

Crook in hand, I cut through the crowd towards the dais. Chapin and his redheaded queen had whirled to a brilliant finish in the centre of the room. Basking in the crowd's applause, they clasped hands and gazed at each other with an expression of utmost accomplishment. Perfect. As the musicians were preparing for the next number, I coaxed the conductor aside by saying I had to make the evening's most important announcement. For I did.

'If I might have your attention!' I called out, thumping my crook on the hardwood floor. 'Ladies and gentlemen, may I have your attention, *please*?' Tap, tap, tap.

While the guests turned my way, I prayed for the right words at the right moment, in the right tone of voice. After all, it was my word against Chapin's; my entire future at stake here. A society wife didn't challenge her husband in public without severe repercussions – but what had I left to lose? Discovering my husband's double identity – the damage it had done to my soul – goaded me to take this last chance. It was either escape, by defaming Chapin, or suffer whatever fate he'd conjured up for Judd Schuck to carry out.

I could only hope that his despicable valet was now bound to the bedpost where I had been: in the arched doorway stood an Egyptian queen and a princess in powder blue, cheering me on with their smiles.

Chapin, however, let out a strangled gasp. His face changed from a sickly shade of pale to an unbecoming flush when he recognised my costume, and as he stepped towards the dais, I too moved forward.

'And what are *you* staring at, Mr Proffit?' I demanded boldly. With another *tap, tap, tap* of my shepherd's crook, I forestalled his interruption. 'Feeling *sheepish*, now that your mama's here? As well you should!'

A murmur arose as the guests speculated about who was portraying the white-faced Bo Peep. This crowd wasn't accustomed to a woman's voice ringing out to challenge a man – but I was only just beginning my tirade!

Chapin recovered, slipping an arm around Antoinette to keep up his ruse. 'Who do you think you are, wearing my mother's –'

'And who do you think *you* are, Mr Proffit? Tying your wife to her bedpost so you can cavort with this – this *floozy*,' I retorted, flourishing my crook at Antoinette. 'Bringing a *spy* into this household – and then threatening to dispose of the wife you've deceived all these years!'

The guests shifted, their whispers slithering around

the room at this too-delicious turn of events. At the buffet table, Fanny Frike's grin widened. When she saw the gypsy king and his Creole consort moving up behind Chapin, she signalled for the two maids in the doorway to get closer as well.

Chapin, however, had focused on me – possibly for the first time in our marriage. 'I don't know who you are,' he bluffed, for how could he not recognise my voice? 'but if you continue this ridiculous display, I'll ask these gentlemen to escort you out. I believe the chief of police is present –'

'Shall we have him tell everyone about Honore Delacroix?' Antoinette spoke up. She raised a whole new fit of whispers, for she was speaking in a male voice while dressed so exquisitely as a French queen – and she wouldn't let Chapin out of her embrace. 'I believe he has a son at the School of Domestic Endeavor –'

'Ah, yes, Miss Delacroix!' I chimed in, my heart dancing with the sissy maid's loyalty. 'Didn't I see her sneaking across the gallery and out through the garden last week? Are those her clothes you're hiding in the attic? Chapin, you've been a very bad boy! Mama really should take you over her knee, this minute!'

'A spanking, ah *oui*,' cried Monique. 'Let me fetch the birch rod –'

'You're going nowhere, you little bitch! It's your fault all this got – got –'

Chapin paled again when he saw she was dressed as Dewel's beautiful mother. He pointed, blinking and backing away as though he couldn't believe his eyes. 'It's been a plot all along! You and my bastard half-brother have – how *dare* you dress like that whore who tore our family apart?'

The guests sucked in their breath, but no one moved

towards the door: even the men were now watching every cue, every nuance, as though the mud-slinging had become serious enough to be interesting.

Chapin realised his future as the mayor of New Orleans – perhaps even his credibility as a cotton factor – was at stake, so he shook himself free of Antoinette's grasp. He marched up to the dais, as though to reclaim his place as the man of the house. The man of the hour.

'Come up to take your punishment – like a *man*?' I taunted, playing to the ladies' twitters. 'Bare that backside and bend over. You deserve a spanking and you know it!'

Shaking with rage – or was it something else? – Chapin whipped off the oversized wig of yellow curls and then yanked the mask from my face. While I didn't like being seen with my hair crushed against my head, I revelled in the fact that my husband was finally paying full attention to me . . . and that the city's golden boy had lost his almighty control.

'Please excuse us,' he commanded in a more courtly voice as he steered me in front of him. 'My wife has taken leave of her senses, and I must remind her of her place.'

The crowd parted. The males nodded approvingly, some of them applauding – or turning to their wives with a similar warning. It was the most ignominious moment of my entire life, being marched out like an errant child dressed to enact a nursery rhyme. Yet I'd never felt better, or more alive. I had taken a stand in my own behalf, consequences be damned. And I wasn't nearly finished.

We entered the schoolroom, which adjoined the maids' quarters and had stood empty since Chapin himself took lessons there. The door slammed with an echoing finality. 'Have you gone totally berserk?' he demanded in a stage whisper. 'I will not –'

'No, I've finally seen the light, Chapin. And don't tell me this doesn't excite the hell out of you!' I exclaimed, pointing with my crook. 'I haven't seen you this hard since – well, never. Now *there's* a story!'

His breath escaped in a rush, while his attempt at covering his fly looked suspiciously like a caress. 'This is not the time nor the –'

'But it's the only time I've got! You're going to throw me out without a penny, remember?' I challenged loudly. 'Maybe I understand your needs now, dear husband. Maybe you ought to drop those pants so I can dish it up the way you like it. Nothing satisfies like a good spanking, right? Cleanses the conscience and purges the soul!'

My pulse was galloping like horses with the finish line in sight, so I didn't dare lose my momentum. I had to strike while the iron – or in this case, my husband – was hot, and hope the maids would step in when I needed them.

'Your *girls* have told me about Honore's naughty little habits. About how she gets so wild and hard while caning them, it takes all three of them to smack her ass afterwards,' I cajoled.

I situated myself in the teacher's chair, patting my lap. 'How was I to give you what you really wanted, when I didn't *know*? Instead of cursing Monique – who certainly got your pecker pumped during your damned home visit – you should thank her for teaching me her technique!'

Chapin was growing more agitated by the moment, looking at me as though I couldn't be his prim, proper Miss Eve – as though I were too good to be true. 'You mean you're not ... you would really take your hand to my –'

'You want my hand, you've got it!' I crowed, motioning him over. 'Right across the softest, most tender part of your pretty little ass. But you know how it works, Chapin. You must show your penitence by taking down your pants and assuming the position, like a good boy. You must *want* this spanking more than anything I've ever given you!'

His taut expression gave way to a sigh of utter submission as he fumbled with his buttons. 'Miss Eve, I'm so sorry,' he mumbled as his pants fell about his knees. 'Not only have I humiliated you in front of our guests, but I've sorely misjudged –'

Whack went my hand upon his backside! It felt so good, I had to give him another one before he fully fell across my lap. 'Damn right you've humiliated me! Prancing around town as a gorgeous woman – all these years just using me as a *cover* for your double life. And then –'

'And then tricking my Tommy Jon as well!' A familiar cry entered the room. 'Grab him, girls! Miss Eve must have her way with him, *non*? High time Proffit paid his dues for deceiving her. For using *all* of us!'

Rushing from the door of the servants' quarters, Cleopatra and Cinderella took hold of Chapin's legs while Monique and Antoinette approached him from the front. The redheaded queen glowered at him as she grabbed his hands between her own, while the Cajun dressed as Dewel's mother slapped his face.

Chapin shook as though trying to awaken from a nightmare. 'You think this is funny now, but when I tell Judd –'

'Sorry, boss,' Cinderella twittered, 'but Stud Fuck is tied up at the moment. Dripping from both holes, because he didn't think two *girls* could get the best of him!'

'So you'll just have to take what's coming to you, and then explain all this to that crowd out there.'

Dewel strode in, closing the door behind him, the powerful gypsy king taking control. He stopped in front of his struggling half-brother, shaking his head. 'The way I see it, you have some decisions to make in these next few seconds, Chapin. If you grant your wife a quiet divorce tomorrow, you can get on with your political campaign by regreasing some palms, and giving some tall explanations to your constituents. That won't include me, however. I'm withdrawing my financial support.'

Chapin blanched, poking my thigh with his prodigious erection. 'You can't do that! If you think for one minute –'

'I think your goose is cooked no matter what you do,' Dewel continued with a shrug. 'Because if you *don't* release Miss Eve from this marriage – which was a farce from the start – I'll tell everyone out there you are indeed Honore Delacroix. And New Orleans will *never* elect a female mayor.'

Dewel crossed his arms, smirking at his half-brother's reddened, bared, quivering butt. 'You'll lose all respect around town, and at the Cotton Exchange. And your school will soon close, because those parents who've paid you to take their pretty little boys will be afraid of this same sort of exposure. So what's it going to be?'

'You have no right – who's going to listen to *you*?' he demanded shrilly. 'All your life, you've been nothing but –'

'Our daddy's favourite,' he replied, leaning low enough to look Chapin in the eye. 'The true heir to real

Proffit property; the plantation owner who works the land while *you* live in this fancy mansion. Just bugs the hell out of you that I've always pulled my weight, while you prissed around in your mama's clothes as a kid, and then couldn't handle being a man!'

'I've got the city's most influential citizens on my side,' he railed, struggling against the eight hands that held him. 'You wouldn't dare –'

'Oh, yes I would. Should've done it years ago.'

Dewel started towards the door, where a shuffling murmur came from a crowd trying to be quiet. He took off that wickedly thin mask to smile at me, his blue eyes signalling that he wasn't nearly finished with his revelations.

'Get your licks in, Miss Eve. Remind this woman of her *place*.'

I didn't have to be told twice. With renewed enthusiasm, I smacked Chapin's puckering butt and revelled in his whimpers. My four supporters kept him from writhing off my slippery, taffeta-clad lap, cheering me on.

'When your hand gets sore, use your shoe,' Cinderella suggested with a giggle. 'The sole of a kid slipper makes the most glorious noise. And it leaves a sharper stripe than a hand.'

Since my palm was stinging and I wasn't nearly finished, I reached down for a slipper. Why wasn't I surprised to see my own shiny, transparent pumps on this princess's feet?

'This is absurd, Miss Eve,' Chapin protested. 'Surely after all these years we can come to an agreement! You can call off that dog at the door –'

'After you set your dog of a valet on me? I think not!'

A couple of slaps with that slipper made his face contort, and I realised Chapin Proffit wasn't nearly as handsome as most people considered him. In fact, he now seemed as ugly and repulsive on the inside as Judd Schuck looked on the outside, which made them a pretty good pair. He was so excited by this spanking, his warm, sticky juice was dribbling down my skirt.

What sort of a man *liked* such humiliation? Required it to become aroused?

Not the sort I wanted to be married to. Seven years of squinting in this golden boy's glare had brought us to this ... cozy moment, where four domestics held him so his wife could administer the discipline he craved. As Dewel threw open the door, acting surprised that so many eavesdroppers had gathered in the hallway, I delivered the last smacks in my brief career as a dominant.

'*That* is for using me as your damn cover,' I stated, smacking the fullness of his fiery cheeks with my slipper. 'And *this* is for mistreating my friends – and for humping my leg like a crazed dog.'

Whack. Whack.

I caught my breath, feeling exhilarated yet ready to cry. 'Let him go, ladies. I can't stand the sight of him any more.'

Rising from the chair, I nearly dumped him before he scrambled off my lap. With all the dignity my unkempt hair and red hand allowed me, I looked at the crowd of costumed figures gawking at us from behind Dewel. I had no idea who wore those masks, nor did I really care: I had always felt excluded from their clubs and cliques, and this display of my exasperation had surely severed whatever surface friendship any of them felt for me.

I exited through the maids' quarters, my steps quickening as I approached the back stairs. Judd Schuck was still in my room, so I couldn't go there – and the house seemed to close in on me with all the heaviness of its Proffit family history, a yoke I'd never worn very well.

So I slipped out the back door into the dark garden, shucking the voluminous layers of taffeta, and those huge, puffy sleeves. I sat on the bench in the shadows of the boxwood hedge, clasping my crook. Drinking in the serene, steady patter of the fountain's waters ... feeling its spray on my face.

I wasn't hiding, I told myself. I was seeking out the Eve who'd yearned for so long to breathe this freely.

25 **Raising Cane**

'Ooh-la-la, Auntie Eve! I've followed a trail of clothes, hoping I'd find you naked, *non*?'

My gaze remained on the dome-shaped streams of the fountain, which sparkled like diamonds in the moonlight as they whispered their gentle benediction. I felt enveloped by a new tranquility: for the first time, I'd stated my case. I'd taken Fate by the hand and run with it, into a future filled with my own choices. I'd made my bed and I'd lie in it – somewhere else.

'The guests, they all left after you did. Chapin's gone now too – with Schuck. Just the three sissy maids and Fanny in there, having a party with all the food that's left.' Monique squeezed my hand. 'Come eat with us, *cherie*. You're our hero now, and we love you.'

My heart gave a little kick, and I shut my eyes. 'Is that why you left me without so much as a backward glance?' I whispered bitterly. 'You – you sent me on that goose chase in my lace, probably knowing Chapin wasn't at the club! Knowing Dewel would – and that I'd probably get caught when – just like every other time –'

Her finger pressed into my lips, forcing me to look into her huge chocolate eyes. 'I had to put on a convincing show for Chapin, *ma tante*. If he thought I'd sneak back, you would've been in worse trouble, *non*? And if you thought I'd rescue you every little time, you'd never be free! You'd keep finding weak reasons to stay with him – to not believe in your own strength.'

Awareness shot through my body. When Monique's round, cowlike eyes pleaded with mine, I couldn't stay angry with her. 'I surprised myself,' I admitted.

'You surprised *everyone* with that spanking, *oui*? Especially Chapin!' she crowed, her laughter ricocheting around the boxwood hedges. Then she held my hand tighter, dropping her Cajun sing-song. 'And I never left you *alone*, Auntie. From the start, after you showed them such kindness, the three maids swore to me they'd look after you. And when I sent Tommy Jon into town to expose Honor Delacroix, Rémy remained close by, in case things got nasty.'

I blinked, trying to absorb this startling information. 'You were *all* in on it? You were –'

'When your husband hired Schuck, Dewel thought he might be catching on to our plan. And once we met that asshole of a valet, *nobody* wanted him reporting our every move – or sniffing after you,' she said with a scowl. 'You were evil only in name, Auntie. No match for Stud Fuck.'

Then, in her inimitable way, Monique sparkled again – kissed my cheek like a playful child. 'And now we want to thank you, for setting us *all* free. Even before Schuck showed up, Fanny thought Himself was becoming a pompous little prick, you know?'

I giggled – but what would happen to me now? Himself would return sooner or later, and I couldn't stay here. 'Did Fanny know he was Honore Delacroix?'

Monique shook her head. Then she fished a cheroot from her skirt pocket and lit it. 'She had suspicions about him wearing dresses – used to find Virgilia's underthings hidden in his closet, when he was little. But she didn't know how much a woman he was until she overheard the maids talking, right before the party tonight.'

I considered this, taking comfort from her quiet conversation and the nearness of her body. She looked breathtakingly beautiful in Maria's clothing – which drove home another point I had to settle for myself. 'And those three didn't recognise Chapin as a male? Even after living with him since they were so young?'

She shook her head again, cigar smoke coiling about her head like an airy snake. 'Honore drilled her femininity into their heads, even as she drilled them that other way, *oui*? And they never knew she lived another life, as a man. Figured any time she was away from the School, she was in her apartment in the Vieux Carré, or seeing to business.'

'The ... apartment overlooking that courtyard where he –'

'*Oui*, with the niece, and with T-Jon. It was Robert Proffit's place in town, away from his wife's clinging bitchiness.'

I thought about these things with a sigh, and came to a momentous conclusion. 'You know, I have no room to point a finger at Chapin's preferences, because – well, here *you* are. The woman who taught me about such things.'

'You are ready for your next lesson then? Right here?' she teased, running a fingertip up my thigh.

I slapped at it playfully. 'I'm saying that had I found out in a different way about his – his taste for young men – maybe I could have –'

'*Non*, Auntie Eve!' she insisted in a whisper. 'No woman wants to measure herself against such competition as Honore Delacroix, and –'

'Come up short.' I sighed again, realising she was right. 'But what will I do? I have no place to stay, no money to –'

'You'll come inside, to eat and drink with us,' she

said, standing me up as she rose from the stone bench. 'We girls stick together, *oui*? When a woman has good friends and good shoes, there's no stopping her!'

How could I argue with that? My Cajun maid was leading me by the hand, insisting I partake of life's banquet rather than snivelling on the sidelines, hungry and alone. And when we stepped inside, where Fanny and the three maids sat at a table loaded with leftover shrimp, and pâtés, and bowls of brandied fruit, they stood up and applauded – as though I were some celebrity, despite my rumpled muslin shift and hair that hung in clumps.

My heart swelled. The evening – my years here in New Orleans – were not a total loss, after all. Cinderella and Cleopatra rushed over to hug me, and even Fanny Frike slung a motherly arm about my shoulders. The housekeeper took a mischievous swig from her wine bottle.

'Couldn't have spanked him better myself, Miss Eve,' she insisted. 'And don't be worrying over me, if Chapin sends me packing. I've squirrelled away enough to go live with my sister in Baton Rouge, like she's been asking me to for years.'

'And we plan to start our own domestic placement service,' Cleopatra chimed in, patting the princess affectionately on her powder-blue bottom. 'Dewel's going to help us get started –'

'So we can give Miss Delacroix a run for her money,' Cinderella finished with a grin. 'By tomorrow, everyone in town will know who she – he – really is. We can capitalise on her notoriety, and on the excellent training she gave us.'

Wasn't it striking, how quickly these women had made other plans? How adaptable they were, even after their lives had been as thoroughly up-ended as mine.

Antoinette sauntered over then, looking . . . less queenly in her velvet gown.

'Had you fooled for a while, didn't I?' she asked. But it was in a lower, mellower voice than I was accustomed to hearing from that bow-shaped mouth. 'You realise, of course, that Chapin had to believe I would stick by Miss Delacroix, once he knew I'd discovered his double life. But now that I've played my starring role, impersonating you, Miss Eve, I'm out of these theatrics for good.'

Cinderella's head swivelled as though she'd been slapped. 'What do you mean, Toinette? You know how lucrative our service will –'

'I mean, I'm done with these damn dresses!' In very short order, he ripped off the gorgeous costume, down to those white panties, and then unpinned his auburn hair. 'It was never the same for me. A necessity at first, when I was hiding from the police and Honore took me in, but no more! My name's Russell, and I'm a man living in a man's world.'

The redhead turned to me then, capturing me with a kiss that went on and on and left my head spinning! Without the padding at his breasts, he had a firm, muscled chest which funnelled down to a flat abdomen, where a long, thick erection rubbed blatantly against my stomach.

'By the way,' he whispered, 'I did *not* set the tenement fire that killed my family. Best I knew from the neighbours' gossip, my mother got soused and kicked over the lamp.'

I drew a shaky breath, stunned by the intensity of the green eyes gazing into mine; a face that was already taking on male contours and a chest that felt broader than I recalled. 'No doubt in my mind you'll set a few other things afire, though,' I said with a shaky laugh.

'It never goes out. Always a slow burn, just waiting to flare.' Russell winked, grinning. 'That other Mr Proffit may have a little competition, once I've got my life in order and my pants in place. Before we leave tonight, I'd really appreciate it if one of you ladies would cut my hair.'

A moment's silence filled the kitchen, while the others looked to me for *my* plans. Rather than disappoint them – for I still felt like a magnolia blossom at the mercy of the next high wind – I found a bottle of wine and raised it in salute.

'To friends, and the future,' I proposed with more certainty than I felt.

'To Miss Eve, who gave us one!' came Cleopatra's response.

Was it my imagination, or were she and Cinderella more openly affectionate now that they no longer lived under Miss Delacroix's thumb? They looked supremely happy, feeding each other chunks of Fanny's finest cocoa cake – so involved in smearing the rich, brown frosting on each other's lips and then kissing it off, I had to look away.

Monique snickered, taking the scissors Fanny brought her. 'You're wanting some of that, *oui*, Auntie Eve? Just can't wait for Mr Dewel to come back, *non*?'

'Who says he is?' I draped a towel around Russell's bare shoulders as he sat in a chair for his haircut. 'I'm betting the party chairmen press him to run for mayor, now that they've caught Chapin with his pants down. Dewel's been involved in their platform planning, and has contributed a great amount to the campaign fund.'

'An astute observation, sugah, but I turned them down. Declared myself completely out of politics.'

We turned to see the man in question leaning against the door jamb, watching us with effervescent blue eyes. He still wore the tight-fitting black pants and flowing shirt, open to reveal a vee of dark curls on his chest; still looked decidedly dangerous with that slash of fake moustache along his lush upper lip.

My throat grew tight. No man had the right to look so damned handsome just standing there, acting as though he had nothing on his mind. Well, maybe *one* thing – but as he let his eyes drift over my short, translucent shift he made no effort in my direction. In fact, he turned his attention to the redhead submitting to Monique's scissors.

'Well, I'll be damned. That little Cajun make a man of you, did she?'

Russell closed his eyes with the first fatal snips, which sent all the hair below his ears slipping to the floor in a shimmering auburn heap. When he – and the rest of us – could breathe again, he grinned and extended his hand.

'She and Miss Eve deserve that credit, yessir,' he said when the Creole's brown hand enveloped his. 'Once they freed me from Honore's clutches, I could reconsider my life outside a maid's uniform. Russell Reed, Mr Proffit – and damn proud of it!'

Dewel nodded, assessing the young man who looked more strikingly male with each snip of Monique's shears. 'I'll be needin' a plantation manager, if you're interested,' he said in a thoughtful drawl. 'Like I told those party bosses, I've got a crop to harvest and a woman to woo. Bet you can guess which one I *don't* want your help with.'

Russell's eyes widened. 'If you're sure I'm the sort of man –'

'Once I know what I want, I go after it. Show up at Bayou Belle, and ask me for twice the money you think you're worth – but give me a couple days to take care of that other thing.' He winked at the younger fellow, tweaking the white ruffle at the top of his thigh. 'After slavin' for Miss Delacroix, I think you'll enjoy our life on the bayou. Workin' hard, but livin' free.'

That slow, molasses drawl had mesmerised us all, until the two remaining maids applauded and proposed a toast to Russell's new life. Mrs Frike was exclaiming over his new look, brushing the little hairs from his shoulders as Monique pronounced him heartbreakingly handsome. The kitchen came alive with their gaiety and the wine, but this revelry was lost on me as Dewel Proffit swallowed me whole with his next gaze.

I've got a crop to harvest and a woman to woo.
Once I know what I want, I go after it.

His words filled my mind, shutting out everything else, yet I wasn't sure I believed them. Oh, Dewel had stated his intentions blatantly enough when we'd made love – and long before that. But things were different now. Before, when Chapin's world was all I knew, I had carefully filtered such messages from this black sheep of the Proffit family: hadn't I been told never to listen to him? Never to trust him?

Dewel's smile sliced through my mental objections as he approached me. The singleness of purpose on his face made me swallow hard; made me hope I could behave as a mature, rational woman rather than laughing – or crying – like a witless little girl if he said he wanted me. Lord knows I needed a man to prove to me, on a daily basis, that Eve Proffit was a woman worthy of love and respect. I'd been living with Chapin for too many years to know anything about the true nature of marriage.

But maybe that's not what he wanted! Maybe Dewel, born on the wrong side of the sheets, assumed lawful relationships were too confining – that they made people behave out of obligation, rather than desire or devotion.

His kiss wiped away all thought. I fell against him, spellbound by his rapacious mouth burning into mine, making silent promises to compensate for all I'd never tasted of love before. He held me captive yet set me free to feel the wondrous, fiery sensations his merest touch could ignite. Through the flimsy shift I felt his heat, his strength, his desire to love and be loved – and to prove it in every possible way, right then and there.

Only after the giggles around us got lewd did he bring the life-altering kiss to its finish. 'You comin' with me, Miss Eve? We've gotta talk.'

Monique let out an unladylike snort, shooing us towards the back door. 'The day Mr Dewel *talks* to his woman will be the day I give up my leather boots.'

Directing our gazes to the bare feet beneath Monique's full skirts, Dewel chuckled. 'Stranger things have happened, Miss Picabou. I'll thank you to stay with Tommy Jon for a few days, since we won't be needin' your help – nor your toys – until we come up for air. Might take me a couple of hours, but Miss Eve *will* be mine.'

Without any visible effort, the bourbon-skinned planter swept me up into his arms and out to his carriage, as though this had been his plan for the evening all along. As he settled into the soft leather seat, holding me across his lap, his driver shut the door. The horses headed down the brick drive towards Prytania at a brisk clip.

Even so, the pace was nothing compared to the rate my poor unprepared heart was thumping. Dewel's eyes were drinking me in with the appetite of a rich man deprived of his brandy and cigars, while he ripped away the layer of flimsy fabric covering my body. He lay me back against his crossed legs then, open and vulnerable to him.

'Dewel, I – what about Chapin?' I breathed. 'I'm still a married –'

'Not for long.' He ran his fingertips lightly along the sensitive skin of my neck and then around my nipples. 'I convinced him to see the wisdom of that divorce, and to visit his friend, Judge Madigan, tomorrow with the appropriate offerin' of cash. It's not like you ever had a real marriage with him, did you?'

I shook my head, for I could count on one hand the times Chapin Proffit had wanted sex, and it was anger or animal release driving his need. Making love wasn't something he did with me. I knew now that I'd served only as the whitewash on a pillar of society's life – a convenience deal he'd made with Daddy, to insure his acceptability.

'And, as I talked to the others, I got the feelin' that once the tongues have quit waggin' over tonight's surprise, Chapin's – or Honore's – cronies will accept him again,' Dewel said with a philosophical grin. '"Proffit" is just another name for money in this town. And in a lot of ways, New Orleans is like a Creole streetwalker: she was embraced by the French, and then the Spanish had her – and now she's an American woman who never met a man she didn't like.'

His observation struck a chord from when I'd first discovered Chapin with his 'niece' – was it only a few weeks ago? Yet my entire world had been turned upside down since then, and I'd been branded by the heat of his blatant brother's desire – for *me*! Dewel playfully turned me around to face the opposite side of the carriage while I straddled his long, solid thighs.

'Lean over, sugah,' he breathed, steadying me with

those strong hands on my hips. 'I'm gonna give you a lickin' you're not likely to forget.'

I glanced doubtfully over my shoulder, swaying with the rhythm of the rolling carriage. 'You're going to spank me?'

Dewel's laughter filled the rich interior of his vehicle; his eyes sparkled like crystals in the dimness. 'I never realised how far gone Chapin was, till I saw him sprawlin' on your lap, desperate for the smack of your hand. Try to take *me* across your knee, woman, and you're gonna be real sorry. Understand that?'

I giggled. 'That whole discipline ritual seems so absurd, and yet –'

I gasped as Dewel guided my hands down to clasp his ankles ... 'assuming the position' in a whole different way. As he spread his knees, he opened my sex to his full view and I was defenceless against whatever he might do next.

'God, would you look at that purrin' pussy,' he murmured, running a finger along my curls and the skin that was growing slick and damp. 'Why a man could want anything else is beyond me.'

'You won't try to put me in my place then?' I queried. The blood was rushing to my head as I clung to his legs, just as it had when he'd scooted my neck over the edge of his bed. I welcomed the giddiness, the sense that this handsome devil wanted to see me from every possible angle – that he couldn't get enough of me!

'Eve, sugah, the only place I want to put you is between me and a mattress,' he said, swivelling a finger inside me. 'Long as you're where I can take you on a moment's notice – long as you want me to meet your deepest needs – we're gonna have a long, happy life together, darlin'.'

I could only writhe in reply, whimpering for more of this incredible torture. His pants rasped against my inner thighs, and when those long, solid legs spread further apart I thought I'd die from the need to be *filled* by something.

He slid two fingers inside me then, maintaining that smooth in-and-out that was racing me towards insanity. 'But you have a say in all this. I'm a reasonable man, and all I ever want is to make you happy.'

With those fingers still probing deep within me, lodged high against that sweet spot, he leaned down to gaze at my face. 'So what do you want to happen now, Eve?' he whispered, in that same mesmerising tone which had led me to new insights about men and marriage, and about the mysterious nature of seduction and sex. 'You're a free woman. All the choices are yours.'

Grasping his ankles to keep from spilling off his lap – a sensation he'd induced to make me easy prey – I couldn't think straight. Nor did I need to. My heart had chosen this man long ago, and had waited until this moment to show me what love and passion could really mean, now that I knew how much I'd missed them before.

'I want *you*, Dewel!' I writhed against the fingers that spread my wetness all around my folds. 'I want you to love me forever – and fuck me right this minute, as though our lives depended on it.'

'Not just yet. I promised you a lickin', remember?'

I yowled like a randy cat at the first slow stroke of his tongue. He started at my clit, circling it with his hard, wet tip, and then drawing it between my folds towards my back crack. Then he did it again – as though he hadn't driven me wild enough the first time.

I shuddered with need, gripping his boots to keep a hold on my sanity – and to keep from pitching forward off his legs, away from this divine torture. Sucking air between my clenched teeth, I endured yet another slow pass of that tongue – but this time, my nether lips and muscles were twitching to the rhythm of the blood that pumped in my head.

'Had enough, sugah? If you can't handle –'

'Don't you *dare* stop! Dammit, Dewel!' I reached between his legs, praying his grip on my hips would hold as I fondled him. 'For a man who swore he'd tame me in a couple hours, you sure are slow!'

His chuckle rumbled against my sensitive, wet slit as he laved it one last time. 'Get over there and spread yourself, hands and knees against the seat,' he said, playfully slapping my backside. 'I won't tolerate a woman bossin' me around, you know.'

He released me, and I assumed that position in time to watch him unfasten his fly. Dewel pushed his pants past a shaft that looked urgent and purple, his blue eyes aglitter in his dusky face as he prodded me with its hot, hard head. As the carriage clattered down the driveway leading to Bayou Belle, he drove his cock home.

I screamed with the intensity of his penetration. In and out he went, thrusting into my cunt as he gripped my hips like he never wanted to let go. My slit quivered around him, sucking him deeper, welcoming the rogue who'd made me glad I was a woman. *His* woman now.

'Askin' me to raise a little cane, are you?' His drawl flowed like warm, sweet molasses as he rocked against my backside. 'Well that's fine by me, Miss Eve. Raisin' cane is what I *do*.'

Visit the Black Lace website at
www.blacklace-books.co.uk

FIND OUT THE LATEST INFORMATION AND TAKE ADVANTAGE OF OUR FANTASTIC FREE BOOK OFFER! ALSO VISIT THE SITE FOR . . .

- All Black Lace titles currently available and how to order online
- Great new offers
- Writers' guidelines
- Author interviews
- An erotica newsletter
- Features
- Cool links

BLACK LACE — THE LEADING IMPRINT OF WOMEN'S SEXY FICTION

TAKING YOUR EROTIC READING PLEASURE TO NEW HORIZONS

LOOK OUT FOR THE ALL-NEW BLACK LACE BOOKS – AVAILABLE NOW!

All books priced £6.99 in the UK. Please note publication dates apply to the UK only. For other territories, please contact your retailer.

LEARNING THE HARD WAY
Jasmine Archer
ISBN 0 352 33782 6

Tamsin has won a photographic assignment to collaborate on a book of nudes with the sex-obsessed Leandra. Thing is, the job is in Los Angeles and she doesn't want her new friend to know how sexually inexperienced she is. Tamsin sets out to learn all she can before flying out to meet her photographic mentor, but nothing can prepare her for Leandra's outrageous lifestyle. Along with husband Nigel, and an assortment of kinky friends, Leandra is about to initiate Tamsin into some very different ways to have fun. **Fun and upbeat story of a young woman's transition from sexual ingénue to fully fledged dominatrix.**

ACE OF HEARTS
Lisette Allen
ISBN 0 352 33059 7

England, 1816. The wealthy elite is enjoying an unprecedented era of hedonistic adventure. Their lives are filled with parties, sexual dalliances and scandal. Marisa Brooke is a young lady who lives by her wits, fencing and cheating the wealthy at cards. She also likes seducing young men and indulging her fancy for fleshly pleasures. However, love and fortune are lost as easily as they are won, and she has to use all her skill and cunning if she wants to hold on to her winnings and her lovers. **Highly enjoyable historical erotica set in the period of Regency excess.**

Coming in April

VALENTINA'S RULES
Monica Belle
ISBN 0 352 33788 5

Valentina is the girl with a plan: find a wealthy man, marry him, mould him and take her place in the sun. She's got the looks, she's got the ambition and, after one night with her, most men are following her around like puppies. When she decides that Michael Callington is too good for her friend Chrissy and just right for her, she finds she has bitten off a bit more than she expected. Then there's Michael's father, the notorious spanking Major, who is determined to have his fun, too.
Monica Belle specialises in erotic stories about modern girls about town and up to no good.

WICKED WORDS 8
Edited by Kerri Sharp
ISBN 0 352 33787 7

Hugely popular and immensely entertaining, the *Wicked Words* collections are the freshest and most cutting-edge volumes of women's erotic stories to be found anywhere in the world. The diversity of themes and styles reflects the multi-faceted nature of the female sexual imagination. Combining humour, warmth and attitude with fun, imaginative writing, these stories sizzle with horny action. Only the most arousing fiction makes it into a *Wicked Words* volume. This is the best in fun, sassy erotica from the UK and USA. **Another sizzling collection of wild fantasies from wicked women!**

Coming in May

UNKNOWN TERRITORY
Rosamund Trench
ISBN 0 352 33794 X

Hazel loves sex. It is her hobby and her passion. Every fortnight she
meets up with the well-bred and impeccably mannered Alistair. Then
there is Nick, the young IT lad at work, who has taken to following Hazel
around like a lost puppy. Her greatest preoccupation, however, concerns
the mysterious Number Six – the suited executive she met one day in the
boardroom. When it transpires that Number Six is a colleague of
Alistair's, things are destined to get complicated. Especially as Hazel is
moving towards the 'unknown territory' her mother warned her about.
An unusual sexual exploration of the appeal of powerful men in suits!

A GENTLEMAN'S WAGER
Madelynne Ellis
ISBN 0352 33800 8

When Bella Rushdale finds herself fiercely attracted to landowner
Lucerne Marlinscar, she doesn't expect that the rival for his affections
will be another man. Handsome and decadent, Marquis Pennerley has
desired Lucerne for years and now, at the remote Lauwine Hall, he
intends to claim him. This leads to a passionate struggle for dominance –
at the risk of scandal – between a high-spirited lady and a debauched
aristocrat. Who will Lucerne choose? **A wonderfully decadent piece of
historical erotica with a twist.**

VIRTUOSO
Katrina Vincenzi-Thyne
ISBN O 352 32907 6

Mika and Serena, young ambitious members of classical music's jet-set, inhabit a world of secluded passion and privilege. However, since Mika's tragic injury, which halted his meteoric rise to fame as a solo violinist, he has retired embittered. Serena is determined to change things. A dedicated voluptuary, her sensuality cannot be ignored as she rekindles Mika's zest for life. Together they share a dark secret. **A beautifully written story of opulence and exotic, passionate indulgence.**

Black Lace Booklist

Information is correct at time of printing. To avoid disappointment check availability before ordering. Go to www.blacklace-books.co.uk. All books are priced £6.99 unless another price is given.

BLACK LACE BOOKS WITH A CONTEMPORARY SETTING

☐ THE TOP OF HER GAME Emma Holly	ISBN 0 352 33337 5	£5.99
☐ IN THE FLESH Emma Holly	ISBN 0 352 33498 3	£5.99
☐ A PRIVATE VIEW Crystalle Valentino	ISBN 0 352 33308 1	£5.99
☐ SHAMELESS Stella Black	ISBN 0 352 33485 1	£5.99
☐ INTENSE BLUE Lyn Wood	ISBN 0 352 33496 7	£5.99
☐ THE NAKED TRUTH Natasha Rostova	ISBN 0 352 33497 5	£5.99
☐ ANIMAL PASSIONS Martine Marquand	ISBN 0 352 33499 1	£5.99
☐ A SPORTING CHANCE Susie Raymond	ISBN 0 352 33501 7	£5.99
☐ TAKING LIBERTIES Susie Raymond	ISBN 0 352 33357 X	£5.99
☐ A SCANDALOUS AFFAIR Holly Graham	ISBN 0 352 33523 8	£5.99
☐ THE NAKED FLAME Crystalle Valentino	ISBN 0 352 33528 9	£5.99
☐ ON THE EDGE Laura Hamilton	ISBN 0 352 33534 3	£5.99
☐ LURED BY LUST Tania Picarda	ISBN 0 352 33533 5	£5.99
☐ THE HOTTEST PLACE Tabitha Flyte	ISBN 0 352 33536 X	£5.99
☐ THE NINETY DAYS OF GENEVIEVE Lucinda Carrington	ISBN 0 352 33070 8	£5.99
☐ EARTHY DELIGHTS Tesni Morgan	ISBN 0 352 33548 3	£5.99
☐ MAN HUNT Cathleen Ross	ISBN 0 352 33583 1	
☐ MÉNAGE Emma Holly	ISBN 0 352 33231 X	
☐ DREAMING SPIRES Juliet Hastings	ISBN 0 352 33584 X	
☐ THE TRANSFORMATION Natasha Rostova	ISBN 0 352 33311 1	
☐ STELLA DOES HOLLYWOOD Stella Black	ISBN 0 352 33588 2	
☐ SIN.NET Helena Ravenscroft	ISBN 0 352 33598 X	
☐ HOTBED Portia Da Costa	ISBN 0 352 33614 5	
☐ TWO WEEKS IN TANGIER Annabel Lee	ISBN 0 352 33599 8	
☐ HIGHLAND FLING Jane Justine	ISBN 0 352 33616 1	
☐ PLAYING HARD Tina Troy	ISBN 0 352 33617 X	
☐ SYMPHONY X Jasmine Stone	ISBN 0 352 33629 3	

BLACK LACE BOOKS WITH AN HISTORICAL SETTING

BLACK LACE ANTHOLOGIES

To find out the latest information about Black Lace titles, check out the
website: www.blacklace-books.co.uk or send for a booklist with
complete synopses by writing to:

> Black Lace Booklist, Virgin Books Ltd
> Thames Wharf Studios
> Rainville Road
> London W6 9HA

Please include an SAE of decent size. Please note only British stamps
are valid.

Our privacy policy
We will not disclose information you supply us to any other parties.
We will not disclose any information which identifies you personally to
any person without your express consent.

From time to time we may send out information about Black Lace
books and special offers. Please tick here if you do <u>not</u> wish to
receive Black Lace information.   ☐

Please send me the books I have ticked above.

Name ....

Address ....

....

....

....

Post Code ....

Send to: Cash Sales, Black Lace Books, Thames Wharf Studios, Rainville Road, London W6 9HA.

US customers: for prices and details of how to order books for delivery by mail, call 1-800-343-4499.

Please enclose a cheque or postal order, made payable to Virgin Books Ltd, to the value of the books you have ordered plus postage and packing costs as follows:

UK and BFPO – £1.00 for the first book, 50p for each subsequent book.

Overseas (including Republic of Ireland) – £2.00 for the first book, £1.00 for each subsequent book.

If you would prefer to pay by VISA, ACCESS/MASTERCARD, DINERS CLUB, AMEX or SWITCH, please write your card number and expiry date here:

....

Signature ....

Please allow up to 28 days for delivery.